One Bossy Night

Iona Rose

Author's Note

Hey there!

Thank you for choosing my book. I sure hope that you love it. I'd hate to part ways once you're done though. So how about we stay in touch?

My newsletter is a great way to discover more about me and my books. Where you'll find frequent exclusive give-aways, sneak previews of new releases and be first to see new cover reveals.

And as a HUGE thank you for joining, you'll receive a FREE book on me!

With love,

Iona

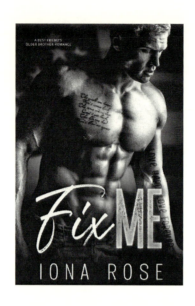

Get Your FREE Book Here:

https://dl.bookfunnel.com/v9yit8b3f7

Chapter One
Hunter

H er scream pierced through the room like shattered glass. I was instantly startled, unsure of what was going on.

I had been in the midst of buttoning my dress shirt as I took in the view of Chao Phraya River from the presidential suite we were lodged in. It was gorgeous in the light of this early morning, the enchanting view of moving boats and shimmering waters reflecting the sun.

I glanced back towards the door connecting her rooms and noted that she had gone quiet. Did this mean that there was no reason to go over? Maybe she had just been startled? I briefly resumed buttoning my shirt, but barely a button into the hole, I was anxious, so I turned around and headed towards her room.

I knocked; however, there was no response. One of the reasons I had insisted on this suite with separate rooms and connecting door was so that, as my secretary, she could have easy and quick access to me, but I didn't expect to be making any trips of any kind to her whatsoever, nor was I the least bit interested in doing so.

There was a line drawn between any interactions between us that weren't related to work, and I didn't want to cross it. However, when I knocked again and didn't get a response, I had no choice but to push open the door and head in. I saw immediately that she wasn't there.

This meant then that she was in the bathroom, and now I was officially worried. Bathroom accidents were the most dangerous, and it made sense now why there was a singular shout and then she had gone silent. She had probably become unconscious after her fall and couldn't respond or call for help.

"Madison," I called out as I stood before her door. "Madison?"

My hand closed around the handle, but rather than hearing a clear sentence assuring me that all was well, I heard a bit of a shrill, panicked response which trailed off into a pained moan that she was obviously trying to hide but couldn't.

"I'm fine. I'm fine," she called out.

To be honest, she didn't sound fine, but since she said she was, I no longer had any business being in her room.

I turned around and took in the messy room with clothes and documents strewn all over and couldn't help but frown. I started to leave, but I stopped and considered. She wasn't coming out and I had definitely heard her scream. It occurred to me then, as I found the dark lace bra lying on the floor, why she could have possibly driven me away despite the fact that she had obviously had some sort of accident. Sighing, I turned and returned to the bathroom. This time I didn't ask her permission and only announced my entrance.

"I'm coming in," I said.

She nearly screamed once again. "No, don't! I'm... I'm fine. I'm just... don't come in, please. I'm fine."

Rather than look at her fully, I utilized the mirror on the wall, and what I found was quite disconcerting, to say the least. She was flat down on the floor with her towel loosely around her body. She was twisted in the most awkward position, and immediately when she saw me, her eyes flew open.

"I'm not decent, Sir," she said and immediately tried to get up as she pulled her towel around her. However, it was too tiny to hide the body that she wanted to hide from me. The body I realized as I stared at her, that she had been hiding from me for quite a long time. And just like that, I was more stunned by her figure than by the fact that she had probably broken a bone or two.

"I'm fine," she said again; however, she couldn't quite turn around to look at me.

I got in then and knelt to the floor, "Can you stand?"

"I... I can, Sir," she said, not quite able to look at me. "It's just that I'm going to need a minute."

"If you need a minute to be able to stand, then you're not fine," I said, quite irritated. I held her then and tried to help her up.

"Now," she squeezed her eyes shut, "my towel is going to fall."

"I'll hold on to it then," I said. "Just make sure to hold on to me."

"That's the plan," but as I tried to turn around, it was

3

impossible not to glimpse the fullness of her breasts and just how shapely her ass was. It was gorgeous and plum, much bigger than I had ever realized. I hated to admit this, but I could feel arousal spiking through me and rushing down to my dick. I had never, in the six months that she had worked for me so far, even entertained such a thought about her, but here I was, ready to spread her open and fuck her so hard she lost her mind.

"I- um... it was a spider," she said. "I'm fine. Really. I thought- I mean, there was a spider behind me, and it shocked me, and I tried to run, but the ground was slippery so - ow." She winced as I managed to turn her around with one hand gripping the towel while she held onto me. "Ow."

"I'm going to pull you up now," I told her. "Let me know if you can stand on your own."

She grew quiet because indeed she hadn't really been expecting to fall, so she had originally grabbed the first towel she could find after she heard me come into the room. Unfortunately for her, it was more like half a towel, barely able to cover her breasts and go around her body, not to talk of her gorgeous ass.

Soon she was on her feet with her arm around me, and I turned to see the wince on her face. Her eyes remained closed for a few moments as she tried to test how her body was, and she soon nodded. She still didn't open her eyes as she spoke, and I understood. She was more or less naked in her boss's arms, and there was little to nothing she could do about it.

" Can you stand on your own?" I asked, and she nodded.

"I think I'm just sore in my knee from the fall, and my

neck is quite strained. It's stiff, almost. I have to be careful with it. Other than that, I'm fine."

"Alright, I'm going to let you go now, alright?" I asked, and she nodded in response.

"Yes, Sir, thank you."

Gradually, I moved away, and her hand instantly shot up to take over the towel, held to within an inch of her life. It would have been amusing, the desperate way in which she grabbed it, if the entire situation wasn't quite grim. The bathroom was dangerous. It was filled with so much glass and marble that if she had truly landed wrong, she could have cracked her skull in two.

I stared at her and couldn't help but worry about her. We had a tight schedule to keep for the day, but we really couldn't do any of that if she was in some crisis, could we? My gaze lowered down to her knees, and I could see the bruise already forming.

"Turn your neck," I said, and her eyes finally met mine. For a moment, I was startled. It felt like I was looking at someone I had never seen before.

She was always in thick, huge glasses that seemed to be the only thing preventing her from being completely labeled as blind, so I had never actually seen her eyes before, nor had I cared. And her hair... was curly. Dark chocolate brown, wet... it surprised me because I never knew she had this much hair. It was always bone straight, tied and tucked into the back of her head, with not a single hair out of place.

It made her look more than anything like a fifty-year-old middle school math teacher, and then of course there were her baggy black and white suits. I knew she was young, but her usual appearance was so stoic that it made me wonder where she had grown up.

She looked like an unattractive country bumpkin who would do nothing but focus on her work and given the experience I had had so far with prior secretaries; this was exactly what I had preferred.

Therefore, everything had gone smoothly ... until now. Her eyes were the most gorgeous hazel I had ever seen, golden with some hints of green in them, her lashes were long and wet and made her seem almost like a doll. I couldn't look away.

"Sir?" she called, and I finally came to my senses.

"Can you shift the breakfast meeting we have with the clients this morning?" I asked. "I think we need to quickly get you to a hospital so you can be checked properly for any signs of more severe injury."

"No, Sir," she immediately refused and tried to shake her head, but she was seemingly dazed.

"Ow," she cried quietly, and my gaze narrowed at her.

"Sure you still want to refuse?" I asked, and this time around she didn't move. Instead, she used only her words.

"I'm fine, Sir," she said. "Really fine."

"Alright," I replied, not wanting to drag this on unnecessarily. "Get dressed then and let me know if there are any complications."

"Yes, Sir," she replied and turned around, exiting the bathroom.

Chapter Two
Madison

"Holy shit!" I heard the voice suddenly say. The sound echoed so much through the room that I jumped again and almost fell down and broke my head for the second time within the space of five minutes.

With my hand to my chest, I went still and tried to calm myself so I wouldn't permanently dislocate my neck. Eventually, when I felt stable enough, I opened my eyes and glared at the phone positioned against the wall on the vanity. Emma's face filled up the entire screen, and her attention was so rapt it was almost amusing.

"First of all, that was your boss, right? And secondly, oh my God, I think he saw you."

Walking slowly toward the sink, I rolled my dry eyes at her drivel.

"No kidding."

"Shit," she was amused. "This is kind of intriguing."

"I almost died, you ass."

"Well, I swear I saw the spider. It was crawling behind you. Didn't you see it?"

"You really want me to turn around to check again?" I asked. "With my broken neck?"

Her smile turned sheepish. "I'm sorry, Maddy. You're right, it could have been so dangerous. When you screamed, my heart was pounding so fast. If you hadn't responded to him, I would have called the police or emergency services right away. That was scary."

I ignored her as I grabbed the robe hanging on the wall and put it on.

"This is what I should have freaking worn in the beginning. I didn't, and as a result, I've just given my boss a show. The show he specifically asked not to have from the first moment he hired me."

"Yeah," she replied. "He didn't see all of it though, did he?"

I gave her a nasty look but had to consider her question. Eventually, I couldn't help but respond, scared for my life, literally.

"You were watching, right?" I asked. "Did he? Did you?"

"All I could see was his back. He's huge and broad. I couldn't see anything else."

My heart sank once again.

I couldn't lower my neck, so of course I can't tell what he saw and didn't see.

"Did you feel a breeze?" she asked.

"Please stop talking about it. In fact, I think it's time for you to leave. I'm already running late, and I can't be late when it comes to him. I can't believe I was looking at lingerie samples with you when I was supposed to be rushing for work."

"I would have said something rude about that, but given that you can't even move right, I'll accept the blame. I'm so sorry."

I went quiet then as I continued rapidly with my skincare while trying my best to slightly turn my neck to wrinkle out the ache. Perhaps it would be fine. It had to be. I was the only one that had come along with Mr. Swift on this trip, so I had to be on top of my game, especially now that I had crossed his one line.

My main problem from all that had just happened should have been just physical, but now when I considered the fact that I might literally get fired for this, my mood plummeted.

"Should I leave?" Emma asked as I quickly moved on to my makeup.

"No," I replied. "My thoughts are spiraling."

"Oh, come on," she said. "Even if he did see some parts of you, that doesn't affect anything, does it? You've called him a monk before. If he is so uninterested in the females that work for him, then why be bothered?"

I shrugged. "Is it strange for me to be? I have literally been dressing like a nun the last few months, all to fit his specifications. How can I not be worried?"

"Yeah," she replied. "I understand. But it will be fine, and if it isn't, be bold, state your case, and tell him that if he fires you for this, you will sue for wrongful termination."

I gave her a look. "Really, and who's going to cover the cost of that?"

"I will," she replied. "I'll handle your lawsuit. Trust me. I might have quit the law firm to start this business, but I'm still legally a lawyer and a damn good one at that."

I couldn't object to this, but it did make me smile at the thought of threatening him with this, not that I could ever. I had worked with him for quite a while now, and still, I got so nervous around him, as stiff as a stick. He was so damn impressive, and with my experience of him so far, I couldn't stop my heart from turning soft when he was concerned, though for my own good, this was and will never be known.

"I have an idea," she said, and I glanced at the phone lens.

"What?"

"Why don't you use this opportunity to pursue something with him?"

"What?" My face scrunched up in incredulity. For someone so smart, she sometimes spoke like an airhead.

"You've had a crush on him forever. At this point, and given how much you know about him, you are more or less in love with him, yet you have never even been able to consider anything between you two."

"He's my boss," I replied in disbelief.

"So? So, you're just going to not try? I think you should. He's seen you naked now, and if he's a man and not gay like I have suspected, then he should have felt something. Now I think more than ever now is your only chance to act."

"And what exactly would you have me do?" I asked, absolutely not taking her seriously at all.

"I don't know," she replied. "You two are also taking this whole conference trip as something of a mini vacation as well, right?"

"Right."

"Well, this will give you plenty of chances to dress a little more alluring. Plus, I'll ship you one of our new lingerie pieces. You can test it out for me on him."

"And how exactly am I supposed to do that?" I asked, absolutely not taking her seriously at all.

"Fall down again, but this time truly be unconscious so he can see my lingerie on your body. Trust me, your body is sick, and the moment he sees my lingerie on your body, he's going to lose it. Plus, you could wear it to the beach as well. Are there beaches where you are in Thailand? Do you both have any plans for it?"

"We have a resort vacation planned in Phuket."

"Perfect, I'll send you something."

"Please leave me alone," I said and reached for the phone. "I'm done; I'm leaving. Go work on your business some more and stop trying to ruin my life. I like my job and my boss. We flew here on his private jet, and my salary is insane. I'm not going to give any of that up just because I have a crush on him. It'll die and I'll come to my senses when he gets with someone, and that's bound to happen sooner or later."

"That someone could be you," she said, and I ended the call. She was always putting these ridiculous ideas in my head, trying to save me from my unrequited love narrative. I wasn't going to listen to her because I truly had spent too much time so far with Hunter not to understand him, and any distraction whatsoever from his work was like cancer that he wouldn't hesitate for even a minute to get rid of.

I stretched my neck a bit more, testing the extent of the strain, and I felt a little better. My prayer was that it wouldn't get worse during the day, so I found some aspirin to take in advance and hurried out of the bathroom.

I had to get dressed and present myself before my boss and pretend he'd never seen me almost naked.

Chapter Three
Hunter

For the first time ever, I waited for her arrival. Not just because she was late, which was understandable given her accident, but because for the first time since she had been working with me, I had finally noticed that she was a woman. From the moment I had left my bathroom until now, it was all I could think about. And I had overheard her with her friend.

I had gone back into the room so that I could offer her some aspirin and overheard a healthy chunk of gossip that had left me quite astounded and a little bit uncomfortable. In the past, and every time I had hired a female secretary who was competent, it had almost always ended the same way. They tried to insert themselves into my life in either a romantic or sexual capacity, which was too much of a distraction to keep around. I hated mixing business with pleasure, and the past few years with the company and its explosive growth had been nearly out of control. So, after firing the last secretary for dressing indecently and all but throwing her cleavage in my face, I had given very clear instructions to the Human Resources department: *"Find me someone competent who isn't the least bit attractive."*

A man preferably, or an older woman with children. And then Madison had entered the picture. She had no experience working in the renewable energy sector, but she did have a master's degree in it and could understand details about our business. This was enough to qualify temporarily as my secretary. I didn't have to explain everything. Eventually though it became clear that she was organized, could learn at a rapid pace and was almost perfect in the role. It was impossible to hide her natural beauty but the way she carried herself made it very easy to ignore.

Until now. Now, and as I had overheard, she was probably doing all of this to fit the role of being as unattractive as possible for me, despite being attracted to me. This was more than enough to clear the lens I had always looked at her with and refocus my attention on her for a moment. I wasn't going to do anything about it, but I was quite looking forward to viewing her in this different light until and if it became a problem.

"I'm here, Sir. Where are you?" I received her text message and immediately raised my head.

"In the corner by the palm tree of the lobby," I replied, putting my phone away. My gaze was focused on the path leading to the bank of elevators, and soon enough, she spotted me.

She quickly hurried over in her dark grandma loafers, bootleg, pleatless flare dress pants, oversized suit jacket, and green button-up dress shirt. I couldn't believe this was the same woman I had seen earlier. In that bathroom, her true self had been revealed, a goddess, and now she had tried once again to veil herself as a dull-looking administrator of some sort. She was hiding... her body, her femininity—she was hiding it all from me!

I took in her thick glasses, and when she finally arrived before me, nearly out of breath, I couldn't help but ask, "Do you actually need those glasses?"

She tried to catch her breath but forewent this effort altogether when it was taking longer than she expected.

"Um, what do you mean, Sir?" she asked as she pushed the glasses up her nose. They were obviously too big for her small face. My eyes went to her hair, noting how straight and tied back and tucked and out of the way it looked. She barely had any makeup on her face, and her demeanor was as unremarkable as usual. She was never flustered, however, not until now at least, and I knew it was because she was late, which she usually wasn't. Her cheeks were flushed, and slight perspiration beaded across her forehead.

I sat up then and replied to her. "I'm asking if you need those glasses. You seem to struggle with them a lot; maybe they're not the best for you. Why don't you try contacts instead? This way, you can always be able to see properly. I suspect that not having your glasses on earlier on was part of the reason you fell."

She seemed to contemplate this a moment, then she nodded. "I'll look into contacts, Sir," she said. "And yes, I do need them. I am more or less blind without them."

"Alright," I replied and rose to my feet. After all, I wasn't one to push, and at the end of the day, it was indeed her business.

I didn't believe her, though. I didn't believe that she truly needed them. I was almost completely certain now that it was all a part of her facade, and I thought of how to reveal this as we got into the waiting car outside of the hotel.

"Good morning, Mr. Swift," our driver, Kit Charnchai, greeted.

"Miss," he nodded towards Madison as well.

"Good morning," I replied, and soon he shut the passenger door behind me.

He was the designated uniformed chauffeur organized for us by the conference team, and we had already met the previous night when he had picked us up from the airport.

"We're heading to Le Normandie by Alain Roux at the Mandarin Oriental," Madison said to him as she got into the seat in front. I had never quite noticed that that was where she usually sat rather than my side, but now my attention was fully on her. I wanted to tell her to switch seats and from now on ride in the back with me, but ultimately and thankfully, I came back to my senses.

"Yes, ma'am," the driver nodded, and soon we were on our way.

"Let's review the schedule for the next ten days," I said, pulling out my phone. "We'll be busy with the conference team at the welcome breakfast, so we might not get the chance."

"Yes, Sir," she peeked and instantly pulled out her tablet from her briefcase.

"For today, the goal of meeting with the conference team is so that they can provide you with all the needed information for it as it officially begins tomorrow. You'll be presenting a keynote speech on "Integrating AI and IoT in Renewable Energy Systems" at the Centara Grand & Bangkok Convention Centre. I've already compiled the notes for all the lectures and speeches you'll be giving at the conference and sent them to you, but just in case, I'll send them again now. Please let me know if there's anything you want me to add, especially for the start of the conference tomorrow."

My phone buzzed then with an alert, and I looked down to see the files she had sent to me. I instantly opened it up and began to peruse the notes she had made for the speech.

I scrolled down even further then to see the remaining topics I would be presenting as well.

"These were the topics I chose for the last three days of the conference?" I asked.

"Yes, Sir, we finalized them a couple of weeks ago."

I went through the details. "Challenges and Opportunities in Southeast Asia's Renewable Energy Landscape," "Sustainable Investment: Financing Models for Renewable Energy Projects," "The Role of Renewable Energy in Achieving Net-Zero Emissions Targets."

"Hm," I said and could sense her slightly turning backwards to look at me. I wanted to stop her when I remembered the strain in her neck, but since she was careful about it, I decided to mind my business.

"Is there a problem, Sir? Do you want me to adjust any of them?"

"No," I replied. "I'll deal with these later. What time is the opening ceremony tomorrow?"

"Just before lunch, Sir," she said. "10 am."

"Got it," I replied and put my phone away. I turned and focused my attention on the brand-new city we were in, trying my best to appreciate the sights.

I had never been to Thailand before, but this was one of the reasons why I had accepted to participate in the conference as soon as the invitation had come in. I rarely ever accepted functions like this, but due to the personal loss I had encountered the previous year, it hit me more than ever how much time was running out and how much of that time I was spending at work.

I loved my work and the impact it was making, but for too many years, I had been too focused on it to the point of cutting everything else out, including functions like this that I could have taken advantage of to take me out of the country. This was the change I had decided on and also why I hadn't brought any staff along despite the fact that this was also a business trip. Killing three birds essentially with one stone.

"What's the schedule for the Swedish clients?" I asked her then, as I recalled.

"We're meeting them later tonight, Sir, at a Japanese restaurant," she replied. "Their secretary sent the details over to me while we were flying over. They said it's the preferred location so that we— you can eat and dine with them as well."

I nearly rolled my eyes at this because eating and dining like this with clients was one of the parts of my job that I didn't enjoy. I liked to eat on my own when my work was done and in silence so I could enjoy it. And I liked to have meetings be solely about meetings. Focused... short, to the point. But in this case, and like many others, I had to adapt especially since there was so much money on the line.

"Do you have any notes prepared or any materials

prepared for the discussions? Were you given anything from the office?"

"Yes, Sir," she replied.

It took a bit of searching in her briefcase, and then she handed over a folder of documents to me.

"They're Swedish founders but based here in Thailand, and their goal is to secure investment and partnership for their renewable energy project to enhance energy efficiency and sustainability in Southeast Asia. They want to be our way into Asia."

I listened to her words for a moment, and then I opened up the file.

"Why did we reject them the first time?" I asked.

"Well, um..." She seemed stumped, and then I lifted my gaze to hers.

"You... weren't interested in dealing with Southeast Asia until recently, Sir. In short, we didn't reach out to them again; they reached out to us when the Renewable Energy Summit announced that you would be flying in to participate."

"Hm," I nodded and continued with my reading.

"Where's their proposal?" I asked.

"There is a summary included in that folder, but if you want the full copy, I'll send it to you right now."

"Do that," I replied, and she got to work.

"Yes, Sir."

And this way, we worked in silence until eventually, we arrived at the breakfast and welcome venue.

Chapter Four
Madison

I fell asleep before we arrived at the venue. And the way I was awoken made me want to die. I heard a knock on the window, and when I opened my eyes, all I could see was my gorgeous boss with his dark wavy hair and blue eyes staring down at me. There was no expression on his face as he watched me, but I was sure it was nothing short of disgust. Instantly, I jumped up, and as a result, both hit my head against the roof and further injured my neck.

"Fuck," I cursed as my hand curved around it, and when I turned to look at him, I saw his eyes narrow. Then, without a word, he turned around and headed into the hotel.

"I thought you'd wake up when we stopped, ma'am," the chauffeur said, "You must be jet-lagged."

"Yeah," I replied hurriedly, got out of the car, and went after him.

The hotel was majestic, not like ours since it was the best and most expensive, but this was just equally gorgeous. I was so distracted by the sights, however, when I saw Mr.

Swift heading towards the elevator. I noticed that even after one emptied, one opened and closed, he remained waiting. I quickened my step, and soon I was by his side, brushing the loosened mess that my hair had become from dozing off in the car.

He turned to me then and watched me for so long I had to turn away. I was sure now that he was thinking of firing me. With what happened that morning and with how sloppy I had been all day; he was now for sure wondering why he had ever even kept me around in the first place.

"You're tired," he said. "I don't need you for this; it's just a networking event. Go back to the hotel, rest, and get ready for the dinner this evening."

I stared at him in shock. Immediately tears started to gather in my eyes because this, for sure, meant I was getting fired, right? How could he attend such an event without his secretary?

"Sir, there are some faces I am able to recognize. I have studied them and gotten ready for the meeting, so I'll be able to help you out."

"No need," he replied. "I don't have to recall any faces. I'm not here for them; they're here because of me. Whoever wants to be acknowledged by me can damn well introduce themselves."

I stared at him, feeling even more terrified.

"Um..." I looked around, reluctant to leave, and to my further surprise, he reversed his offer, but this time, what he did was even more outrageous.

"If you don't want to go all the way back to the hotel, then why not just get a room here?" he asked.

My eyes widened.

The elevator dinged open again, and without a word, he headed in.

"You have my card, don't you? Use it as you wish."

I instantly darted forward and slammed my hand against the steel doors to keep them from closing.

"What is it?" he asked.

"I'm not sleepy, and I really don't want to sleep right now. I want to work."

He watched me, and then he sighed.

"This is not a discussion. If you don't want to take a nap, then find something else to do. This hotel should have a spa and a boutique or whatever. Get a treatment to get rid of those bags under your eyes and buy a dress. It shouldn't be a bulky dress. Buy something alluring and let your hair down or something. Not a bun like this."

I was so confused at his instructions.

"What? I mean, why, Sir?"

"Don't we have a dinner with the Swedish clients tonight?" he asked. "That's what your preparation is for."

Stunned, I removed my hand from the door and could only stand in confusion and awe.

"Also," he said before the door fully closed. "Don't wear your glasses. You obviously don't need them at all."

The door slid shut, and as always, I reached to push the lenses up my nose but found absolutely nothing there.

"Holy shit!"

I spun around and once again winced at the pain in my neck. By the time this day is over, I am pretty sure that my head is going to completely fall off. But that soon became the least of my worries when I realized that my glasses were nowhere to be found. I thought about this and soon concluded that they had fallen off back in the car when I had been startled awake. And since I truly didn't need them, I hadn't even noticed that they were gone.

I slapped my hand against my forehead and nearly sunk to the ground.

Not only was I sloppy, but I had also been caught lying and seen naked. All in one day and after six full months without an accident.

I looked around the gorgeous golden hotel and wondered if it was just me or if Thailand hated me?

Sighing, I turned around and began to wander away. I passed by a reflective surface then and stopped to stare at myself. With the briefcase and the oversized, ill-fitting suit jacket and pants, I looked so unremarkable. Almost like a poor kid that was trying to fit in. But this had worked, for the longest time it had worked, so why was everything changing now? He was so predictable, and it had given me a measure of safety and peace. Now that he wasn't, now that he was suddenly barging into my bathroom, seeing me naked, and saying the strangest things, I felt as though the ground underneath my feet would be pulled out from under me at any time, and this was a disconcerting feeling to say the least.

Sighing, I continued wandering. Pretty soon I found the spa. It looked so luxurious that I couldn't help but consider what he was asking. Still, doing this in the middle of the day when I was supposed to be working was unfathomable to me, so I could only take a seat outside the place and call Emma.

She was as usual at her kitchen table, hard at work on

her new business. But she set the phone up in a corner and continued working.

"I just received a new sample," she said. "You won't believe how bloody upset I am; they messed up my design, and they used cheaper materials than they showed me. I'm just having the worst day. How's your neck?"

I watched her and only had one question.

"Can I come work for you? Be your project manager or quality control guy or whatever?"

She gave me her full attention then.

"What's wrong?"

"I think I just got fired."

She went silent.

"Um... what?"

I explained what had happened, but to my surprise, she burst out laughing. I watched her, upset, as she held her chest and tried to control herself.

"What the hell is wrong with you?" I asked.

"You claim to be able to read people well, Maddy," she said. "You claim to know your boss really well, but do you know him at all? I think he's really not as rigid as you think he is. You fell earlier this morning. And you both arrived just last night, and before then you've been practically living in the office for over a week, trying to get materials ready and itineraries booked. He's taking this as a vacation as well, isn't he? You planned it all. You think he didn't notice? You think he's surprised that you're falling asleep in the car?"

My frown loosened.

"Take his advice, please? Go to the spa, fall asleep on the table there as they massage every inch of your body with oil and perfume. Go to the sauna afterward or something and then get a facial. After that, find a salon, do your hair for once. Get your makeup done, and then go get the most stunning, sexiest dress you can find for this evening. Just like he advised. How does him asking you to do any of this mean that you're going to get fired?"

"You don't know him, Emma," I said, and she shook her head.

"I'm hanging up. I'm the one with the real problems here. So, you go have your wonderful luxurious day and leave the rest of us struggling through ours alone. He's not going to fire you, and if he does, you can apply to be my personal chef. I'm adding weight from all this takeout I keep buying."

"Agreed," I replied and rose to my feet for no reason. "I'll be on the next flight back now. I'll cook all the healthy meals you want for you."

"Rejected. I don't want to be poisoned, plus my big lawyer salary reserves are depleting with all these road-blocks and destroyed designs. They're draining me like a sink. Soon enough I'll be your roommate, and then I'll need a job from you."

This made me smile, but I did listen to what she was saying though. And then I sighed. She ended the call, and I looked around. First of all, I took a few pictures and then took a selfie of myself. One look at my reflection and I almost threw up. This was possibly the real reason why he had turned me away. I looked as basic and unremarkable as a concrete wall. Almost lifeless even. Maybe in my quest to be unremarkable physically in his eyes, I had just ended up as embarrassing, and so now more than ever, I was tempted to follow his instructions. Glancing back, I stared at the big bright signage of the spa and the two women walking out of it at that moment with huge smiles on their faces.

I thought a bit more, pulled out his card from my wallet, and then I made the decision. They had the ultimate package: everything Emma had mentioned, and it was incredibly pricey. However, I was aware that this was because we were in such an expensive hotel, but I didn't want to leave their premises while he was still here. I wanted us to head back together.

I most definitely didn't want to use his card for this because that was something for him to use against me in the future. Perhaps it would be evidence he could use to say it was the reason why he suddenly fired me when I sued him. *'She used my personal card without my permission.'*

Absolutely not. I was remaining spanking clean until the very end.

And so, I used my card instead and felt even more pain run through my body as soon as it was charged. About an hour later, however, I was running through a vineyard, plucking grapes from the trees and chasing butterflies. I was fast asleep and surrounded by endless barrels of wine as the masseuse gave me the most wonderful facial and face massage, and then she massaged every inch of my body like I was a loaf of bread.

By the time she was done, I couldn't get the smile off my face. My neck still slightly ached, but overall, I felt much better, and she gave me something for the bruise on my knee. By the time I got off that table and headed into the sauna then took a shower, I felt as though I had just been reborn. My problems seemed far away and inconsequential, so when I got out, I kept strolling and found a salon not too far away, I couldn't help but go in.

I didn't need anyone to do my makeup, but I did need my hair properly taken care of. It was clean, but it needed some styling, and as he said, I couldn't come to the dinner with it pulled back and tucked out of the way like usual.

Thankfully, the attendants spoke great English, so I was able to explain myself properly, and pretty soon, I was in the chair with warm soothing water on my scalp. I didn't even bother telling them I had done my hair that morning as they shampooed and conditioned, and then I was put in a chair. I didn't need any highlights. I loved my hair, but they did ensure that the waves and curls popped, and in just under an hour, I looked like the brunette version of Carrie Bradshaw.

My hair was parted in the middle, layered, and flowing all the way to my back.

I looked gorgeous, and I didn't even have any makeup on. The stylist seemed so excited to see my face, and then she asked if I wanted any makeup done for the full makeover effect.

"No thank you," I replied. "I loved the clean feel of my face after not putting on makeup for so many months, but I did have one more request to make."

I turned around then to watch the gorgeous guy that had more or less turned me into a goddess.

"Do you know where I can buy a dress?"

He clapped his hands together in excitement, and then he nodded so hard I felt the pain in my neck for him. I got up then, and after paying exorbitantly once again, I was given clear directions to the hotel's boutique.

Chapter Five
Hunter

By lunchtime, the networking and welcoming party was drawing to a close, but I was invited from there to various other places for lunch. I declined them all when I realized that just like my secretary, I was exhausted from all the working and traveling, and this was a vacation for me, so I was going to take my well-deserved rest.

After rejecting them all, I left the venue and pulled out my phone to call my secretary. I wondered if she had done as I had told her, and a part of me almost expected her to not have. I was going to be furious if this was the case, I was sure, so as her phone rang, I hoped to God, she hadn't defied me.

"Sir?" she asked.

"Where are you?" I asked.

"Um... in the lobby waiting. Reception."

I sighed. Of course she hadn't left.

"I'm ready to leave, are you?"

"Yes, Sir," she replied.

"Did you do what I asked?"

"Yes, Sir," she replied, and I was a bit surprised.

"Alright, get the car arranged. Let's head back."

"I have lunch scheduled, Sir," she said. "Do you have anything in particular that you want to eat?"

"Have whatever it is delivered to our room. I want to go to bed. Wake me up in time for the meeting." She seemed slightly surprised by this.

"Um, of course. Sure, Sir, I'll handle it."

I headed down to the lobby, and soon enough, I spotted her. I almost didn't recognize her. Her hair was gorgeous and flowing, and just so striking that I couldn't look away. Her skin was a bit oily, and she still had on those wretched clothes, but most importantly, she was without her glasses. She looked the same but yet unrecognizable, and I realized then that she had indeed listened to me.

I saw the tote bag in her hand and didn't need to know that she had indeed bought a dress. With a nod of acknowledgment, we headed out together and found the chauffeur waiting with our car.

A little while later, we were back at the hotel, and we went our separate ways. It was the presidential suite with separate doors, even though they were connecting, so we didn't need to enter together. Given the encounter we had had earlier that morning, it would no doubt feel awkward now to do so.

Soon she disappeared and was out of sight, and after completely stripping off, I shut the blinds and napped for the first time in almost a decade without any guilt whatsoever in the bright and sunny afternoon.

A few hours later, I woke up to the setting sun. It wasn't

a new sight, since I was able to catch it from wall-to-ceiling windows in my office in Manhattan but seeing it here in a completely different country and continent was interesting, to say the least.

So, I remained in bed and watched until eventually, my thoughts went to my secretary. It would be time for dinner soon, and I hated to admit that I couldn't truly wait to see the dress that she bought. I wondered if she would look the same, and if she didn't, I wondered even more what I was going to do about it.

I still didn't want to be distracted by any females but given that I was on vacation with her and had overheard what she had said to her friend, I had to admit that I was playing a very dangerous game. Soon enough, my phone began to ring, and even though I wanted to go back to bed, I couldn't, and so I retrieved it from where it was charging on the nightstand and tried my best to avoid looking at emails and simply read the text message she had sent to me.

"We have to leave in about forty-five minutes, Sir," she said, "So that we won't be late."

I was more than aware of the schedule, but I didn't need that long to get ready. Still, I found myself shamefully excited to see her, and so I got up and headed over to the bathroom.

In there, I took my time with the warm shower and basked in the kind of ease I hadn't felt in years. Unfortunately, however, I couldn't help picturing her body as well... at least what I had seen of it that morning, and it was stimulating, to say the least. Glimpses of her that I had seen kept flashing through my mind throughout the day. Even when I was in the breakfast meeting, sometimes conversations would get too boring, and I would zone out, the fullness of her gorgeous breasts and her ass coming to mind. It had been such a while since I had noticed any particular woman. The last couple of years had been hell, but now I was coming up for air and couldn't help but recall just how insane my libido used to be.

Now it seemed as though it was back to life. Now, with these mere thoughts about her, I gazed down and saw that I was hardening. I wondered what to do about it. The sane thing was not to pay it any attention, but what was the point in restricting myself? What was the harm, since she would never know? And so, holding my girth length, I began to stroke myself until pleasure began to simmer through my veins. I felt heated all over, excited, especially as I thought about what it would feel like to suck on her breasts, to feel her ass bouncing on my cock as she rode me reverse, and my hands went even faster.

"I needed to fuck her."

This was all I could think of as I came closer and closer to the edge. It was inappropriate; it was something I would never do in my right senses, and I was out of control. However, I couldn't stop. So far, she had been so proper and professional, but I didn't want that anymore. I wanted to see the real her. I wanted to see just how wild she could be and how early she could scream my name as I made her come. I wanted the heat of her mouth around my cock, and I wanted her sucking so hard on the head that I blanked out.

"Fuck!" I cursed as cum spurted out of my dick. It splashed against the glass wall before me and stained my hands. The release was incredibly sweet, though brief, but I felt lighter, more in control. However, the fact that I had

just jerked off to her was alarming, to say the least, as I regained all my senses. I needed to be careful, or else I was going to get carried away. This was one of the wiles of vacation, but I decided that perhaps it was time to let loose. It was only ten days, and I could be a little bit unrestrained.

The problem, however, was that she was highly competent with her work and knowledgeable about the field, and I really didn't want to lose her and have to start all over again in finding someone who could understand all aspects of my business and me in order to coordinate things as wonderfully as she had so far.

Sighing, I got out of the shower and made my final decision.

Work was always more important. Being disciplined was always more important, and so from that moment on, I wouldn't push her into looking more feminine even though it was nearly impossible to keep my mind from recalling just how indescribably gorgeous and fuckable she had looked naked.

Chapter Six
Madison

As I stared at myself in the full-length mirror at the entrance to the room, it was almost hard to recognize me. Coupled with the hair, the makeup, and this gorgeous green satin dress that clung to my skin, I felt breathtaking. Since it was a business dinner, I had gone for decent, but of course, it was still a little bit sexy. The slit was much, much higher than I had remembered, going all the way to my upper thigh. And then the top...

It was sleeveless and had a turtleneck halter cut. Back at the boutique, I had seen it on the mannequin and instantly fell in love, but I hadn't had the time to try it on because he'd called me just then.

Now, however, I was slightly panicked. It fit perfectly, but it was tight. Every curve and dent of my body was accentuated, and then the chest area was bordering on lewd. Turns out, Asian sizes were a little bit different from Western sizes because they had for sure not made the top part for a woman with ridiculously huge breasts. My nipples were already hard from brushing constantly against the material. I filled it out so completely that even I was turned on, and I was going to a business meeting.

Instantly, I called Emma and went into my luggage still lying open on the ground to search for the biggest, most oversized suit jacket I could find. I grabbed it and moved it where I had positioned Emma, and before I could say a word, she gasped.

"Oh my fucking God!"

My heart dropped into my stomach. I was so screwed.

"It's too much, right?"

"If by too much you're asking if you're going to make every man that sets their eyes on you tonight so horny that they might commit a felony against you, then yes. Jesus. We told you to buy a dress to turn into... I don't even know."

"And the hair... it flows, girl, it flows. And the makeup. So light, so perfect. And that dress... your bloody breasts, Madison!"

"This is all your fault," I accused completely despaired as I began to pull on the jacket. "If only you hadn't called me this morning, my life wouldn't be about to run off the train tracks."

"Oh, come on, don't be dramatic," she said. "You don't see the opportunity in this?"

"How the hell could this possibly be an opportunity?" I nearly cried, as I began to pull the blazer all the way up. "I'm attending a business meeting."

"And you look exquisitely elegant," she said. "This, I am sure, was the most decent dress in that entire shop. Everything is covered due to your neck. The only allure here is that it fits you so perfectly well that you might as well not be covered. If the fabric was tan colored, you would literally look naked."

She laughed out loud, and I could only be even more upset.

"I'm going to get fired," I shook my head slowly as I turned around. "You know what, I'm going to offset the whorish vibe of the dress with some sensible loafers."

"You better not try it," she said. "How embarrassing. Didn't your boss tell you to dress this way in order to impress the clients?"

"Up until this morning, he didn't care that they existed so I don't think that's the case at all. If anything, they're the ones to impress him."

"Whatever," she said. "Just don't wear loafers. Wear heels. Sandals. You took some along, didn't you?"

"Just in case, I brought a black pair."

"Not the best, but it's what you have, and you'll be able to walk in it so go with those."

I quickly put them on as per her instruction but had no further time to chat.

"Okay, I have to go now," I said.

"Take off the jacket," she yelled, but I ended the call, grabbed my briefcase, and headed toward the connecting door. I pushed it open without thinking and just then saw him seated on the bed and on a phone call in nothing but a towel around his waist.

At first, I was confused because I couldn't understand what I was doing here and why I had come through this door. I wasn't thinking straight, but now that I was and at his annoyed look, I immediately retreated and apologized profusely. I slammed the door shut and locked it behind me.

Then I leaned against the surface and tried to catch my breath.

What was wrong with me today? It was as though I had lost all of my brain cells along the way. I literally couldn't think straight and avoid mistakes, and it was freaking driving me nuts.

I didn't know what to do now, so I headed over to the bed and took a seat dejectedly. About ten minutes later, there was a message on my phone.

"Where are you?"

Instantly, I jumped up, headed out through my own door this time around, and met him in the hallway waiting. I lost my breath.

He was in a tweed blazer with a crisp dress shirt and dark pants. They fit his muscular body in a way that couldn't be explained, and I found my nipples hardening even further at the sight.

His hair was a bit damp but slicked away from his face, and his blue eyes were so piercing and intense that my heart began to race.

Fuck, he looked good. He looked so good that all I could think about was blowing off this dinner and getting down on my knees to suck him off. I had imagined it several times in the past. Too many times, even, but I couldn't stop. I would do anything to suck his cock as long as it didn't involve losing my job, and then I would thank him for the opportunity afterward. That was how incredibly infatuated and impressed with him I was.

"Why the jacket?" he suddenly asked, and I immediately came back to my senses.

I looked down then but couldn't quite say the truth.

That the dress I was wearing was too revealing and that it covered me up.

"Um... it fit," I said. "Plus, I'm worried that I might get cold later on."

"No, you won't," he said. "It's the middle of summer. It's pretty warm."

I stared at him then and didn't know what to say.

"Take it off," he said, "and if you get cold, you can have my jacket."

With that, he turned around and continued heading down the hallway towards the elevator. I watched him walk away then but truly had to wonder why he was suddenly so interested in my appearance. Was this because we were in a different country? Did he care that I was more or less as stiff as he was, and he was just trying to get me to let my hair down like him? I couldn't understand. However, as always, he had given the order, and I had to obey. So, quickly so that I wouldn't keep him waiting, I reopened my door, tossed the jacket inside, and hurried over to join him in waiting for the elevator.

Chapter Seven
Hunter

She was breathtaking. Whatever I had imagined she would look like when dressed up, she blew all of my expectations out of the water and exceeded them. I couldn't quite believe this was the same person who had been wearing the dreariest and most oversized clothes since the day she had started working for me. In a way, I almost regretted insisting that she do this because after seeing her in this way, I didn't know how I would be able to revert to not noticing her as a woman. Thus far, she had simply been my secretary, but now... well, that had been blown to bits.

Still, I had ample control of myself, so I didn't gawk or stare, but it was difficult to not notice the curve of her body. She seemed like she worked out. Her arms and abdomen were so impressively toned, and I was even more astounded.

. . .

"Do you go to the gym regularly?" I asked as the elevator headed down towards the ground floor.

She turned to glance at me then but couldn't quite meet my gaze.

"Yes, Sir, I do," she replied. "A couple of times a week, and I try to run each morning."

I nodded, impressed, and couldn't believe she had hidden all that work behind dreary clothes. Well, it was paying off now in monumental ways because I couldn't keep my eyes off her ass. She was closer to the buttons than I was, so I could look at her and appreciate how the dress clung to her so much better. It was just so much more than I had expected, and my mind still didn't quite know how to process this. Tonight was going to be interesting, to say the least, and truly, I couldn't wait.

We met the Swedish businessmen and women about half an hour later when we finally arrived at the venue. It was an extremely traditional Japanese restaurant, which meant that we had a private room and had to sit on the floor. It was comfortable, though quite the experience for me, so I soon settled in, and she did the same by my side. It was incredibly hard not to notice the slide of her slit up her thighs, so deeply that for a second, I was sure I glimpsed her underwear.

I shook my head to control my mind and thoughts, but I couldn't help but notice the Swedish CEO's complete focus on her.

"Have you ever been to Thailand before, Miss...?" he asked. She was a bit startled he was speaking to her, so she couldn't help but glance at me. I didn't mind, so she responded.

"It's Miss Parish," she replied, and the man nodded in response.

"Lovely name. What's your first name, though?"

"Madison," she replied, and I grew impatient.

"We should get started," I said, and the man instantly came to his senses and sat properly as well as the others present in the room.

A Japanese attendant then came in with liquor and the food that had been selected and reserved ahead of time for both parties and calmly began to serve them. Realizing just how famished I was since I had skipped lunch, I dug into the meal immediately and managed to relax despite how serious the conversation topic was.

. . .

We talked extensively about technology deployments and their adaptation of our novel AI-driven software in increasing the efficiency and output of renewable energy systems. We talked about local partnerships with like-minded firms and the government, some of whom I had met at the welcome breakfast earlier in the day. All in all, our visions were aligned, and they seemed to be able to build the reach, so it was one to consider. I was so engrossed in all of this that it took me a while to realize that he was incessantly filling Madison's drink cup from across the table.

Wanting to be polite, she couldn't refuse and had to down it, but pretty soon it was hard not to notice that he was getting her drunk. Especially when she very vocally tried to reject him, and he refused. It was all under the guise of being friendly and hospitable, but pretty soon, I grew immensely irritated with him.

However, I didn't want to step in because I wanted to know more about his character, especially when it came to personal relations. So, I allowed him to do whatever he wanted to her until she was barely managing to stay upright. I couldn't help but turn to her then and feel pity. I was quite upset, though, because I didn't like how weak she appeared. I knew, though, that she was probably trying to endure for the sake of the company.

. . .

I understood and really appreciated the consideration, but the moment she came to, I was for sure going to give her a huge scolding. Nothing ever should come at the detriment to her well-being, especially in the midst of strangers and in a foreign country.

The liquor was potent and strong, even for me, and I knew how to hold mine on a normal day.

Suddenly, she got up to her knees, and it startled me. I wondered what she was doing until I realized that she was reaching for my cup. I had set it down earlier after picking it up because I had found that it was empty, and I didn't want to drink any more.

"I'll refill it for you, Sir," she said, her speech drowsy and her eyes constantly trying to close shut. She was fighting it and so unstable yet trying to do her job.

I said no, but she didn't hear me. Instead, she smiled and stared into my eyes, and something in my heart shifted. She looked like a little kid, yet with the gorgeous body of a woman that no one else could take their eyes away from. It made me wonder just how old she was. I had been so disinterested in her for so long, so unable to see her for so long that I didn't even know what her age was. This was disappointing, to say the least for me.

. . .

"No need," I repeated, but she was so clumsy that the tiny cup overturned and spilled across the table. It went downwards and almost began to pour onto my crotch, and she shifted even further. Without thinking, she grabbed the nearest cloth that she could find and began to dab it all over my crotch.

"I'm so sorry, I'm so sorry," she cried. "Sir!"

If we were alone, I would have allowed things to continue because one touch of her hands to that private area and I was immediately having a reaction. Perhaps the alcohol was not just bad for her, but for me as well.

Sighing, I grabbed onto her arm and settled her down beside me. The ride of her dress and how it revealed the black underwear she had on was impossible to miss. All I could hope was that the Swedish creep across the table, enjoying the show, couldn't see it. I wanted to fix it, but when I found that I couldn't, I decided it was time to go. I rose to my feet then, and as I did, it hit me that perhaps she had allowed herself to get so wasted because I was here, and she trusted that nothing untoward would happen to her. Whether this, or she didn't feel the strength of the liquor, which I was convinced was hard to do. It was fruity, but the second my tongue had tasted it and felt the burn down my throat, I knew it was not an ordinary drink. Too bad she wasn't able to detect this and had instead gotten carried away.

"Why would you be leaving now when we just got started?" all four of them instantly rose to their feet as well. The one literally trying to poison Madison continued, "We've just gotten the boring stuff out of the way, and now we're about to get to the great part."

"No," I replied. "As you can see, she's not able to control herself anymore, so I need to get her to bed."

At my words, the room seemed to suddenly go quiet, and I knew what the problem was. I knew what I had said and how it came off. And I didn't care. I just truly wanted to get her out of here before it was too late. With my hand around her waist, I allowed her to lean against my shoulder.

"Here, a bottle of water," one of the women offered. "She'll feel a bit better after this, and a good night's sleep will have her back to new."

"Hopefully," I replied because we had a lot of work to do. I started to head out of the room, but just as I had stepped out, the man came over to me. He shut the door behind me so that the others wouldn't hear what he had to say.

. . .

"Mr. Swift," he said, "I was just wondering if you have a personal relationship with your secretary here?"

I watched him, my temper rising, the desire to set Madison down somewhere so that I could have all the strength and focus in punching the living daylights out of him.

"No, I don't," I replied dryly, and I was only able to catch myself because despite his creepy ways, he was actually a prominent client whom, if I indeed collaborated with, could expand our business even further out of the west.

"I would like to pursue her, then," he said. "I hope this won't be a problem with you."

I stared at him, wondering if I had heard him correctly. At my darkening expression, he further clarified his sentence.

"I hope I'm not offending you; it's just that since you're not interested in her and I am, I would like a chance to pursue her. I would have liked to spend more time with her now, for instance, but you're sending her back to her room."

"You can't see that she's drunk?" I asked. "That doesn't mean anything to you?"

.   .   .

He laughed. "These drinks were really strong, weren't they? I didn't expect that she wouldn't be able to handle it."

"You kept feeding it to her," I replied.

He stopped, then, the smile dissipating from his face. However, I continued to push.

"Was your plan to get her drunk? And were you expecting me to abandon her as well so that you would have free access to do whatever you wanted to her while she was so drunk and incoherent?"

"She doesn't—she seems fine," he replied. "Drunk, definitely, but not incoherent."

I turned to glance at the woman by my side and noted that she had straightened and was staring at the man.

"He's right," she slurred. "I'm fine."

.   .   .

Smiling, she tried to pull away from me, and I rolled my eyes.

"She's not," I told the man. "I know what a normal state is for her, and this is not it. So, while she still might not be incoherent to you, she is to me, so I'll take her back to the hotel and to her bedroom to get some rest, and you can try your hand at propositioning her next time when she's actually awake, alert, and sober."

He glared at me, but I didn't care. I turned around then, but before I left, while holding her hand in mine, I had one more thing to say to him.

"Your character so far has not been particularly pleasing to me. If you know anything about me, then you'll know that the character of a business partner is equally, if not even more important than the product or service they're actually providing to me. I think you need to reconsider our collaboration because if this is the way you try to take advantage of people, then I will definitely not be interested in collaborating with you."

"Mr. Swift, please don't take things too far," he said. "Millions of people will benefit from our collaboration, and I was just asking you about your secretary and honestly putting forward my interest in pursuing her if you didn't have anything to do with her."

I wasn't going to remain here arguing semantics with him, so I simply ignored him and headed out to fetch our waiting car.

Chapter Eight
Madison

After drinking the bottle of water he offered me in the car, and rolling down the window so I could get some fresh air, I somewhat became sober. However, I still felt a bit dizzy and disoriented, but one thing that I could sense very clearly was his presence beside me.

"You feeling better?" he asked, since I went silent and did nothing but just stare out the window. However, my face burned with shame. I recalled everything clearly but still felt so weak that I wasn't sure I could handle myself right around him. The best thing for me to do now, I supposed, was to just be as I was until I was able to get to my bed.

I nodded, but then I turned to him with a smile.

"Cute evening, right?" I asked, and meant every word, though I couldn't exactly decipher why I had said. It made sense to me, though. He eagerly waited for a response.

"Cute?" he asked, and I nodded.

"Yes, cute. You."

He frowned, and I felt fear strike me.

"Oh, no. Did I offend you?"

He remained silent.

"Shit!" was all I could think, and the overwhelming rush of emotions barraged me. I couldn't help the tears that filled my eyes then as I stared at him. "I'm going to get fired, right?"

"What?" he asked.

"Because of all I've done. Today was messy, but I usually don't mess up, and it's your fault."

He was taken aback, and I hoped he could understand what I was saying. It made sense, what I was saying, but I couldn't quite grasp the words. My mouth was moving, and I was letting it, but why was I crying even harder? I felt so embarrassed because he was watching me with his perfect face, and I was turning into a mascara-streaked mess. So, I buried my face in my hands and let loose.

I tried to cry as quietly as I could, but I had no clue if I was able to achieve that. What I did know, though, was that at some point, as I sat up, I wiped my face. I grabbed the bottle for another sip of water, and then I stared out at the passing buildings and blinding lights.

We were quiet as we continued on the drive, and I tried to get my bearings right. I couldn't remember much, but what I did know was that I wanted him. Perhaps it was the cold night or the alcohol, but my nipples were so hard and sensitive. I tried my best to ignore it, but I couldn't. So, I looked down at them and with the pad of my thumb, decided to massage them. I hoped he wouldn't see, or maybe I hoped he would. I didn't know, and I didn't care. I just felt so fucking horny.

"What are you doing?" I heard his voice then.

I turned to him and replied, "It's too sensitive. It's been like this, alright."

He was silent again, and I didn't care, but there was something about completely rubbing them that became quite overwhelming. It felt good, and so, for a moment, I shut my eyes and lowered my head against the backrest. I wanted to stop. I knew that this was inappropriate, however, I couldn't. It felt too good.

I grabbed my breasts then, and I was sure that I moaned. I became even more restless, and my hands headed towards my dress to hike it up. My clit was so swollen, so needy, so sensitive. I needed to soothe it. I needed to fuck.

"Ahh," I breathed. However, before I could touch myself, a wrist circled around mine. I turned around then and was surprised to find him so close to me.

It was my boss! Hunter. Hunter Swift.

At first, I felt scared, but the concern in his face melted me so much that it made me smile. Maybe he cared for me. Maybe he wasn't that oblivious to my existence. I was sure now that all of this was a dream. So, I leaned forward and kissed him on the lips. It was soft. All I had wanted was a taste, but then I was struck. He tasted too good, so much better than what I had been thinking earlier. My eyes widened. I couldn't believe it. And so, I tried to kiss him again, but his hand flattened against my face and stopped me.

"We're almost back at the hotel," he said quietly as he leaned back against the chair. "Behave yourself."

"But..." I felt on the verge of tears. I shifted closer to him then. If I couldn't get him in real life, then I could get him now, right? I had to be able to do that. I couldn't be shy.

However, I was. I shifted, still, our bodies were melded together, and yet I couldn't make the first move. All I did was shake my head, but I could feel his gaze burning into the side of my face.

"What are you doing?" he asked, and I turned to look at him.

God, he was handsome! Beyond what I could describe. And those eyes of his.

I said then exactly what I had been thinking about from the first moment, but just in case someone else overheard and leaned forward and whispered into his ears.

"I want to suck you off."

I leaned away then, our faces barely an inch from each other. He watched me, and then he turned away.

"No thanks."

Emotions gathered in my heart again, and tears filled my eyes.

"It's all I've ever wanted."

"What?" he asked.

I stomped my foot, but I was so startled by it that I had to stop. What was happening?

"Madison," he called, and I turned once again to meet him. Our faces were so close. It was wonderful. And his lips, they were so soft... so sweet. I had tasted them before, right?

I was sure I had, though I couldn't quite remember. Would he tell me if I had? Could I ask? I was too shy, then I realized, so I turned away. But then an idea occurred to me. I could just kiss him again. If I did, I could confirm if this was true or not, and if he complained, I would just tell him I was trying to test a theory. Everyone was entitled to a test, right? Was it a test or taste? I couldn't figure it out.

"Madison," he called again.

"Is it test or taste? I asked.

"What?"

"Kissing someone. Is it a test or taste?"

He continued to stare at me, but then I couldn't wait; he was too slow, so I leaned once again and kissed him. This time it was longer, deeper. My tongue touched his; however, before I could glide against the velvety smoothness, he caught me by the arm.

"Stop," he said. "I'm begging you."

"Why are you begging me?" I asked, shocked. "You don't have to beg me, I'll do anything for you. Anything at all, all you have to do is ask."

I turned to him, but now he looked mortified.

"What do you need? Tell me," I asked.

He continued to watch me, and then he sighed. He seemed tired. Deadly exhausted, in fact.

"Was that it?" I asked. "Do you need to rest? Do you need a massage? I'll book one. She can come to the office."

I turned then and began to search for my purse and my phone; however, I couldn't find it.

"Madison, please stay still," I heard him call from behind me. "You're going to hurt yourself."

"I've almost found the phone," I said, but then he grabbed me once again and turned me to face him.

"Can you just please keep it together till we get back to the hotel?"

It took me a while to understand what he was saying,

but soon the word 'hotel' registered in my head like bright neon lights.

"Hotel? We're going to a hotel together?"

"Yes, yes, we are," he said, and my heart burst with joy and excitement.

"Really? So, we're going to—you know?"

"You know what?" he asked.

I turned then and finally noticed that the driver was in front. He couldn't hear what I wanted to say. It would be inappropriate. So, I leaned in then and whispered exactly what I thought into his ears.

"We're going to fuck, right?" I asked. "You're going to fuck me? I've imagined it for so long. I masturbate at least once a day to you. I've done it for months and you never looked at me. It's fine; I forgive you, but you have to fuck me hard, okay? I want to scream. I don't want to be disappointed."

At the thought, I felt emotional once again, and I couldn't help but sob. I buried my face in my hands and cried my heart out.

Chapter Nine
Hunter

I was speechless. Truly. I had no idea whatsoever about what to say or do. And most importantly, I couldn't believe that someone so completely lifeless when completely sober was this insane while drunk. I wasn't even sure she was drunk. One second she would seem coherent and then the next she wasn't. And what she had just said in my ear? She was going to drive me mad.

"You do know that when you get sober tomorrow and remember all this you're going to want to quit, right? You're either going to want to quit or you're going to want to shoot yourself in the head. Whichever it is, don't. Let's just blame it on the dress and since I was the one who told you to get it, let's just blame this entire night on me as well."

Sighing, I shook my head and waited, however she didn't respond. Instead, she remained in the position she was in until I became certain that she had fallen asleep, there was no question about it, and in many ways I was relieved. Eventually, her hands fell down to her sides, and then her neck began to droop. I watched her for a moment, recalled her complaint earlier about her neck, and guided her head down to my shoulder.

Soon, we arrived back at the hotel, and I considered just lifting her in my arms and carrying her in. If I told her to walk and given the heels she was wearing, she just might very well injure her ankle, and the last thing I needed was a limping secretary for the rest of my time here. This was supposed to be a vacation, but so far, it felt as though I was being punished for not noticing the real her all these months.

"We're here," I lightly tapped her shoulder. It took her a while, but eventually she came awake. She was groggy at first as expected, but I truly hoped that the little additional sleep she got would help her out.

"Where are we?" she asked.

"Back at the hotel," I replied.

"Okay," she replied, uninterested, and then she returned to resting on my shoulder.

I pushed the door open and then tried my best to get her out. She could walk somewhat fine, but I had to put my hand around her shoulders. Truly, I would have carried her, but I didn't need the extra stare and alarm that was sure to come with me carrying a woman into my hotel room. The authorities were bound to come knocking at my door trying to confirm if she was okay.

Soon, we were heading up to the last floor in the elevators, and I couldn't help but watch her. She was still leaning against me, but she seemed a little bit more awake now. And quiet. Incredibly quiet. Maybe too quiet?

"You okay?" I asked.

She turned then and stared at me, a little bit more

calmly, and then without responding, she looked away. I didn't let her go. As soon as we arrived back on our floor, I held her hand, and we went over to our suite together. I didn't bother opening her own door since she could just go in through mine, however when I tried to push the connecting door open, I soon found out that it was locked.

"You locked it from the inside?" I asked.

She didn't respond, and so I turned to see that she was watching me.

"I'll take you to the front," I said and grabbed her purse. However, this time around she didn't follow.

"Your key is somewhere within here, right?" I asked. "Do you use the same one as mine?"

She still didn't respond until I looked at her again to watch her.

"You need to cooperate with me here," I told her. "You need to get into bed so you can rest and sleep all this drowsiness away."

"I don't want to rest," she said, and I sighed. She truly was like a baby in her current state; however, I was in no mood whatsoever to baby anyone. I just wanted to get into the shower and go to bed.

"Why didn't you say anything about my dress?" she suddenly asked.

Her voice was clear now, and so were her eyes, but I was sure that she was still somewhat intoxicated, maybe a little less than she had been earlier.

"I don't know," I replied as I headed back to take my seat on the bed. "Was I supposed to say something about it?"

I took my jacket off as well as my shoes and was immensely relieved.

"Yes," she replied, and I looked at her.

I took in her figure then for the umpteenth time that night and realized that we were alone. Finally, we were alone. There wasn't anyone around, no Swedish asshole trying to take advantage of her...

I looked at the gorgeous dress, recalled how she had grabbed her breasts and nearly masturbated right in the car...

It immediately made me smile because I knew for sure when she remembered this the next day, she was going to want to jump off the building. It was a good thing we couldn't quite locate her key yet; perhaps it would be good for her to spend the night here so I could prevent any accidents from happening.

Although with how alluring and moody sexy she was looking right now, I couldn't help but hope that I would be able to keep my hands to myself. As I got up and headed over to stare out the window to consider this, I knew that I would because my working relationship with her was at stake, and that was more important to me than any momentary rush of pleasure.

"You're laughing," she said. "Am I... am I that ridiculous to you?"

At her words, I turned around then, wondering if she was still drunk.

"Aren't you clear-headed yet?" I asked.

She didn't respond. All she did was stare at me, and I really couldn't take this anymore.

"Please search for your key card in your purse so you

can go to your room. Your purse is over there by the entrance. And please take off your shoes; I don't want you spraining your ankle. You managed to make it up here with them, and that on its own is incredibly impressive."

I settled into the single chair beside me then and shut my eyes for a moment. I truly needed a drink and a cigar. This really was not the kind of vacation I had in hand, but perhaps this one would be more memorable than anything else.

"What's the schedule for my remaining time?" I asked. "After the speech I have to present at the conference tomorrow."

I looked up then and received the shock of my life because although she was still standing before me, she was completely naked. Well, she had stripped off her dress and now the silk fabric was puddled around her legs. She only had on her black lace underwear, and her breasts were completely exposed before me.

I was shocked to say the least, but I managed to keep a cool head.

"You're still drunk, aren't you?" I asked.

"No, I'm not," she replied, and I shook my head.

"Please go to bed. It's been a very long day and an even longer night. You're really going to regret this tomorrow."

"I'm not," she said. "I know you're going to fire me after today, so why not just do now what I've always wanted to do."

I watched her, so completely captivated that I had the eerie suspicion that I just might never be able to look away ever again.

"What exactly do you want to do then?" I asked.

"I want to be me," she replied. "I want to... I'm tired of dressing so badly all the time. That's not me."

I nodded in agreement, unable to keep my gaze from going down her body.

"I understand," I said. "And you're right. You don't have to dress that way. But I never told you to dress that way before. That was how I met you."

"They were the instructions given to me by HR," she replied.

I was taken aback. "What? Who? Derek?"

"Yes," she replied. "He almost didn't give me the job. He said that I had the qualifications and would gel well with you, and that I was what you needed, but that I was too attractive, and you hated those kinds of distractions. He said that every time you—"

She suddenly stopped then and shut her eyes.

"Hm," I replied. "Are you okay?"

"No," she grumbled, and I couldn't help my amusement.

"Stop laughing," she nearly began to cry once again. "This is humiliating."

"Please don't cry," I said. "We were talking now. What did Derek say about my past experiences? I mean, I know, but I just want to clarify."

She looked at me as though I had stabbed her, and I wondered once again what was going on through that head of hers.

"What is it?" I asked.

"You really..." she croaked. "You really don't care for me, do you?"

"What do you mean?" I asked.

"I'm standing before you naked right now, and you don't even care. Am I that unattractive?"

I stared at her and had to admit to myself that she was one of the most beautiful women I had ever met. I just hadn't realized it till now, and beauty like hers wasn't something I usually paid attention to. However, with her theatrics for the night so far, I couldn't help but notice. I noticed a lot of things about her. She was hilarious, intelligent, and so out of control when she was drunk that if it wouldn't hurt her, I wouldn't mind seeing this side of her more often. And a part of me felt kind of guilty now that I was settled enough to think things through because the fact of the matter was that I had allowed her to get this drunk. I could have stopped him from pouring her drinks way before it was too much, but I didn't. And I felt deeply apologetic about this. However, I didn't know how to fix this now.

I gave all of this a thought, and then I sat up.

"You know everything could go back to the way it was," I said. "All you have to do is put your clothes back on and go to your room."

At my words, I realized in an instant that I was going to regret this for the rest of my life. Her expression turned instantly vile.

"Don't tell me to go to my room!" she yelled, and I was startled. And then, I burst out laughing. God, she was fucking adorable. I leaned into the chair and truly hoped that I could record this because when I told her about it the next day, there was absolutely no way that she was going to believe anything that I was saying.

To my surprise, however, she started to head towards me. She wobbled and almost fell, but then she managed to catch herself and thankfully finally kicked off her shoes. She arrived before the chair and instantly sank down to her knees.

"What are you doing?" I asked as she grabbed my belt.

"You know what? I'm young," she said. "I'm not going to wait anymore, and I don't care if you fire me."

"Trust me, you'll care tomorrow, Madison," I said. "And if you don't stop right now, I will truly fire you."

"I don't care," she said, and then my zipper was pulled down.

I grabbed her wrist; however, she refused to budge. Eventually, and as I watched her, I let go. What came across my mind was what she had said earlier to her friend about me completely sober. How attracted she was to me. Without her getting drunk like this, none of this would have happened. I stared at her gorgeous face and breasts, and all I could think of was grabbing them just the way she had and sucking on her nipples.

In little time, she had pulled my zipper down, and I was surprised at how surprisingly gentle she was with me. Her hand wrapped around my cock, and I wondered if she would remember this the next day. If she did, well, it was sure to change the entire trajectory of our relationship.

However, as she smiled at the sight and then leaned forward to cover the head with her mouth, I decided that I didn't care. She was drunk. I should have forced her to stop, but this was happening, and I couldn't muster the will to stop it. And so, my head fell back at the sweet warmth and heat.

I loved how she sucked me. She licked up and down my rock-hard shaft as she fisted me, and the wet feel of her tongue along the satiny smoothness was so fucking good. I wanted her to go faster, but I couldn't force her, so I savored every second as she took me in. I loved how she took me deep in her throat, going all the way down till she couldn't anymore.

Sucking the precum off the head and licking her tongue across it was a complete mind trip, and by the time she established a rhythm with her hands and mouth, I was just as inebriated as she was.

I loved her moans. She sounded like she was doing this for herself more than anyone else, as though she was finally living out a dream. She smiled and licked and slobbered on my cock, and I couldn't believe how reactive I was to this, how much I was enjoying it. Unable to control my breathing, I pushed her hair out of her face to watch her, and she began to jack me even faster. Her hands pumped up and down as she sucked on my head, and in mere moments, I was on the verge of coming. I tried to pull away, though, but she wouldn't let go until it was too late. A loud satisfying moan came out of me as I shot my load into her mouth. She didn't pull away, refusing to let a single drop go to waste.

I watched her lick me completely clean, and then she straddled me. She still had her underwear on, but my cock settled between her thighs, and I could feel the warmth and heat from her sex. I stared at her as she grabbed onto my shoulders, and then she began to rock against me, seeking her relief. I enjoyed every bit of this, but I knew that we couldn't go further than this. However, if she remembered this at all, I wanted to give her something pleasant to recall. And so, I grabbed her chin and kissed her.

The kiss was deep, intimate. I could taste myself on her,

and the filthiness of it caused pleasure to begin simmering once again through my blood.

I loved the way she kissed, I realized. She was intentional about it, willful, intense, and I couldn't get enough. I couldn't help but think about grabbing her completely naked, and now that I was seeing it, it was hard to take in, but it all felt so good. I hadn't felt like this in so many years, and so I didn't want to restrict it, but I couldn't get carried away.

Still, considering how she had grabbed herself earlier in the car and rubbed her nipples, I wanted to do the same. So, I leaned forward and took a nipple in my mouth, licking across the gorgeous pink bud, then moved to the other, taking my time in sucking each as well as the swells all around. I loved the way she tasted. I couldn't get enough, and of the way she couldn't control her breathing. She was panting and moaning and writhing, and I just couldn't keep things under control for too long. I decided then, however, that there was one more parting gift that I wanted her to remember the next day. And so, I rose, and she clung onto me instantly like a monkey. She hooked her legs around my waist, and I carefully carried her over to the bed.

"You're going to fuck me?" she asked, doe eyed. It made me feel the kind of affection for her that was terrifying, but sweet warmth filled my chest for her. I really liked her, more than I had thought was possible when I had gotten up that morning. But now, as I slid her flat and got on my knees before her, I realized that I did like her, beyond this and beyond today. I had severe issues with secretaries being unable to perform like I needed them to in the past, but she didn't seem to have any problems whatsoever with this.

She had been efficient, professional, and I had come to depend on her and even trust her more than I did any other executive or employee in the office. For someone who had learned how to be constantly vigilant and alert, this had been a huge weight over my shoulders. And so, I wasn't surprised that the moment she had changed her appearance today and revealed the vixen she was underneath, albeit currently a drunk one, I had latched on like a moth to her flame.

Right now, all I could think about was eating her out. I didn't know what the future held, especially these ten days, and we had now reached the point of no return. I didn't know if we would ever be able to work together the same after this, but since we were at this point now, I didn't want it to be uncomfortable. I couldn't fuck her, even though it was what I wanted, and I didn't believe she was conscious enough to consent to that, even though it was all she had practically talked about and pleaded for all evening.

But I could make her come the way she deserved, the way she had been wanting all evening long. And so, I spread her legs apart, and I loved the way she writhed across the bed. She kept calling out my name, like a wish, and moaning, and I loved the sounds. They would stay with me for a while, I was sure, but nothing quite compared to the sight of finally pulling down her panties and seeing just how soaked she was.

"Focus, Madison," I said as I slid my thumb through her damp, pulsating sex.

"Is it the alcohol that did this, or are you usually this way for me, even in the office?" I leaned forward then and gave her a good lick, and the sound of her moan reverberated through the room.

"Oh, fuck, Hunter," she pleaded.

"Answer me," I said as my mouth closed around her clit. "Answer me if you want more."

"Yes, yes!" she cried out, unable to stop writhing and thrusting her hips towards my lips. I licked her again, savoring her taste and opening her up with the pad of my tongue.

"Be specific with your answer," I said as I appreciated just how pretty, domed, and greedy her sex was. "Do you usually get this wet when you're with me in the office? Have you been like this when I was working?"

"Yes," she breathed, "all the time."

"Guess I truly haven't been paying much attention then," I said as I slid a finger into her. She clenched hungrily around my finger, and I couldn't help my smile. Another finger soon joined in the sweet assault, and I watched as she slid her fingers through her hair and gripped the roots.

I started slow, enjoying watching her just as she had enjoyed sucking my dick earlier, but then I aimed to drive her crazy. So, reaching forward, I settled over her and sucked on her breasts while I increased my pace. I thrust so quickly into her that she cried out, and then I grabbed her sex to give her some relief.

I loved seeing her torso tremble in response, and when she reached out for yet another kiss, I couldn't resist. I drowned myself in her taste and continued to rub the sweet knob of her clit. All I wanted now was to be inside of her.

I could feel just how tight she was, how turned on. She couldn't stay still or lessen her tone, and I just knew that fucking her would be the wildest of rides. However, I had to control myself till tomorrow. Or until another chance arose. Till she was completely sober and could clearly decide if she wanted to continue with me. If she wanted to go all the way.

I broke the kiss then, as she gasped, and I kissed down her body, tasting every bit of her skin that I could reach. Soon, I returned to her sex and once again covered it with my mouth.

Her hand found its way to my hair, and the sting of her brutal pull of the roots spurred me on.

I didn't let up until she was coming into my mouth. Her thighs clenched against my sides, and her legs curled around my back as she trembled and moaned.

It was the sweetest sound.

Soft yet tortured... endless... breathless... gratifying.

Afterwards, I got up and collapsed by her side. I laid flat on the bed and tried to catch my breath. For a moment, I wondered if I was drunk as well because I felt like I was. I shut my eyes; however, before I could drift off to sleep, she turned and draped her legs on my body. I couldn't help but go completely still, especially as she buried her face in the crook of my neck and kissed above my pulse.

"Thank you," she said and fell asleep.

This time around, and thankfully, she didn't wake up.

Chapter Ten
Madison

I woke up completely naked.

This was unusual for me because I would never go to sleep naked. When it was too hot and I didn't want to run the air conditioner, I would take my tank or t-shirt off but never my underwear. Little else made me feel as vulnerable.

"Ow..." My hand went to my forehead as it occurred to me that there was more that was unusual. I had a splitting headache and all sorts of strange funky tastes in my mouth. What the hell had happened? I opened my eyes, and the sunlight nearly killed me. Instead, I turned away from the window and was at least consoled that I was underneath warm, white, and very clean sheets. I tried to comprehend all that had happened and where I currently was and why I felt like death. Only a few minutes passed before my eyes flew open.

A few images flashed through my head, but they didn't make sense. I had given someone a blowjob. That was impossible. But as I allowed my mind to continue its patchy attempt at recollection, the strange taste in my mouth began to make some sort of sense. I sat up then, as my heart began to thump in my chest.

"Ow," I complained again at the throbbing pain. However, before I could even say anything else, the alarm went off.

"Fuck!" I cursed. I tried to search for my phone; however, it was nowhere close. It wasn't in the sheets; it wasn't on the nightstand. I pushed my hair out of my eyes and looked around the room.

I knew where I was. I was in Thailand with my boss, Mr. Swift. We'd had the dinner thing in the Japanese restaurant.

I'd worn the dress. It had been an amazing dress, and so I should feel confident... I should feel good right now, but I felt like absolute shit. Absolute shit that my ringing alarm was soon going to send me into an asylum.

I scrambled to my feet then, dragging the much too heavy blanket with me as I had the good sense at least to search for my purse. It didn't take long because on the shelf right in front of the TV, there it was.

I rummaged through it, found the lit-up phone, but couldn't for the life of me remember my password. I tried face recognition one more time, failed it, and then tried to think. However, as I did, more images from the previous night came to mind. I stopped dead in my tracks.

Unfortunately for my phone, however, it fell from my hands and landed on the floor. It was carpet, so I wasn't worried. And even if it wasn't, and the overpriced iPhone had shattered into a thousand pieces, I wouldn't have given a damn because what I had just recalled was mortifying. In fact, it was so mortifying that I was sure it wasn't real. It couldn't be.

Right?

How could it be that I had... said the most obscene things to Hunter? I couldn't even think them out loud when I had been in my right mind, but now... It replayed as clear as day, a brief moment in time and then it was interrupted by the phone ringing once again.

I picked it up to check the time, and it was just as I had set it for 7:30 a.m. All the reminders for the day were already waiting as well, and at the top of it and most important was the conference starting at 10 a.m. There was also breakfast which was at 8 a.m. and –

Holy freaking shit, I had a breakfast meeting with my boss in thirty minutes. The breakfast buffet the hotel offered ended at 9:30 a.m., and so we had decided to meet there ahead of time to get some food in and head over to the venue for the conference and his speech.

Once again, I threw the phone aside and hurried over to the bathroom; however, I was so fuzzy and unstable that I staggered and nearly fell. The wall saved me, however what I couldn't understand in that moment was why I was rushing when I had set my alarm for that time.

It took a great deal of suffering to recall, but I had to because it seemed as though I was losing my mind. Soon enough, the answer came. I always showered the night before so that when morning came, I was practically ready to just jump out of bed and go. I didn't wear makeup... didn't take particular care with my hair and outfit. It was always the same boring dreary suits to discourage his interest, I wore every day, with sometimes just a change in the dinner wear. No one noticed anyway, especially not him, so I'd never needed to try.

"You still don't need to try now, you moron," I muttered under my breath, but even my jaw ached. The image of literally sucking someone's dick came to mind once again, and I was so terrified. Whose was it - it couldn't be... it couldn't be my boss, could it?

"Why the hell had I drunk so much?" I lamented as I finally made it to the bathroom.

It was a mess, and it drove me wild since I couldn't stand bathrooms and kitchens being a mess. Every other place was ignorable, but not these two. In my hurry and desperation to get ready and look as beautiful as was possible the previous day, I had spent at least more than an hour on my makeup. It still looked minimal and effortless, at least that was what I had hoped, and apparently it had worked since I had ended up on my knees sucking someone off.

I couldn't believe it. I wanted to call Emma so that she could assure me that it was a bad dream, but I had woken up naked. I still didn't want to know the explanation for that, but I was sure that sooner or later, it would come to me.

I started brushing my teeth but couldn't quite look at myself in the mirror. Only after I was done did I look to see the state of my hair. When I, however, saw the mess my eye makeup was, I nearly fainted once again. My mascara and eyeliner were smudged all over the place, lipstick stained my chin, and my lips slightly swollen. I looked like a crack whore. What exactly had happened the previous night? I had a feeling that my boss was completely aware since I had made it to my bed at least. Perhaps he had helped me take my clothes off? I nearly screamed. Everything inside of me did shrivel up, however.

"That couldn't be the case," I shook my head as I headed over to the shower stall. *"That was impossible. He would never do that."*

After adjusting the temperature, I turned the water on and tried to wash away all of my bad decisions from the previous night. From wearing my dress and letting that Swedish asshole get me drunk. But more importantly, I was angry with Hunter for letting him. He was too smart not to have noticed what he was doing, and now I couldn't help feeling betrayed.

I also couldn't help the stark realization that I had remembered all of these. This was new information, and so I felt relieved that the memory coming in fragments wasn't at least gone forever. Okay, I do remember this part. The Swedish asshole had gotten me drunk, and Mr. Swift had allowed it. Ass. The ass I needed to meet now in twenty minutes or else I was fired. Given all that I was slowly recalling from the previous night, however, I wasn't sure I would be surprised if I was fired. Ten minutes later, I was truly out of time. I was his secretary, and something like tardiness he couldn't contain, so I turned the last ten minutes into a game show and got dressed at the speed of light.

I was a mess. I felt a mess. I didn't even have the time to do my hair. It was the first freaking day of the conference. I couldn't believe it. Perhaps I could wet it and run my fingers through it. We still had till ten a.m. However, with him, I couldn't quite really leave his side. I had to be on top of things and think of these trivial matters on his behalf.

I had no choice, no other way, so I grabbed my shoes, sprinted down the hallway, and put them on in the elevator. Neurotic, I almost crashed into some people who were nice enough to understand. I was almost taken aback. The elevator doors binged open, and I headed out toward the breakfast area.

I prayed he wouldn't be there so I would be able to look human. However, when I got in, I quickly looked for the farthest corner with a view and found him already raising a cup of coffee to his lips.

He... looked wonderful.

I looked like a train wreck, most certainly, but not him. He looked rested and invigorated with not even a single hair out of place, and I couldn't understand it. How was this the case? Hadn't we got out together the previous night?"

He lifted his hand then to check his watch, and my heart jumped. I was at least three minutes late; that wasn't small by any means. He would notice; he would complain, and I would feel even worse. But I had no choice but to walk forward.

"Good morning, Sir," I greeted.

I gave him a brief smile, pushed my hair out of my face, set my briefcase on the floor beside me, and then mustered up the courage to look him in the eye.

He seemed casual enough, and to my surprise, he didn't mention the fact that I was late. It wasn't as though he had the very few times I had been in the past, but he had never failed to make me understand that he was deeply displeased. I had put close attention into reading him and understanding him, so it wasn't strange to me that I could very clearly interpret his mood.

"You should get some food," he said.

"Yeah... right," I replied. However, eating was the last thing I wanted. Instead, I was so freaking thirsty. I rose to my feet then and headed over to the breakfast bar.

Chapter Eleven
Hunter

I had looked up recommendations for what she could eat to take care of her hangover. Congee had been recommended, a mild porridge, as well as ginger soup. And of course, eggs. Toast was mentioned as well, but I didn't know which to tell her to go for. For beverages, coconut water was recommended as well as orange juice. I turned and watched her by the dispenser as she drank cup after cup of water. I had never seen her so... disheveled.

There was no makeup on her face, her hair had definitely only lightly seen a brush, but her clothes, though, were prim and proper. They were also a complete and total reversion to whom she had been before the previous night, and upon seeing her again this morning, I truly couldn't decide which version of her I preferred. Did I want who she was the previous night? Who we were together, or was it time to revert? Did she even remember?

I had woken up long after midnight with her body still draped over mine. I was so damn exhausted that the reasonable thing was to fall right into bed, but if she had woken up in my arms, perhaps things would be even more awkward and complicated than they currently are. I'd taken her to her room, and seeing her wrapped underneath those covers, so warm... so beautiful, I'd wanted to be beside her. Even now... I wanted to ask how she was doing. I had hangover medicine; I'd contacted Mr. Kit to get it for me before the sun had even risen, but I didn't know how to hand it to her without outrightly shifting the dynamics of our relationship.

Sighing, I lowered my head and started on the fruit salad I had previously rejected. She came over then with water and sat down.

"I'm ready to leave whenever you are, Sir," she said, and I lifted my gaze to hers. She reached into her briefcase, and I watched as she retrieved a hair tie and tied her hair away from her face.

"You need to eat something."

Her movement stopped, and then she looked at me. The ghost of a smile curved her lips, and then she looked away again.

"I can't hold anything down. I, uh... I went past my alcohol limit last night." I returned my attention to my fruit salad.

"They have congee here," I said. "Rice porridge. It's bland... it's suiting. It'll help you get through the day." She watched me, and then she nodded slowly.

She got up again and returned a few minutes later with the steaming bowl. When she set it down, however, I sighed.

"That's too bland; you might not be able to eat it. You should have added some meat or sauce. They have chili oil."

"I can," she said. "I'm fine... I can go through today,

but... I literally cannot handle salt right now. I'm just going to try this because you recommended it."

I couldn't hold back anymore. I reached into the pocket of my jacket and retrieved the bottle.

"Take some of this. Your head must be killing you."

"It is, Sir," she replied. She stared at the bottle, and then looked at me again.

"Don't worry; I've done the research. It's safe for you to use."

She smiled. "That wasn't what I was concerned about. I- "

She shook her head, refusing to continue, and I decided to leave things the way they were.

"What's our schedule for today?" I asked when I saw that she was barely eating her meal. She would taste it, pull away, and then she would try again. It was a torturous, endless cycle.

"Well, um..." She tucked her hair behind her ears. I didn't miss the slight tremble of her hands.

"Conference at ten. We'll be heading there after break-fast. Networking lunch afterward in the same venue, and we left the evening free in case any new appointments came up from the networking lunch. There's also the option of going out for a traditional Thai theater performance later on tonight. I've arranged for Kit to be available to drive you there. I've already secured the tickets in advance so I can come along as well if you wish."

I listened to her words, and then I nodded.

"Do you like watching theater performances?" I asked. She seemed a bit startled by the question, but soon enough responded.

"Not exactly, Sir," she said. "But I'd love to see it, so I'd be more than willing to come along so that I can assist you as well. Plus, this is Thailand, and I'm pretty sure it's going to be a very unique and enjoyable experience for you."

I watched her until eventually she pushed the bowl aside and picked up the medicine instead. She looked behind to read the instructions, and then she opened the bottle herself.

There was nothing else to say, at least for now, but I couldn't stop talking to her. For all I knew, there would be close to literal alternative chances to do this for the rest of the day, so I couldn't help but want to take advantage of this short but quiet time we had together. If more time passed, perhaps we would both altogether forget that last night had even happened.

My heart clenched with worry even at the mere thought. I didn't want her to forget. I also didn't want to forget either, but with the way she currently was with me, it felt as though her entire body had been turned into ice.

She was so distant... so unreadable. Maybe she truly wasn't feeling well and needed the rest.

"Why don't you take today off?" I asked her, "You might not be able to handle today if you keep feeling like this."

At this, any sign of weakness immediately left her face as she stared at me.

"You sent me away yesterday as well, Sir," she replied. Her words didn't shock, and her gaze filled with concern.

I wondered briefly until I replaced all that I had said to her the previous day.

"I'm not going to fire you," I told her. However, she picked up her spoon again, completely distracted, and obviously forgetting to realize that she had already set it down and rejected the food.

"You need the rest today."

"And yesterday?" she asked. She faltered. "I am-"

She stopped, and I knew what she had wanted to complete the statement with.

"You got drunk working," I said. "You didn't just decide to suddenly go out drinking and then return late this way. I know how efficient you are and how seriously you take your job, so don't worry. Take the rest you need, and I'll handle the conference today."

"Can I say no, Sir?" she asked. I was a bit startled to hear this because what employee in the world ever rejects a few days off?

"We're flying to Phuket tomorrow, right?" I asked, but she shook her head.

"No, Sir, the conference continues tomorrow." she replied. "You have another keynote to give tomorrow, and then the rest of the day is free. There is a jazz performance though late in the night. It is at a bar not far from the hotel. It's a really famous place, so I included a note to it in case you were down for attending after dinner."

"So when are we flying to Phuket then?" I asked.

"The day after tomorrow. You have the entire day free, and the next as well before we have to return for the conference."

"Hm," I replied. "Alright. Sure you don't want to eat something else before we leave?" I asked. "You won't get access to food again before lunchtime."

She lifted her gaze once again and watched me.

Chapter Twelve
Madison

Things were just too uncertain... too strange. We were talking, but we were saying nothing. I needed answers, but I wasn't getting any. I needed food, but I couldn't eat. Perhaps I really should take his offer of a break because I didn't think I was going to survive the day. But I couldn't be useless two days in a row. I had prepared for this conference to assist him. If I was going to be this incompetent, then he would have brought another staff along, but he had trusted me. Sighing, I shook my head and instead opened the bottle of medicine and drank from it as directed. It was absolutely the worst, but I managed to bear the acrid taste because it was my only hope now. Before we left, however, there was one question I wanted to ask him.

"Sir?" I asked as he pushed his bowl aside and picked his phone off the table.

"Yes?" he replied.

"Last night..."

I watched him go still.

"Last night, the Swedish investor-"

"Yeah?"

"He was - I'm sure he was deliberately trying to intoxicate me. He kept forcing me to drink. Why didn't you stop him?"

I met his eyes then, however, my confidence soon faltered.

"I mean, it's not your job to protect me or anything; it's just-"

"No," he replied, and I was surprised.

"What?"

"It is my job to protect you, and I was sure that I was going to."

Fear instantaneously struck my heart as I couldn't quite decipher exactly what he was saying. So, he hadn't protected me? Did that mean-?

"I wanted to see how you'd be when you weren't completely in control," he replied. "Yesterday was quite interesting, and I... I was curious about the other side of you. The other side that wasn't so prim and proper all the time. I didn't know, though, that he was doing that because he was interested in you. I just thought he was nervous and being overly hospitable."

I shut my eyes then as my arms around his shoulder came to mind at the recollection of his shoulder. I was a bit unstable, but he had more or less told the man to fuck off. And then he had taken me down to the elevators and back to his room. I recalled him stripping off his pants, sitting on the bed, and then sucking him off... that had happened on the chair by the window.

"There was a disconnect."

"I need to know the rest of what happened," I said. I trusted that it would come, but I was becoming restless. I truly needed to know now, or I was going to lose my mind.

"I, uh- I hope I didn't do anything too inappropriate last night. For?" I asked. "If I did, I truly apologize. It wasn't my true intention."

He stared at me, and then he rose to his feet without a further word. I grabbed my briefcase then and hurried after him.

In the car, I stared out the window at the beautiful but unfamiliar city as we drove past. The conference center was about twenty minutes away, so it would take a while for us to get there, and I couldn't stand the silence. So, I pulled out my phone and texted Emma.

My prayer was that she would be awake so that she could keep me company. I really needed it right now... something familiar to ground me to reality, and she was it. So, I sent the message.

"Hey!"

A whole five minutes passed before she replied, and I was so upset that I almost didn't reply to her.

"What's up? Was your night as magical as I expected?"

"I woke up hungover and naked," I wrote back.

"Wait, what?" she replied. "Is that in a bad way or a good way?"

I glanced at the man beside me. "I'm not sure, either."

"Oh my God," she said. "I mean, I was going to tell you not to miss the chance and to take this whole holiday you two are on to make him notice you, but it seems you're doing a whole lot better than I had expected."

I instantly frowned.

"I'm not trying to get him to notice me, what the hell are you saying?"

"Why aren't you trying to get him to notice you?" she asked. "After all, you tried so hard for six months to ensure he didn't notice you. And now that that's changing, why wouldn't you take the chance to be bold?"

"No!" I nearly yelled. "I'm not doing this right now. I fucking woke up naked and hungover. My life has started going downhill since I spoke to you yesterday."

"So it's my fault?" she teased.

"Yes!" I nearly yelled back.

She sent a few laughing emojis. "What do you remember though? Do you know if he was the one that stripped off your clothes and tucked you in? That would be so wonderful if he was the one that did, but a little creepy. Why did he have to take your clothes off?"

At her question, I thought even further about what had happened, and just then it all came back to me. How I had completely embarrassed myself in the car... in this very car, trying to get him to fuck me. How I hadn't relented even when I had returned to the hotel, and finally, whose dick I had ended up sucking at the end of the day.

But it hadn't ended there. I felt sensitive when I touched myself. In the shower. I knew something happened but not quite; however, now it hit me like a ton of bricks. He had eaten me out.

"Holy fucking shit!" I cursed out loud.

At first, I didn't care that he was right beside me. I didn't even realize it, not until I met Mr. Kit's widened and shocked gaze in the rearview mirror. Instantly, I realized where I was and who was beside me and turned to look at him, completely apologetic.

"I'm so sorry, Sir, I just-"

I couldn't even complete the statement as I stared at him. He had –

I remembered every word, and I didn't know how to feel. And best of all, I remembered just how hard I had come. How I had screamed and held onto him. And how I had thanked him afterward.

He turned away without a word, and I couldn't believe it. How could he - after yesterday - how could he not say anything at all? How could he just return to business as usual? How could we just return to work as usual and not even acknowledge that we had crossed every professional line down to man the previous night? In fact, the line didn't even exist anymore. What the hell was happening?

I stole another glance at him and saw that he was scrolling through his phone, a slight frown on his face. Now, I truly wanted to escape. I needed to process this. I couldn't handle the demand of the event we were heading to and have this on my mind as well.

I picked up my phone once again and texted Emma.

"He ate me out. Last night - he ate me out."

This time around, when she took time in replying, I understood that it was due to shock.

"You're joking, right?" she asked.

"No, I'm not. I just recalled it all now, every single excruciating minute and second of last night. I was completely loose. I completely lost my mind. I all but forced him onto me, Emma. I begged and cried and forced him."

"And he gave in?"

"He said he was reciprocating the favor for me... going down on him, and so he ate me out, but he didn't go any further. He said I wasn't sober enough."

"That's good, right?" she asked.

"I don't fucking know. This had been my dream for so long, and now that it happened, it has taken me several hours to process, and now I truly don't know how to feel about it."

"Has he said a word?" she asked, and I replied.

"No. Isn't that weird?"

"It is weird," she replied. "Maybe he wants to forget as well?"

"Why the hell would he want to forget? It was amazing!"

"For him, it might not have been," she said, and all sorts of thoughts barraged through my head. My confidence plummeted, as well as my peace, and I only had one response for her.

"You're an asshole."

Chapter Thirteen
Hunter

She was so unstable; it was truly beginning to worry me. Had she recovered? Had she not? Did she remember everything? How did she want things to proceed from now on between us? How did I want things to proceed from now on between us? Perhaps I was over-thinking it? Perhaps I wasn't?

I turned to her, and she continued to stare ahead as though she had just seen a ghost. I could have asked her. I wanted to ask her if she had remembered, how she felt about it. However, I couldn't bring myself to, so I ignored talking to her and looked away. One thing was for sure, and it was that last night everything had shifted between us. I couldn't look at her anymore and feel nothing. I couldn't look at her anymore and feel the same. I wanted her.

Just the reminder of what it had felt like the previous day to have my cock in her mouth hit me every minute, how she had sucked me off with such enjoyment, how she had looked doing it, and afterward, and how I wanted... us to go all the way. I wanted to taste her, I needed more, but I couldn't decide if more was the right way to go.

Soon we arrived at the conference, and I was shown to my seat amidst the other speakers. I lost her along the way, but there was a table for the staff if the speaker so hoped, so she was able to settle herself. She handed me my materials and gave them a look through. I had already found the time to do that this morning when I had spoken up a bit earlier, so plus, the topic was something I was ordinarily deeply immersed in on my day-to-day basis, so there was nothing truly to think about.

Soon enough, I was called on stage, and I began speaking. What I found, however, was while my mouth moved and I said what I knew, all I could do was search with my eyes for her. I wanted to be discreet about it just in case she was watching me. However, and when I truly couldn't spot her, I slowed down, worried. Had she gone to the bathroom to throw up?

Just then, however, I finally looked behind at a round table in the corner, and then our eyes met. There were over three hundred people in the room, and I hadn't even been able to spot her because I had been looking for a woman with crazy, down hair.

Now, however, she was back to the way she usually was. It was as though she had taken the time to go to the bathroom and put herself in order. Now, her hair was slecked back as it always was, without a single strand out of place, and she was back to the Madison I knew.

I couldn't help but feel a little sad at this because I wondered if she would ever come back. I wondered if the girl that had sobbed into my neck the previous night and begged for me to fuck her would ever come back.

Temporarily, and as a result of stray thoughts, I forgot my words and had to pause for a little bit. I picked up the glass of water before me, took a sip, and then glanced back at the slide behind me so that I could continue.

Chapter Fourteen
Madison

"Is he single?"

I was startled at the slight prod by the woman seated before me. She was so gorgeous I couldn't look away, with bangs that didn't seem to move and the most perfectly shaped lips I had ever seen.

"What do you mean?" I asked.

"He's your boss, right?" she asked, smiling, "I saw you come in with him earlier."

"Um... yeah, yes, he is," I replied as I glanced at the stage once again. He was indeed mesmerizing to watch; the way he spoke, the way he was measured and intentional with it made me so mesmerized by who he was.

Seeing him up here, captivating the entire audience with every word that came out of his mouth, made me understand why I was so head over heels for him. It had been this way from the very moment I had met him, and last night had all but solidified my desire for exactly what I wanted with him.

The woman prodded me once again. "Is he single?" she asked.

I stared into her eyes and replied, "No, he's not. He has a girlfriend. Their relationship is incredibly serious."

"Oh really? How long have they been dating?" she asked. "You're sure about this?"

"Over three years," I replied, even more confidently. "They'll be getting engaged soon. He's already discussed engagement rings with me. I mean, jewelers."

She gave me a peculiar look, and I didn't need to interpret it to know that I had just messed up. Not only had I just lied about my boss, but I had basically exposed his secrets and thrown him to the wolves, so of course she would think I was crazy. Who would release that kind of information about their boss? I panicked even further when she leaned over to the woman next to her and whispered into her ear.

I sighed because once again, I had done something that clearly indicated that I was risking my job. There was no other explanation for my behavior and attitude.

I returned my attention to him, but just then Emma sent a message once again.

"Hey, how's it going?" she asked. "Has he said anything about last night yet?"

Needing the distraction, I replied immediately.

"No," I replied. "He's up on stage giving his keynote speech, looking gorgeous as always, while I have just lied to someone behind me and said that he has been in a relationship for three years and now he's about to get married, so basically, she needs to back off."

"Is that true?" she shrieked.

"Of course not. I've never even seen him with a woman in that sense in the six months I've worked with him. He's obsessed with his work. It's all he ever does."

"No wonder he's attracting suitors as he talks on stage," she said.

"Yeah," I agreed. "All eyes are on him while he just looks like he's quite uninterested in being there. It's a little bit funny because he doesn't like crowds at all. I bet he cannot wait to get back to the hotel."

"I, on the other hand, sure can. Maybe it's best I try to avoid him as much as possible until things calm the hell down between us".

"I said it before, and I'll say it again," she said. "I don't think you should avoid him at all. It's already too late. You guys have gone intimate. Maybe not all the way yet, but it's only a matter of time. So why try to shy away from it? He will never just be your boss anymore; he will also be the man you've been intimate with, who you quite possibly are in love with, although you'll never admit it."

I truly didn't know what to say. She was right. I guess the sooner I accepted it, the better. It was either things went uphill from here onwards or downhill. It would never be the same.

I watched him for a little while longer and thought about her words from earlier that morning.

She was right. If I could spend six whole months dressing so nerdishly so that he wouldn't notice me, why then couldn't I do the same in the opposite direction? Why couldn't I get him to notice me? I adored him, and he seemed to be attracted to me, or rather, he was immensely attracted to me, at least enough to give in last night, so why was I so scared?

From his last story rampant around the office about how his previous female secretaries came onto him and how he threw them out like trash. He hadn't thrown me out so far, and I... I wanted the assurance from him about why.

I put on a sly grin then and replied to Emma's message.

"I know him," I wrote. "I know so much about him that you would find it creepy, truly. More than you need to know. More than even he knows. I used to wonder where all this was headed, and at the end of the day, I just accepted that it was headed nowhere. But after last night... for now, I will admit that I want more. Maybe I'm too scared to say anything about him being the love of my life just yet, but I at least want him to be the man that I have been intimate with and not just my boss. I can at least strive for this. It's not as though we can go back."

I sent the message and then shut my phone off. A few seconds later, however, it lit up with a message.

It was from Emma.

"Where did you go? Why aren't you responding?" she asked.

I frowned at her question.

"What do you mean by why aren't you responding? I sent you a message."

Just as I sent it, however, I looked down and realized that all the messages I had just sent hadn't gone to her.

"Shit, I think it didn't send, maybe the network was bad."

I left the chatroom and was about to turn the screen off, however, when I noticed that I'd just recently exchanged messages with Hunter. It was less than a minute ago, and I couldn't understand why. Had he tried to talk to me? That couldn't be, he was still on stage, staring directly at me now, I realized.

Something knocked into my heart with a staggering blow as I finally read the first sentence and then the second. I pulled the chatroom open and nearly screamed. Instead, I was so shocked that I jumped to my feet in the middle of a room with more than three hundred people.

Thankfully, I didn't curse back as I just might have ruined the entire event if I had.

I wasn't sure though that I hadn't when in the next moment my chair fell down behind me to the ground, showing the force with which I had stood up from it.

I immediately tried to right it quietly; however, I didn't carry on speaking until I was seated again, and with my head so lowered down, I wondered if I would ever manage the courage to straighten up enough to look him in the eye once again.

I couldn't look at him now. All I could do was try to delete the message and truly hope that he hadn't seen it. I was so terrified that I immediately did this and then had no choice but to wait for my fate because now more than ever, I was sure that it was headed to nowhere but doom.

Chapter Fifteen
Hunter

I could feel the vibration in my pocket as I spoke, and for a moment, it distracted me indeed. I wondered who it was, but I didn't really care because even though I tried my best not to watch her from across the room, no one else stood out like her, especially in a completely makeup-less state. She was quite enigmatic, though, and I found it strange that I wasn't the only one to notice her sudden interruption of the conference simply because she had been startled by something. I wondered what it was - was it good news or bad news? Why had she been so shocked?

I couldn't help worrying about her, and it made me anxious to wrap up my speech even more. Soon, I was done and returned to my seat, barely even realizing that I was receiving hearty applause. I bowed politely in appreciation and then pulled out my phone to slyly check if she had been the one to send me a message.

It turned out it was, but the content of the message left

me shocked to say the least. I didn't bother unlocking my phone to gain access to it; it was right there on my screen, and I just continued to stare. It made sense why she had suddenly jumped up. I was sure she had deleted it in the chatroom, so if I had any chance in hell whatsoever of seeing it again, I had to take a screenshot of it. I did so, and truly, afterward, it was a feat to control my amusement.

I wondered who she was talking to? What friend of hers was she sharing all this personal information with? It occurred to me then that I didn't know. I didn't know anything whatsoever about her, and this had always been the way for me with staff, but as I read that message over and over again, I knew that I wanted to know her. I wanted to know exactly what she meant - that she was too sane to conclude me as the love of her life yet. How much exactly did she know about me... more than I knew. And she wanted me to at least be the man that she had been intimate with.

Well, turns out that I want the exact same as well. We were more or less on the same page, so I couldn't help my smile as I put the phone away.

Other speakers came up to the stage to speak, and soon enough, the morning event came to an end. I was incredibly pleased because I got to see her. I had a feeling that things would become even more eerie between us, that she would do all that she possibly could to hide, and that it would be hilarious. I truly couldn't wait, so I turned around, but instead of her, I was met with the Swedish investors that we had dinner with the previous evening.

Everyone was standing to their feet and mingling, the

hall getting rowdy, and I wanted to try to leave. However, he stopped me, and I couldn't help but be even more irritated as I saw his face.

"Mr. Swift," he smiled at me. "I sent you a message last night and this morning, thanking you immensely for allowing my team to host you. We hope to continue our discussion today, and I also have some officials that I am personally connected to and who are vital to our project."

I watched him, and truly, I didn't know what to say. I was interested in what he was offering, but the way he had acted yesterday severely pissed me off.

"My secretary is still hungover from all the drinks you fed her yesterday," I couldn't hold myself back, and this was how I knew I was losing it just like Madison because under normal circumstances, I would have put my goals and focus first. But I liked this side of me. I liked this more human side that she brought out where everything was not always simply about achieving. I wanted to have a little fun, just as she was telling me to, and so I decided to take my own advice.

At my words, his smile immediately faltered, and then he began to stutter. I couldn't stand him, so I turned around, but before I could leave, I was surrounded once again by a different crowd.

I shook more hands than I could identify faces, and more often than not, the questions they asked warranted automatic responses. It was my field. I knew what to say and when to say it; however, suddenly someone said something out of nowhere that completely stumped me.

It was the organizer of the conference. He had come over amidst those gathered around me to determine how the networking lunch happened. He was hoping that I would move away from the conference hall so that it would encourage the rest of the attendees to also move, so that we could talk instead as we had lunch, since the conference had to be returned to in the afternoon.

And then he added a sentence that I had never even thought I would ever hear.

"Congratulations about your engagement?"

I was sure he was talking about something related, but it still didn't make any sense to me.

"Excuse me?" I asked.

"Oh, it's spreading around the women," he replied with a smile. "They're all devastated. Don't you see how many of them are here? They all thought you were still single, so none of them wanted to miss this event for the world. But now, I don't know if even a single soul will be here come the afternoon session."

He said it as a joke, and the majority laughed in amusement, but I wasn't amused at all. Instead, I was incredibly confused, especially as I understood the context in which he was espousing this now.

"Who said I was engaged?" I asked, and the man seemed quite taken aback.

"You're not?"

"It was your secretary," the woman beside him said, smiling. "She was asked if you were in a serious relationship, and she said that you were close to being engaged, if not even engaged, so all of us have to back off, except there's still a chance?"

Everyone laughed at this, but I wasn't the only one not amused. It wasn't that I was angry; I was just confused. I turned around then, and it was as though she had overheard everything. She turned away, and all I could see was the back of her head. Shaking my head, I almost felt sorry for her. She was most definitely having the absolute worst day ever. As to their inquiry, I didn't respond. There was no need to, and just as quickly, everyone moved on.

Chapter Sixteen
Madison

Everybody in the tearoom wanted to talk to him. I completely understood. He was the talk of the conference - his expertise, his success, his youth, his scarcity. He never went anywhere, but this time around, he was here, and everyone wanted a piece of him.

I stayed just close enough, and at first, he didn't notice me. But I noticed soon that his eyes kept wandering, and I pulled out my phone to send him a message. But when I recalled what I had written earlier, I lost my confidence. I was clinically insane. At this point, it was official, and I wasn't exactly keen on reminding him of this fact. So, I simply tried to stay within his line of sight until eventually, our eyes met. His gaze lingered on mine, and I couldn't help but notice that even though everyone was trying to talk to him, there were a few seconds where his complete and total focus was on me. It made my heart flutter, even though I was sure he was just staring at me because of what I had written. Sure, I had deleted it, but the notification had come to his phone, so I was a hundred percent sure that he had read it.

But I had already worked up a couple of ways to salvage this, and I knew just how to use it the second we found a moment alone together. My only question now was if he would actually believe it. That was indeed the question.

But now, as I overheard the entire exchange, I knew that I was dead. I had only told one person. It had been a complete in-the-moment lie, and now the entire conference was celebrating him for being engaged. And he hadn't refuted it. I wanted to run away. At this point, I couldn't even feel fear again. All I could do was feel amusement. At least I knew it would be a funny story to tell after I had gotten royally fired.

He had said that he wasn't going to move, but now I had no doubt about it. I was messing up his perfectly ordered life, and there was no need for him to bear it. I wondered what to do now. I couldn't leave him in the middle of the event and just head back to the hotel unless he explicitly asked me to, so I stayed put and tried to avoid his eyes. If he needed something from me, he could text me as he usually did.

But then, we would have to be alone soon because we had to head over to the lunch venue. It was three stories down, and I wondered if it would be weird for me not to take the elevator with him. What was sure, though, was that we wouldn't be alone, so I was counting on quite the number of people between us to buffer his wrath and my embarrassment.

Shaking my head, I followed behind as we left the hall, with people trying to keep up and talking to him while he did his best to answer. Soon, the elevator arrived, and I watched him from behind. However, just as everyone went in, he didn't. He stopped and was searching for me. I couldn't run away then. I hadn't expected it, and it was too late for me to take cover. Our eyes met, and then he gestured. Tears rushed to my eyes.

"What are you doing? Come over."

I did as he asked, and then the elevator filled up.

"I'll take the next one," he said, but about five people immediately got off. "No need, no need. You'll have to wait. You're the guest of honor, Mr. Swift."

I hoped to God that he would listen to them and go and leave me to my misery, but he didn't. Instead, he headed in, and when he turned around to see that I hadn't followed along, one sharp, angry gaze from him, and I knew I was on the verge of being yelled at. He had never done so before, but I knew that look in his eyes. He was rapidly losing his patience.

And so, I headed in, and he quickly introduced me, most probably to dispel that I was the alleged fiancé.

"This is my secretary, Miss Parish - Madison Parish."

"It's incredibly nice to meet you, Miss Parish," I had greetings from all over. I turned to accept some hands while others it was simply impossible to. As the elevator began to head down, soon enough, we arrived at the lunch networking venue. It seemed there were even more people here than those who had actually attended the conference, which was quite amusing to me, but it was to be expected. Free food always drew a crowd like nothing else in the entire world.

We soon found our seats, and once again, I wasn't

seated at his table. However, the way we were positioned, I was directly in his line of sight at the next table. He watched me while I turned away, unable to bear it. Soon, the event started with some gorgeous musical performance, and I focused my attention solely on the food and the entertainment.

Chapter Seventeen
Hunter

She was avoiding me, there was no doubt about it. She seemed embarrassed for what she had done, for all the things she had done so far that she couldn't meet my gaze. In a way, she looked so sad, and it worried me. She watched the performance and even smiled at random times, but I could tell that there was no truth behind her smile and enjoyment of it. She was just trying to pretend just long enough for me to figure it out. I had thought of waiting till we returned to the hotel to ask her about what was going on, but I knew then that I couldn't. I was too antsy; I was beginning to care.

"You told everyone I was engaged?" I sent her a text.

At first, she pretended to ignore it, and then I sent another.

She looked down then, and though she didn't lift her head to meet my gaze. I shook my head.

"I'm so sorry, Sir. I, uh... the message was actually meant for a friend of mine. She wanted to write it to someone else but wanted me to check how it sounded, so I edited it and mistakenly sent it to you."

This almost amused me. Almost. But I hated the fact that she was lying to me. There was nothing I hated more than people lying to me, and so I found that I couldn't quite accept this or even continue on with the conversation. I had wanted to chat casually with her, but instead, I put the phone away and focused instead on what was happening in the hall. There was more than enough conversation around to distract me, but before we could even be served, the Swedish man, I think his name was Felix, came over once again. He lowered to speak to me, and I made sure to glare at him very clearly, revealing my displeasure that he was truly irritating.

"Mr. Swift, I know we have some wrinkles to iron out, but the officials at the table over there have invited you over. They're seated, and they're very excited about working with you. I truly hope that you will honor their invitation so that a relationship and a further partnership and development with the government can blossom."

His words were incredibly attractive, and I couldn't quite say no. So, without a further word, I nodded and rose to my feet.

He was all smiles, so I turned away from him and focused instead on heading over to the officials' table to speak to them. This was what was important. This was one of the major reasons why I had chosen to attend this conference, but I couldn't help but feel as though I was getting distracted.

She was distracting, but maybe this was a good thing?

I mean there were other ways for an exit. We could

enjoy ourselves and our vacation together in every sense of the word to the minute, and if we discovered later on that we weren't a good match, then I could have her transferred to another department and to ensure she didn't get the short end of the stick, her pay would remain the same.

And if she chose to remain as my secretary regardless, then I would accept that as well. I didn't need to analyze this perfectly like I did everything else in my life in order to judge the perfect outcome.

There were solutions, but this holiday and our involvement with each other was a rarity that I didn't want to lose. In order for me to go this route, however, I couldn't care much about her or whether she lied to me or not. I needed to keep things strictly transactional with her. And every time I did otherwise, I was going to be reminded painfully, just like this, that getting annoyed was the price to pay.

With my decision made and my resolve renewed, I continued on with eating lunch and communicating with the officials. There was a translator present to help out with the language barrier, so all in all the process was quite slow, but it was just the distraction I needed.

Eventually, though, not too long after, I needed to contact her once again, but this time around, I didn't send her a message.

I instead tried to catch her attention as I glanced towards her table and found her watching.

I called her over and in seconds, she was by my side.

"We need to make time tomorrow for some golfing with these officials," I said to her.

She didn't hear me. The hall was too noisy, and so she had no choice but to lean further down, and I whispered into my ear. This, to any onlookers, was just a simple incon-sequential move; however, I couldn't help the stirring of my dick as I took in her scent.

It was of something that smelled of berries and mango. She smelled absolutely divine, and being this close to her physically, so many moments from the previous night came to mind.

When finally, she understood me, she turned and stared right back into my eyes. I hated to admit it, but my heart for a moment stopped. I realized then that perhaps my attempts to keep things anything but professional between us was a fruitless and pointless endeavor. But still, I had to try.

For my own sanity, I had to try, so I ignored this and returned to the men at the table when all I wanted to do was stay by her and stare even more into those gorgeous hazel eyes of hers. Perhaps it was because she had been my secre-tary for quite a little while, but there was a certain level of safety and comfort I felt with her around. Especially now that I was in a brand new place meeting brand new people and using a translator to communicate.

Chapter Eighteen
Madison

A part of me always knew that if somehow, we got together, I would be a bit more affected than I had been back when he didn't personally or sexually, for that matter, care for my existence. But now, after what he had done the previous night, after the fact that I wanted to recall how many times he had kissed me and realized that I didn't know because it was so many times, I suspected that I might be in trouble. The craving had started to intensify, and since I had told everyone that he was engaged to protect my nonexistent territory, it was obvious that I was out of control.

Nothing, however, hit me like when we were that close in proximity to each other, like we had been when I had leaned down to hear what he was trying to tell me. Being his secretary, these kinds of situations occurred more frequently than not, and I could still remember the first time it had happened. He was so oblivious. He was trying to find information that he had mentioned earlier in the day and couldn't find on an agreement I had typed up for him, and I had to lower down to check on account of the fact that my ridiculous thick fake glasses sometimes obstructed my clear view.

Then I could feel his heat, inhale his scents, and look into his gorgeous eyes. To him, it was like what it had been like staring at a wall, but I truly wondered what it felt like to him. For me, I had been convinced in that moment that I was falling in love with him. This wasn't going to be a smooth situation wherein I had complete and absolute control of myself. From what I suspected; he was going to make me lose it from time to time.

Sighing, I received the instruction he had given out about the golf invitation, so I returned to my seat and began to take notes. I was seated with a few men and women, and just then, the woman by my side nudged me. She was much older, so I didn't expect to be barraged by questions about the rumor I had spread about my boss. However, this was karma coming for me, so I couldn't help but smile when needed and pretend when prompted.

"How is she?" The woman asked, and I was taken aback at first. She soon explained, "His fiancée, you said he was engaged, right?"

"Yeah," I replied. "Um, yeah."

"So, how is she? I imagine she's incredibly beautiful and smart, right? Is she just a pretty girl? Men like him tend to just go for the woman that will give him the least trouble. The others here are so jealous and heartbroken. You hurt a lot of people today."

I smiled at her and really wished that I could roll my eyes, but she was too close to mine to catch this, so I quickly turned away and returned to work. After readjusting his schedule, I started to count down the minutes until this ended and I could go back to bed. How I had survived this day so far, I didn't have a clue, but I was done trying, and all I could think about now was my bed.

There was, unfortunately, an afternoon left of the conference for the day, and he had said that he would be attending. I would usually never ask, but I was sure at that moment that what we needed from each other was space, and since I didn't see how we could go to work after all of this together, then there was really no point in hesitating to ask for more. So, the moment the conference was over, I found him and informed him of what I wanted to do.

He seemed quite surprised to hear my request. Twice his lips parted as though he wanted to say one thing or the other, but then he stopped himself at the end.

"I can remain if you need me," I said, feeling even more incompetent than I already did. "I'm fine. I just need to rest. The hangover's all but gone now."

"Two minutes ago you said that it was taking its toll," he said, and my guilt worsened.

"You're lying a lot," he said. "I don't like that. I've never once considered you a liar, and I think I'm only now realizing that this is what kept you as my personal secretary."

I stared at him, completely taken aback, and then I felt even worse.

"I'm sorry," I lowered my head, "I just... it's difficult for me to ask for this time off when it's the middle of the day. But I need it. I didn't want to admit weakness to you, so I have to... it's not alive. Earlier, I was trying to be strong, but now... I just want to rest for a little bit."

"That's okay," he said, "and you can go. We can talk later."

"Thank you, Sir," I said, and he nodded. His gaze lingered on me for a moment, and then he turned and continued on his way. I was finally free, and I couldn't believe it. As fast as I possibly could, I hurried out of the venue and met Mr. Kit, who was waiting to take me back to the hotel.

As soon as I got in, I stopped thinking. I shut off my brain, took off my clothes, got into bed, and pulled the covers over my head. The room had been cleaned by staff, so it was a relief to me that everything had been stowed away and brought to order. And I shut my eyes and tried my very best not to think of everything that had happened within the past several days.

Chapter Nineteen
Hunter

Barely ten minutes after she left, and I regretted that I hadn't gone with her. The conference had been bearable when she was there, but now all I could think about was returning to the hotel. I wouldn't see her, but I'd know she was in the next room, and to me, that was more interesting than remaining here. So, the minute we had a break, I got up and walked out. I sent a message to the organizer apologizing, saying that something very urgent had come up, and then I found Mr. Kit and was driven back.

When I reached my door, I couldn't help but wait before it for a moment. Just a few steps to the right, and I would be at hers. I wanted above all else to find out if she was doing well. This was what I wanted to ask back in the restaurant, and instead, I lashed out and scolded her for lying to me. I just didn't know how I was supposed to show care for her, even though I had set down the rule that I wasn't to relate to her personally. Maybe that was just the decent thing to do as a human being? However, I couldn't help but think that it was going to make things even more complicated between us. And so, I'd lash out instead.

Now... I wished I had checked whether or not she had eaten during lunch. She needed food if she was to recover, and I was sure she hadn't had any. So, after some thought, I placed those orders with room service, got in bed as well, and fell asleep. A few hours later, I woke up to the sight once again of the sun setting. It was beyond magnificent, and I wondered if I had ever appreciated it like this back when I was in New York. I was always so busy, always so occupied with one meeting and nearly late to the next. But this time around, for once, there was only one thing on my mind, and that was her.

I tried to go back to bed, but I couldn't. She needed to eat, so I picked up the phone and sent one of the hotel staff to her room to ask what she needed. There were too many options, and I didn't want to pick something that she would be forced to eat. Afterwards, I laid down in bed and recalled the plan she had for us to go to the theatre. She hadn't yet reminded me of it, though there was still about two hours left to go. It only meant that either she was still asleep, or she was awake and waiting to remind me as well.

. . .

I considered the option and decided that I would stay in instead. I tried watching some television, but five minutes in, and I recalled why I hadn't watched television in over ten years. Completely unengaging. So, I pulled out my laptop instead and started on an email that I had to respond to from the office back in New York. The time flew, and darkness descended over the city, but I couldn't stop thinking about her.

Chapter Twenty
Madison

The knock on the door startled me awake from my dreams. I was so deeply asleep that not until my phone began to ring, did I jerk awake. Initially, I thought it was my cell phone as I hurriedly reached out for it, but eventually, I realized it was the hotel phone.

I grabbed it and found that it was from the restaurant. "Miss Parish? This is Miss Madison Parish?" the voice on the other end asked.

"Yeah, yeah," I replied groggy and immensely disoriented.

"We were sent up to ask what you wanted to have for dinner. There's a restaurant staff right outside your door, so he can take your order."

"Um..." It took me a while to process it. "Who sent him or her... I mean, I didn't send for anyone. I didn't send for food; I've been asleep."

"Mr. Swift?" she replied, and the exhaustion was immediately wiped out of my eyes. I pushed my hair out of my eyes, understood what they were saying, and nodded.

"Um, yeah, let me call you back."

"Sure, ma'am," the woman said, and the call ended.

I had no idea what time it was. I had drawn the blinds before I had gone to bed, and they had blocked everything out. I hurriedly grabbed my phone again, and when I saw that it wasn't yet time for the performance, I released a heavy breath of relief. I wasn't screwed. Phew. I still needed to get up then, so I could feel human, get my brain working, and a few minutes later, I knew that I needed to call him.

Earlier on, I had been certain that he was so monumentally pissed at me that besides work, and until we could get back to the city and he could fire me, he wasn't going to talk to me. But now he was ordering food for me? This was how he was. One moment he would be cold as ice, and the next he could make you feel so warm that you didn't know what to do with yourself. I loved this about him, and so, more than ever, I was even more confused. What was I to do now?

I headed over to the bathroom, and after brushing my teeth and washing my face, I decided to get dressed. I sent him a message.

"Sir, the performance starts in an hour. Do you need any further preparations for attending? I'm available to help you as needed."

I sat down on the bed as I waited, and then my phone buzzed with a message. "Come to my room," he said, and my heart nearly jumped out of my chest.

I stared at the message and had to check it several times to make sure it was right and that he was the one that had truly sent it. Why did he need me to come over? He usually wasn't one for processes or meetings. He was brief in every-thing that he did... straight to the point.

Sighing, I rose to my feet, and I couldn't help but wring my hands. When I arrived at the door connecting our rooms however, I stopped. I had to be professional, so I headed out the front and then went over to his to knock.

Getting this room had been his idea, and at the time, I had been nearly heartbroken. I had brought up the booking for separate rooms to him, but when we found out that they weren't next to each other but were instead at the opposite ends of the corridor due to availability, he had then decided for us to just get the presidential suite.

"In case we're working late and need quick contact with each other, there's no reason to be that far apart. Our major business in Bangkok is the conference and networking."

That had made sense to me, but then I cried myself to sleep that he didn't even see me as a woman enough to care that we'd be sharing interconnected doors. Nothing was for sure going to happen between us. I was certain that it hadn't even crossed his mind.

Now, as I waited in front of his door, I couldn't believe how much things had changed—or had they? Had yesterday and today all just been a fluke because we were in a different country and had gotten carried away?

I didn't know what to believe in or even hope for, and this was the most unsettling part about all of this. So, he came to the door and opened it. He was dressed in the dress shirt he had worn earlier, but this time around it was completely unbuttoned, revealing his gorgeous, unbeliev-able physique.

For the first few seconds, all I could do was stare, almost

with my mouth agape. He eventually realized this and turned away without a word.

"Why did you come to the front? Is the interconnected door locked?" he asked as he returned to the chair by the window and took his seat. He was dressed in dark slacks, barefoot, his wavy hair neck-length and all over the place in the most gorgeous way possible.

My heart was weak. I remembered all that had happened the previous night, starting from right there on the chair he was still seated on and working with his laptop, and then to the bed. He had on his glasses. It was rare he wore them at outings or even in the office. I had only seen them when I'd stopped by his apartment. But now they were on, and the gorgeous dark rims around his eyes gave him the kind of appeal that made me want to do exactly everything I had done the previous evening, but this time around, completely willing and sober.

"Did you get something to eat yet?" he asked. "You need to eat now so you can fully recover,"

I replied, even though he wasn't looking at me but instead had his gaze on his screen.

"I think that sleep was what I needed the most, so I'm fine."

"Choose something with a soup base," he said. "It'll make you feel great."

"Yes, Sir," I replied and continued to stand before him. He didn't look up again, so I knew that I had to move the conversation along.

"I was wondering if you wanted me to order you some- thing to eat as well. I could join you, or maybe you want to go to the restaurant before the theatre performance. We still have about an hour left, so we need to leave soon if we're going to make it."

He continued typing, which was quite typical of him, so I knew that soon enough, he was going to finish and face me. And this was exactly what he did. He shut the laptop off, and then he lifted his gaze to mine.

"I don't want to go out for dinner or the performance. I'd rather stay here. Plus, there's a situation I'm monitoring in New York, and I'm waiting on responses that I don't want to miss."

"Alright, Sir," I replied, wondering what responses he was waiting for. I knew almost everything about his business, so if he was communicating with the office, I should be aware, right?

I frowned then, as fear struck me. Did this mean that someone else was handling his affairs? What was happening? I immediately moved to apologize.

"Sir," I called. "First of all, I want to apologize deeply for spreading the rumor that you are engaged. I will ensure that this is straightened out and corrected by tomorrow. It just slipped out. I was—"

I stopped in my tracks when I realized that once again, I was so obviously lying. I lifted my eyes to meet his, and as he folded his arms across his chest to look at me, he asked, "Is this a Thailand habit you've picked up or something? Lying through your teeth."

I lowered my head. "No, Sir, I just... I'm sorry. There have been a lot of changes that I'm not sure how to process yet, so I'm not really willing to completely reveal them to you either."

"I understand," he said. "But you don't have to lie to me.

So, let's start with correcting the first lie you were about to tell a minute ago."

I watched him, not even sure if I remembered what I had been about to say. Soon, though, it came to me, and I realized that I had to admit it. What was the point in lying now, truly? We had already given food for thought.

"I... uh," I began. "With the amount of attention surrounding you, I just thought that—except I said that they would swarm you throughout the entire afternoon, and that this would get impossibly annoying for you."

He narrowed his eyes at me. This was a simple and reasonable excuse, and so I waited with bated breath for his response.

"Is that so?" he asked, and I lifted my gaze to his, hoping he'd believe my half-truth.

This was obviously a lie, but it wasn't his business to know this, so I wasn't surprised when he turned away and didn't pursue the matter any further.

"Do you want to eat here, or do you want to go out?" he asked.

Going out sounded wonderful. It would be a wonderful way to experience the city, but when I thought of us being alone in the gorgeous room together, I really couldn't compare it to being out in public and acting as platonic as possible.

"I'd prefer to stay in, Sir," I replied.

Glancing down at my outfit, I truly wished then that I had put in more effort to look feminine. But after what had happened between us, I wasn't really looking to appear promiscuous before him. More than anything, I had wanted to be presentable, so I had simply donned a pin-striped pajama set that was as decent as they come.

"Alright," he said, and rose to his feet. There was also something about him doing this that was always so exciting to me. He was tall... much taller than me, with a gorgeous build, so every time he did this, every time the full impact of his presence in a room was felt, it made me feel this way. I stepped out of the way, but then he did something that made me nearly lose my breath for a minute. He held me and moved me gently out of the way. This was completely unnecessary. I could walk, but now, after this, it was as though I had turned to stone. I stood exactly where he had put me until he returned with the menu he had retrieved from the drawer by his bedside.

"Options," he said as he returned to the seat. He started to peruse through them, and all I could do was watch him until eventually, he noticed.

"Aren't you going to sit down?"

Like a robot, I instantly plopped down on the bed. But then I realized that this might be considered rude, so I rose to my feet once again.

"Sorry, I, um... I'm sitting on your bed. Is this chair, okay? Can I sit here?"

I was referring to the seat before him, but it soon occurred to me just how close and in direct vicinity of each other we would be as a result, and I didn't really think he wanted to see me that closely, or that I wanted him to. I didn't have any makeup on, and it felt like I was encroaching on his space. Maybe it was best I returned to my room.

I truly didn't understand myself, because the analysis

was grating me to bits. It was just that until recently, he was my boss, and this was how careful and cautious I was around him. The need to be more, but not having the confidence to ask or even act this way, was what was screwing with my brain.

"What's wrong with sitting on my bed?" he asked, and I lifted my gaze to his.

"Um... it's where you sleep?"

He was immensely amused, which made me feel a bit lighter.

"It's where you slept too, last night."

"Ah..." I stared at him. "Yeah."

"Do you remember?" he asked, and it took a while before I could respond, because even though I knew that sooner or later, we would have this conversation, it wasn't really something that I wanted to have right now... that I was ready to have right now. But I couldn't lie and say I didn't, even though technically earlier that morning, it would have been the truth. Why the hell hadn't he asked me then?

"Yeah... I mean, yes, Sir. I do remember."

"Take a seat," he said, and I settled down on the seat before him. He watched me, and then he picked up his phone to take the call. I listened to the smooth, quiet way he placed his order, and then he handed the phone over to me.

I immediately panicked. Answering his phone was more or less my job, but it wasn't something that I wanted to do in front of him, because I was sure to sound like a blubbering idiot. So, I lowered my head and my tone as I accepted the menu from him as well and placed my order. After the call ended, I returned the phone to him.

"Have you had Thai food before we came here?" he asked.

"Yes, Sir," I replied. "My, uh, friend put me onto it. Emma. I mean, you didn't need to know her name; I just wanted to humanize her, so it wouldn't seem like I was lying."

"What would make me think you were lying?" he asked.

"Um, I... I've, uh, it has seemed as though I have been lying so far today, but I don't lie. I mean, I usually don't lie at all; I just try to work around the truth a bit when I'm in a tough spot. And Emma is not a lie. She used to work for a law firm, and they always went out to fancy restaurants and whatnot, and she got introduced to Thai food, so whenever she came over to my house, she always... I mean, not always, usually ordered it, and that's how I was introduced to it."

I finished my entire message and wanted to shoot myself in the mouth, because what had prompted me to say all that? He usually didn't talk this much. He usually didn't like people who talked this much.

He nodded at my response, and suddenly, I had to get out of there so that I could breathe. So, I rose to my feet, nearly startling him.

"What's wrong?" he asked, and I smiled.

"Just a moment, Sir. I left my phone in my room. I'll just be a second; let me grab it. I didn't want to miss anything important."

"Alright," he replied, and I started to head for the connecting door. But then I recalled that we were supposed to be professionals, so I started to go through the front door. I thought he would stop me to discourage me from being so formal, but he didn't say a word. He had most probably returned his attention to his phone.

Turning, I returned to my room and found my phone. I immediately called Emma because in many ways, it felt like I was spiraling out of control.

Thankfully, she immediately picked up.

"I think something broke inside of me yesterday," I said.

"How so?" she asked.

"Ever since all that happened, I have literally turned into a blubbering, rambling idiot. I'm answering questions he didn't ask me, talking too much, acting weird, and generally neurotic. What the hell is happening to me?"

"Of course," she almost died laughing in amusement.

"You really don't know what's happening to you?" she asked.

I headed over to the bathroom to check and adjust my appearance, since I would be sitting just a few feet away from him for the next half hour at least.

"Do tell," I replied sarcastically as I pulled dried mascara off my lashes.

"You're trying to win him over," she said. "You're trying to get him to know you and to like you."

"What?" I asked incredulously.

"You know exactly what I'm talking about," she said, and I had no choice but to eventually admit that she was right.

"So, I'm saying more and talking more because I'm hopeful."

"Yes, you are," she replied. "And that is wonderful because it will mean that you will listen to me when I say this. He is what you want. He has been what you've wanted for the longest time, and you have denied yourself that.

You're not timid, and you're not that unattractive woman with bright green oversized dress shirts and Salvation Army oversized blazers."

I rolled my eyes at her, but every single word she was saying was hitting me straight in the heart.

"My point is, don't hold back. He's wonderful, and all that, as you've said, but you're just as awesome. I don't want you to cower anymore before him, and since you two have already crossed that invisible line, then please don't settle for less."

"It's so easy to say all you're saying right now," I said. "But you should see how I am around him. You wouldn't believe it."

"And that needs to change," she said.

"Again, easier said than done."

She sighed.

"I'm leaving. Do whatever you want."

I didn't argue. I needed to end the call as well because there was nothing further left to say. I knew what I wanted, bright and clear, and I had found the confidence to not shy away from it. So, with this resolve in mind, I grabbed my phone and returned to his room.

Chapter Twenty-One
Hunter

The food arrived just as she returned. I had just laid it out when the door connecting our rooms opened, and I was a bit startled because I had expected her to come to the front. With a smile, she settled before me, and I handed her a pair of chopsticks. Something seemed different about her. She wasn't as nervous as before and seemed to be in control of herself, and I wondered why. Or perhaps I was just paying too much attention to her?

"Tell me about your philosophy," I said. She had just put a bit of meat to her lips, so she paused for a moment to look at me.

"My philosophy?"

"Yes," I replied as I relaxed against the chair with my full plate in hand. "Why do you sometimes go through the front door and sometimes go through the connecting door? I need to understand so I can gauge what state you are in depending on the door you use."

This made her smile, but it took her a while longer to respond.

"You really don't want me to lie to you from now on?" she asked. "Even little harmless lies designed to save me from embarrassment and to keep our working relationship stable?"

At her words, I paused. She wasn't looking at me. Instead, she had returned her attention to her food and was calmly eating. I knew exactly what she was asking in every sense of the word.

For a moment, my mind went to my bed and the clear memory of us the previous night flashed through it. I made my decision then, and it had to be one of the riskiest things that I had ever done in my life.

"Yes," I replied. "I hate being lied to. Tell me the truth to the best of your ability without any deflection or sugar-coating."

"Alright," she replied, but she still didn't respond right away. Instead, she continued eating, and I knew that she was still deep in contemplation. And so, I allowed her the time she needed until eventually she was ready to speak.

"In very simple terms," she replied. "I go through the front door when I want to remind myself that you're my boss, and I go through the connecting door when I want to forget that you are."

Her words, though brief, which was unexpected, were incredibly clear and self-explanatory. I didn't need any further clarification from her because I too had these times of battle with myself.

Now that she had put it in this way, I truly couldn't help but smile.

"We really caused a lot of damage last night, didn't we?"

"Six months' worth," she replied, and I nodded.

I liked where this conversation was going, but before anything, I needed to confirm something with her.

"I'm sorry I gave in," I told her. "When you were insisting. I'm not sure if you remembered that. In exchange, I tried to reciprocate, but I didn't go any further. I'm still not certain if you were okay with any of it."

"For the record," she replied even as we ate. "I am okay with all of it. More than okay."

At this, she lifted her gaze and met my eyes. And then she smiled and lowered them once again.

"Hm," I said in thought.

"So... where do we go from here?" I asked.

"For starters, can I stop dressing like an old middle school teacher?" she asked, and I almost spat out my food in laughter.

"I never asked you to dress that way."

"Well, it's the standard uniform around you, since no woman with a working libido can keep their eyes and hands off you."

I shook my head as I kept eating. It occurred to me that it had been quite a while since I had had a personal conversation of this sort with anyone. It was always solely business-related, and this change in pace and topic was quite thrilling, to say the least.

"Did you hear of the previous secretaries that came before you?" I asked, and she smiled.

"Cassandra and Leila?"

"Yes, them."

She laughed. "I heard Leila showed up at your gym."

"Showed up?" I asked. "You mean she signed up at my gym. And because she was my secretary, of course, she had access to both the building and my schedule. When I asked, she said she lived with a friend there, which was obviously a lie. Imagine training at night after work and seeing your secretary's ass right in your face? She managed to skirt the indecent dressing at work bit and decided that I couldn't fault her for this at the gym, and she wouldn't stop hitting on me either."

"Wow," she said, and I wondered for the first time ever if I had said too much.

"Wow, what?" I asked.

"That sounds like something I would have done. It sounds like something I should have done."

Once again, I was amused, but I didn't know what to say to this.

"If I - do you think we crossed the line because of a change in location and pace?"

I contemplated this response. "I think we got here because you gave me the time to notice you. It could also be because rather than getting me to notice you, you simply just did your job and did it well. And there was no need for the extreme dressing. The Human Resources head was just being over the top. The other girls were either intentionally provocative, so with you, he just went overboard."

"So I can wear skimpy strapless tops and miniskirts to work now, Sir?" she asked. "Yes! Thank you."

At this, I narrowed my gaze at her, and she immediately changed her tune.

"I didn't mean that, Sir," she said. "I was kidding. I don't dress like that on a normal day, not to talk of in the office."

"You're going to keep calling me Sir even when I'm with you like this?"

She looked at me.

"We're not working right now," I pointed out.

Smiling, she lowered her head. "I'm sorry, force of habit."

"It's okay," I replied.

We continued eating further in silence, and then she asked.

"So... where do we go from here - Sir?"

I lifted a brow once again at her and chuckled my chest in laughter.

"I'm sorry. I just can't drop it that easily. It's been six months; every single day I have called you boss. In your presence... you have no idea how imposing you can be."

"I'm imposing?" I asked, and her smile reduced. She lowered her head.

"You are. I mean, besides the fact that you could fire me, which would technically and almost immediately make me homeless, by the way, and -"

"Wait, why would firing you immediately make you homeless?" I asked. "Isn't your salary high enough for your role? I thought we were paying a premium salary compared to other offices in the city. Is this not accurate?"

It was as though she had frozen in place from all the questions.

"Uh... so, this is where things might get tricky between us," she explained. "I mean, you're paying me a very high salary, and I won't technically be homeless immediately. This wasn't a lie, but I was just trying to point out that in case you were considering firing me, it really wouldn't be a good idea. I mean, you can do what you want; you're the boss, but I was trying to use a bit of -

I was just trying to exploit this into securing my job. I'm sorry."

She lowered her head and released a heavy breath.

"We have to set very clear boundaries, or else this won't work, right?" she asked in a low tone.

"Yes," I replied.

"All right, one boundary is that I wouldn't ever try to use our personal relationship for professional courtesies or favors, whether directly or indirectly. I'll put this in writing."

"Can you manage it?" I asked.

"The alternative is that I eventually get fired, as a result, right?" she asked.

I held her gaze but didn't confirm nor deny her assumptions.

"I'm going to take that as a yes. Therefore, this is one boundary that I will never cross again."

"Okay," I replied.

Chapter Twenty-Two
Madison

I was messing up once again. Rather than steer the conversation towards the most beneficial route for me, I was probably making him doubt me. Making him doubt us. I mean, there was probably currently no "us," but he for sure had an idea in mind, and that was what I wanted to find out about. Or rather than find out, which would make me no doubt appear manipulative again, I decided to simply just state to him what I was capable of.

"I can keep things as platonic as possible between us, Sir," I replied.

"What do you mean?" he asked.

"I can..." my gaze glanced towards the bed.

"I can do this with you, and when it comes time at work, I can also solely be your secretary. I won't mix it up, and I won't cross lines. And when that part of our relation has run its course, then we can amiably call it quits. If it becomes difficult for me to work for you as a result, I'll resign, but I don't think it will be. The guidelines and expectations are set from the very beginning with no miscommunication whatsoever."

He watched me, and then he set down his fork. I watched as he picked up the bottle of red wine we had ordered and poured both of us a glass. We had completely forgotten about it and had just started eating. I awaited with bated breath for his response, although I pretended to resume eating, and soon enough, it came.

"Okay," he said as he set the bottle down.

He raised his glass of red wine, and I knew immediately to do the same. We clinked to it, and it was settled. For a moment there, it felt as though the world around me had shifted.

Perhaps it was just my perception, but my entire body was no longer brimming with anxiety. It felt as though I had just won something invaluable, and I couldn't wait to start enjoying it. I tried to taste the rest of my food, but it was pointless. Food wasn't what I wanted, and for the first time in my life, I complained about the portions being too damn sizable.

We continued in silence because there was absolutely nothing else to talk about, and there was no point in filling it. We both knew what we wanted and had concluded our agreement, and I was going to honor it. So eventually, I set my chopsticks down. It would be incredibly awkward to afterward sit and remain there watching him, so I excused myself and headed over to the bathroom. I let my hair down, cursed about not having any mouthwash, but had found the courage to open up two buttons from the top of my chest.

I wished I was like Emma. So much more unrestrained and fearless. However, for now, and for a start, all I could let peek through was my cleavage and a sliver of the lace of my bra. I could only hope that he noticed.

When I returned to the room, I found that not only had he was not tired, he was eager as well. The plates were all returned to the cart except for the dessert and the bottle of wine, and he was pushing it all towards the door.

"I'll leave these outside," he said.

I watched him, and then headed over to the nightstand to call the restaurant. In the next minute, they were sending a staff over to pick up their utensils.

Afterward, he returned and headed into the bathroom while I stood by the window, sipping on my glass of wine. Soon, I heard the door click shut and couldn't help holding my breath. I didn't turn around, and soon enough, I felt him behind me. The view before me was beyond magnificent, yet all I could give my attention to was the man behind me. Towering over me... enticing me.

The first thing I felt was his arm sliding around my waist, strong and warm. This instantly sent my eyes fluttering shut. And then his breath was in the crook of my neck. I felt the sensation of the heated wet kiss of his lips against my skin, and my already racing pulse jumped.

"Are you on birth control?" he asked.

"Um... yes, Sir," I replied, and I could feel his smile. "I mean, yes."

"Do you know my first name?" he asked, kissing me again.

Just before I could answer, however, he held me by the neck and turned my head, and then our lips were pressed against each other. It wasn't a soft or gentle kiss. Instead, it was a ravenous one. Deep, hungry, insatiable. By the time I pulled away, I had completely forgotten what he had asked me prior. All I could do was stare into those gorgeous eyes in disbelief.

He was going to fuck me, and I would be sober this time around to enjoy every single minute of it. I couldn't wait. And so, without any further prompting, I began to unbutton my shirt. In no time, I was done and pulling it down my arms, leaving me standing before him in my bra. He leaned down to kiss the swells, and I watched him.

"You have the most gorgeous breasts I've ever seen," he said. "You know this, right?"

"Right," I replied, and then it occurred to me what I was saying. "I mean, I didn't mean right... I wasn't coherent."

Smiling at my nervous self, he kissed me once again and it melted away.

"How do you want me to take you?" he asked, and my heart nearly stopped in my chest.

At first, I was sure he was teasing, but when I saw the intensity in his eyes and remembered who he was... remembered how he handled his life and affairs with such precision and intention, I realized that he meant every word.

"Like last night," I said, remembering just how hard I'd come, how hungry he'd been for my sex. I hadn't been able to get the memory out of my head or down below either. My clit was pulsing, needing the heat of his mouth, hungry as the previous day.

"You want me to eat you out?" he asked, and I nodded, unbelieving that this was my boss. That this was Hunter fucking Swift.

"Alright," he said, "but you'll have to do something for me first now, won't you?"

"Anything," I replied, much too eagerly. It was too late to catch myself, but I did try to reduce my embarrassment, though I was sure this was fruitless.

Smiling, he nodded his chin towards the bed, and then he escorted me to the bed, helping me sit then I watched as he took his seat beside me.

"Last night, you mentioned wanting me for so long," he said. "Can you show me?"

At first, I was sure I hadn't heard what he said about my wanting him for so long and when I confirmed that he wasn't going to repeat himself, I truly had to consider if I wanted to do this, if I wanted to go this far.

One more second of additional thought, and I grabbed the waistband of my pajama pants and pulled it down my thighs. It puddled around my feet, leaving me in the dark lacy panties I had donned earlier.

His gaze shamelessly went down my body, taking in every inch of my skin. Even though I knew he had already seen it all, this time felt different. I was fully aware and conscious, and the torture was immaculate. I could read in his eyes that he really liked what he saw, and this brought an indescribable thrill to me.

"Slide back on the bed," he said, and I didn't need to be asked twice. I did as he asked until I couldn't go any further. I knew what he wanted.

"Show me," he repeated.

This time around, I had the perfect truthful excuse.

"I don't have the right equipment here," I said.

It took him a while to process this, and when he eventually did, he threw back his head and laughed. It made my heart dance. When he looked at me again, there was a certain sparkle in his eyes.

"That was only half the truth, wasn't it?" he asked. "I mean, you could always use your hands. But I am curious..."

He rose to his feet and came over to me.

"What exactly is this equipment you speak of?" He pulled his shirt off and tossed it away.

"Can you show me?"

My gaze went down to the already prominent and very obvious bulge in his pants.

"Yes, I can," I replied.

He stood before me, and my hands flattened against the hard ridges of his abdomen. I couldn't help but feel him up. I couldn't believe that he had given me free rein and access to him, and I didn't waste it.

"Show me," he repeated, and I complied. I unbuttoned his slacks, pulled the zipper down, and soon enough, he was in nothing but his briefs. I mouthed him through the cotton fabric, and then with my hands on the band, I pulled his briefs down to reveal his gorgeous, erect length.

I had thought about it over and over in my memories, and it had been fuzzy at best. But now, seeing it once again in its full glory, my throat slightly closed up, fighting a choke. He was huge in girth, pink, and perfect. I looked at him and shook my head.

"What?" he asked.

"Sometimes I think the universe is very unfair," I said. "You're you, and you have this?"

He was amused. "Maybe I'm me because I have this. Have to match the outside with the inside, don't I?"

Now it was my turn to laugh out loud. He was so ridiculously funny, and having a sense of humor like this was not something I had expected from someone who had always been so stiff.

Here, he was making the entire atmosphere as light as possible, and as a result, my reservations and defenses were instantly gone.

I held his gorgeous length, stroked it, tasted it, licked it, and through it all, I enjoyed watching his breathing quicken. I stared up at him, needing to see his reaction, needing to see the effect that I had on him.

He didn't hide it, but I wished it was more, so I took him in all the way to the hilt, and then I began to suck him off, just like I had done the previous night.

Throughout the day, I had tried to remember what it had felt like, and all that came to mind was that it was fun. But now, I realized that it was more than fun, it was unbelievable. I enjoyed every moment of it more than I could recall ever enjoying anything else, and I knew that it was because this was him.

Slightly, his knees shook, and I loved so much that it was because of me, because I was attending to the head of his cock and sucking him so hard that pleasure was pummeling through his body.

He grabbed my hair and held my head in place, then he said words that just might have made me come right there.

"I'm going to fuck your mouth," he said, and began to move his hips. I tightened the grip of my mouth, relaxed my tongue and throat, and allowed him to take what he needed from me. By the time he pulled away once again, my lips were stained. He leaned down and kissed me, long and hard, and I was near trembling with excitement.

With one hand against my chest, he pushed me down on the bed, and I didn't resist. Then he spread my legs apart, and I shut my eyes as he pulled my panties down my thighs.

"Hmm," I heard him purr from above me, his voice filled with appreciation. "You're gorgeous down here," he said, the warmth of his breath tickling against such a sensitive place. "You know this, right?"

He didn't even give me a chance to respond. I had no problems with it, and so when his tongue and lips connected with my sex, I let out my long, tortured moan, the exact way that I felt it. That first lick and caress seemed to be heaven on earth. Afterward, it seemed to be even better than I had recalled. The way he applied pressure, kissed my clit, and sucked on it drove me wild. And then he would slide his tongue into me to lap up all of my desire.

But at this point, I was writhing across the bed, unable to stay still, unable to contain the heat and sweetness. I didn't care that people could hear us; maybe they could, and maybe they couldn't. It didn't matter. All that mattered was that, almost certainly, he was just trying to push me so hard that I fell apart right before him.

I willingly submitted. I wasn't going to put up a fight because what would be the point? I wanted to fall apart over and over, but most importantly, I wanted him to be the one to put me back together. That was the hard part. Reaching forward, I slid my hand into his hair as I worked my hips against his mouth, and I couldn't believe I was holding onto the gorgeous strands. I had always imagined it would feel like this, silky, soft, romantic. I cried out at a particularly good suck, and I could feel his smile between my legs. I pulled his hair in retaliation.

Just then, he lifted, and I watched his eyes glazed over with pleasure. I wanted to feel all of him on top of me.

I wanted to feel that wonderful weight of his entire being pressing against my body, so I reached for him with desperate fingers. Smiling, he didn't respond. Instead, he took his time kissing up my stomach till he got to my breast and then he unhooked my bra. I wasn't small in any way, but the way he grabbed me and squeezed made me feel like I was. I loved the way he held my breasts and sucked on my nipples with feverish abandon. He treated me like he had been waiting just as long as I had, and as though he couldn't get enough, and when he moved even further and kissed me, I nearly believed it.

"Ready," he whispered to me as I grabbed his body and pressed it against mine.

I nodded because this was a fucking dream. He felt so good, smelled so good that emotion clogged my throat. He grabbed his length, and I could feel him as he stroked the head up and down my sex. The teasing was pure torture, but I couldn't refuse it. It felt so incredibly good, and so I tried my best to be patient.

He positioned himself at my entrance, and then he began to slide in. I loved how gentle he was with me. I wished he would go faster, but I knew that he was trying to give me a bit of time to get used to his length and width, and I appreciated him so deeply for this. Smiling, I savored the feel of him stretching me open bit by bit, and then he impaled me all the way to the hilt. I purred like a satisfied cat and could feel his smile against my face as he kissed down my chin.

I loved the way he grabbed my hips, then he positioned himself slightly sideways, and then he began to fuck in and out of me. Just like he had started in the beginning, he thrust in and out of me with utmost care. It was torturous, but it felt so good. Soon, however, and just like I had hoped, he lost control of himself. He began to move even faster, and I held on for dear life. I loved the sounds that he made. At first, I knew that he tried to hold back, but as the minutes passed and as he fucked me, I could hear and feel them growing harsher.

I felt the sting of his hands as they dug into my skin. Desperate, euphoric.

"Fuck," he cursed into the crook of my neck, and I held him even tighter to me. I understood. My entire body felt as though it had been set on fire from the inside out. It felt so good; I felt like I was being coiled like a spring, the pleasure flowed through every inch of my body like great wine, and I wanted to scream.

"Hunter," I called his first name. "Hunter, oh God," I moaned as his thrusts came harder and faster, and soon we were both teetering close to the edge. I could feel it from the force of his pummeling. Earlier on, he had had a rhythm, and now he seemed as though he had tossed it out altogether. It was as though he had his own rhythm now in his head that I couldn't follow, and it made me grab the bed sheets so hard I nearly pulled them from the frame.

He would go slow and then fast, do that rolling thing he did with his hips that always temporarily blinded me and prevented me from seeing anything else. My hands grabbed at the roots of his hair as my thighs dragged across the sheets, curled, clenched.

I felt as though when I broke apart, it would be into pieces that I would need a while to put back together, and I was beyond looking forward to it.

"God," he kissed me. "You're so perfect, Maddy," he called. "So gorgeous, so sweet. Fuck. I could do this all night; I can't get enough of you."

I couldn't get enough of him saying all these words to me either, and it was more than enough to push me over the edge.

"I'm coming," I cried out, and afterward, the loudest, most intense moan spilled out of me. I could feel his entire body clench hard in response too, and I knew that my release had also provoked his. He shot his seed inside of me with a shout that reverberated through my body, and I reached forward to grab his ass.

He came endlessly while I writhed my hips to wring out every bit of pleasure left between us. The aftermath was magical. I could barely feel anything, and yet I felt everything. The sweetness, the pleasure, the intimacy. I felt as though I was trembling all over, and I loved it. As long as he didn't pull away and he didn't just then but eventually, he did roll to his side so he could get his weight off me, and before I could feel the coldness of his absence and our separation, he rolled me with him till my back was pressed against his entire body.

I felt as though I was in a magical cocoon of warmth and contentment that almost brought me to tears.

"We need to stop falling asleep diagonally on the bed," he said, and I couldn't help my smile.

"Yeah, do you want to move up?"

He grabbed his cock then and slipped it back into me, and I knew my answer without him needing to say a word.

"No need," he said. "We'll move up when we need to. Do you need to right now?"

"No," I replied.

I didn't need to do anything besides enjoy these very special and unbelievable moments with him.

"That was wonderful, Hunter," I said, and he seemed to hold me even tighter in appreciation.

"So, you do know my name," he whispered into my temple, and I couldn't help my smile.

"Of course, I know your name."

"Use it more often when we're alone together then," he said, his tone groggy from sleep.

"Yes, Hunter," I replied, and shut my eyes so that I could completely drown in the bliss that he was.

Chapter Twenty-Three
Hunter

Our phones both began to ring at the same time. At first, we both ignored it, but the amount of racket in the room eventually pulled us both awake.

"I'll get that," she said, however, she didn't quite move away from me. Smiling, I pulled away and headed over to the table by the window to find mine. The fact that it was ringing by this time told me one thing, and that was that there was trouble in New York. I wasn't surprised. It had been too quiet the past few days, but now it was time to really get back to work. My only hope was that it wouldn't be something so severe that the few days in Phuket weren't affected as well.

"Hello?" I answered.

"Hello, Sir," Meredith Shaw, my Chief Technical Officer, answered. "I'm sorry for bothering you. I know it's almost midnight there, but there's a situation."

"What happened?" I sighed as I stared out of the window.

"Data Breach."

The moment she said this, my heart dropped into my stomach.

"Fuck. Do I have to come back?"

"No, Sir," she replied. "We're handling it. We're sure we can handle it, I just wanted to keep you in the loop."

"We've only had one data breach so far," I reminded her, "and it was a small one, so I'm not exactly sure you can handle it. I'll let you be in charge, though, but I want to be involved."

"Yes, Sir," she replied. "I tried to reach Madison, but I think she might be asleep. I have to liaise with her, so that she's aware. This throws off your schedule?"

I turned then to look at the gorgeous woman who was now wide awake and sitting on the bed, staring at me. Her hair was all over the place, and although she had the sheets over her chest, it wasn't too difficult for me to picture just how gorgeous she was stark naked.

"Sir?" Meredith called, and I returned my attention to the issue at hand.

"Alright, um, we're prepared for this, so I need a meeting with senior management right now, as well as the legal and Public Relations teams, so I can be briefed on what is happening, the actions taken thus far, and our public relations strategy. When did this breach happen?"

"About half an hour ago, Sir," she replied, and I shut my eyes.

"Is it under control?" I asked.

"We're working on it, Sir."

"Alright," I replied and turned once again to look at Madison.

"Try to reach Madison so she can handle all of this. I'm ready when you are."

"Yes, Sir," she replied, and the call came to an end.

I returned the phone to the table, and by the time I looked up again, she was on her feet.

"What happened, Sir?" she asked.

This made me smile because of course, she was back in work mode. I, on the other hand, was in an incredibly good mood, because I could still smile when something so detrimental had happened. But after the way I had come so hard inside her, I didn't think anything could upset me for a while unless the building was on fire.

"Data breach," I replied, aching to go over to her but needing to maintain some element of distance for my sanity. Going over to her would make all of this seem too romantic, and I didn't want that just yet. I was already crossing the line by falling asleep with her, but there was no way that I was going to come and then have the energy to kick her out of bed. If she wanted to leave on her own accord, then she could, but I wasn't going to kick her out. Plus, there was something so restful about having her warmth and scent around me. It was so freaking wonderful, and it made me sleep better. I didn't want to let go of that, at least not yet.

"They were trying to call me as well," she said. "I think my phone was ringing from the other room. I'll go check it."

She started to hurry away toward the front door, but she remembered that she was practically naked and stopped midway. Then she turned around and returned. I shook my head at her, and as our eyes met, she seemed a bit startled at the smile on my face. Her expression was one of confusion for a second, and then she was on her way. But I needed to understand what that had been about, so I stepped out.

"Wait," I said, and she tried. "Come over here."

She stared nervously at the door, but then ultimately, she came to lie next to me. I was completely naked, so I ensured she was pressed up against me so she could feel how excited I was beginning to get just at the mere sight of her. Leaning down, I kissed her and wove my tongue with hers. She melted into it, grabbing my arms to stabilize herself.

By the time we parted, she was once again calm, and perhaps even a little disoriented.

"What was your expression about?" I asked.

"What expression?" she replied.

"Before you headed out the door. You seemed surprised and confused."

She stared into my eyes, and then she replied.

"I was a bit surprised that you seemed so calm. Data breaches are code red, aren't they? It's extremely serious, or... maybe they already have it under control."

"Barely," I replied, and her eyes widened even further. "Don't worry," I smiled. "We'll handle it, plus I was somewhat amused because of how comical you looked when disoriented."

Her eyes widened then as her hand went to her hair.

"Holy shit," she swore. "I look a mess, don't I?"

Before I could even respond, she was out the door and scrambling into her room.

Shaking my head, I picked up my phone once again and stared out of the window in thought. I deeply suspected who was behind this breach, and now, so focused on it, I realized that I was slowly becoming upset.

I picked up the phone once again and called the head of our IT department, Marcus Leigh.

Chapter Twenty-Four
Madison

I had trained for this. I was ready for this, but it was unfortunate that my sex-hazed brain kept tripping over the bed sheets until I eventually just had to let go of it completely and grab a robe instead. I found my phone and laptop sitting on my desk and immediately returned Marcus's call. He didn't pick up, so I called Meredith, and she immediately did.

"Why the hell are you unreachable?" she instantly lashed out.

I tried to control my temper, mainly because I was still groggy and because I wanted to remain in a good mood, but I could tell already that she was going to make this as difficult for me as possible.

"It's late; I was asleep."

"What do you mean it's late? It's not even midnight there, and your boss is still up."

Sighing, I waited until her annoyance had passed so that we could continue on with our work.

"Do you know what to do?" she asked.

I wrote down on my notepad as I thought.

"I need to arrange an emergency meeting with the boss and the senior management. I'll contact Grey in legal and Cullen in Public Relations to join as well. Has the breach been leaked? I'm wondering if we'll have to contact the shareholders as well."

"Not now," she replied. "Just make sure that Hunter is able to attend the emergency meeting now without it messing up his schedule too much. And of course, whatever materials we need, you can arrange before Stephen and whatever we send and hand it over to him."

"Alright, got it," I said, and the call came to an end. I immediately set up a real-time crisis management dashboard and sent Hunter the link as well as to the other members of senior management so that they could include notes to be shared by everyone and so that they can also track updates and news and actions in progress or to be completed.

Thankfully, Marcus picked up, and I was able to liaise with the cybersecurity and IT teams as well to join the dashboard so that their updates would be included. This was all I could do now until the meeting began in twenty minutes, and so I took the moment needed to take a breath. I was still in a robe, my hair was a mess, and we had a conference call in a few minutes.

So, grimacing, I got up and headed over to the bathroom. After finding a hair tie, I pulled my hair back, put on some clothes, and then changed into an oversized dress shirt and shorts. Afterwards, I took my laptop with me, and I couldn't believe how nervous I felt to knock on Hunter's door.

"Come in," he called out, and I met him once again dressed in the shirt from earlier, though it was still completely unbuttoned. I wanted to lick across his glistening skin. He was so fucking gorgeous; my mind couldn't contemplate it, especially in this moment when his very existence seemed so effortless and even exciting.

He appeared completely calm and was instead running some tests on his computer. I watched the numbers as they scrolled through his system and couldn't help but notice the frown that was now on his face. He was no longer in as good of a mood as he had been earlier and was now instead focused on resolving this issue.

I headed over and hesitated even taking the seat before him. This was working time, and there was no room for familiarity as we had agreed, so I stood until he offered me a seat.

"Sir, the meeting is in ten minutes. You've opened the board, I see?"

"Hmm," he replied as I watched him rapidly type a text message to the department. Suddenly, he stopped typing, and then he picked up his phone and rose to his feet. He headed over to the window, and soon enough, he was in deep conversation with IT.

No longer needing to be asked, I took my seat on the chair opposite him, and prepared for the meeting. I listened to what they had to say and couldn't help feeling slightly relieved.

Soon enough, it was time for the meeting, so I joined the conference room, and after confirming that everyone was present and had been able to join, I called him over.

"Sir?"

"I'll be right there," he replied.

He finished his call, and a few seconds later he came over and took his seat in front of his laptop. The meeting soon started, and we were all put in crisis aversion mode.

Half an hour later, more than half the attendees had been kicked out after being given instructions to handle things that needed to be immediately. The rest had reports to be given to Hunter later on, so I took note of all imminent milestones and deadlines. Finally, the meeting came to an end.

Afterward, his attention returned to his laptop while I, on the other hand, focused on adjusting his schedule for the entire day. He was so focused that even after more than half an hour had passed, he was still solely focused on resolving the issue. I watched him and felt as though we had been transported back to New York. This was the Hunter I had fallen in love with. Unlike any other man that I had ever met, he could remain in this position for the several hours and not even bother moving from where he was.

He kept working while I tried to stay awake, but eventually, even with the chill of the room and the extreme silence, I couldn't help but lean into the chair and fall asleep.

Chapter Twenty-Five
Hunter

It was nearly an hour later before I looked up, and the moment I did, it was almost amusing to see that she was asleep. I was exhausted, though, and I was sure she was as well, so I rose to my feet and took her laptop from her. It was mere seconds away from crashing onto the carpet, and that in itself was another set of problems waiting to happen. As soon as I touched her, however, she was instantly startled awake. Her eyes met mine, huge and startled, and as it registered that I was there, she instantly got up and nearly hit my head. I had anticipated it, so I had ducked just in time.

"I'm so sorry, Sir," she said. "Um, I fell asleep. Sorry. What's happening? I, uh, I had some questions to ask you."

She quickly reached down for her notepad, and then without even pausing to take a breath, she immediately went through her notes.

"Most importantly, I wanted to ask if you want your schedule cleared tomorrow so you can focus on this situation."

"Don't we have the golf game tomorrow? With the government officials?"

"We do, Sir," she replied. I began to stop once again and for a moment, she was distracted as her eyes went to my body. I, on the other hand, focused solely on her face.

"Who exactly are the officials I will be meeting with? Were you able to identify them?"

"Yes, Sir," she replied. "I just checked now, and the first one is Mr. Somchai Preechawong, who is the Minister of Energy Development, and Mr. Supaporn Liangprasert, who is the Director of Renewable Energy Division."

"Alright, well, I definitely can't cancel that, so I'll just have to depend on you to be up to date on the situation in New York. If they need me urgently, then you can, of course, come pull me away. My hope is that all will be resolved by morning."

"Yes, Sir," she replied, and then I dropped my pants.

"I'm going to take a shower," I said, and she nodded. I continued to watch her and couldn't help but note how she tried her best to avoid the fact that I was naked before her.

"The crisis is averted for now, and the emotional atmosphere in the office is calmed, so can we go back to being casual with each other?" I asked.

I turned around then to leave and could hear her silence.

"Join me if you wish," I said and headed in.

In there, I wondered if she would come in. My eyes went to the bathtub, and for a second and in pride, I considered running a bath so that we could both relax, but I didn't think it was possible for me to relax now, so I decided that it was best to just shower so I could be somewhat more refreshed to be ready for anything if they needed me.

The water was just the right temperature, and as it cascaded down, I shut my eyes and tried to enjoy the heat beating down on my head. It was a bit sore, which made me realize just how hard she had pulled my hair during sex. Once again, all the precious, wonderful moments flashed through my mind, and I couldn't help but wish that she would come in to join me.

I turned towards the door then, and suddenly, it creaked open, and I couldn't help my smile.

"You have more questions to ask me?" I asked when I saw the pen and notepad in her hand.

She looked down, then surprised.

"Oh, I forgot to put them down."

"You came to take me up on my offer?" I asked, and she nodded.

"Come in then," I said. "The pressure and heat are wonderful."

She didn't waste any further time. She stripped immediately and in under a minute was pulling the glass stall open and joining me. The steam instilled encapsulated us both. My arms went around her slim, gorgeous waist, and the feel of naked skin against naked skin was mesmerizing, to say the least.

Feeling her this way seemed more intimate. I didn't know what it was, but it was as though if I squeezed her just enough, she would melt into me, and this was what I wanted more than anything in that moment. Touching her felt even better. And kissing her made my fucking heart race. This was indeed turning out to be a much more interesting vacation than I could have ever anticipated.

I loved the way she grounded against me. Her ass was full and plump, and my cock fit right into the crevice. She rolled her hips as she angled her head behind to catch my lips, and every cell in my body came alive. I grabbed her mound, causing her to gasp into my mouth and writhe even harder against me. I hadn't exactly been planning to fuck her in here, but now our bodies were so sensitive that I felt as though I would quite possibly lose my mind if I didn't.

And so, without wasting any time, I directed her to flatten her hands against the glass, and then I spread her thighs. It was too easy to slide into her, and the smoothness nearly did me in.

I leaned forward then and whispered into her ear because I needed to let her know what her sex did to me.

"I love the way you clench around me," I breathed. "So fucking hungry."

Reaching down, I began to stroke her clit, and she cried out. I started thrusting then, going slow at first to allow her to get used to the sensation, and then I lost myself to our uninhibited pleasure. Slamming into her repeatedly meant that her body also slammed into the glass.

I was worried about hurting her, so I grabbed her hips instead, and this route made me nearly lose my mind. Holding her in place as I pummeled into her made my legs, as well as hers, begin to shake. But we had to finish, and so I kept going until she was slipping from my arms, and I had to grab her.

She cried into my mouth, kissing me and even biting down on my arm.

"Oh, Hunter," she writhed and ground against me, pushing her hips backwards even harder to meet the intensity and speed of my thrusts. We couldn't prolong our time here. The sensations were too intense, and so in minutes, we were both coming at the top of our voices. I grabbed onto the handle of the stall to keep us both balanced as I poured into her. My head was thrown back, my lips apart, and my eyes staring blankly at the ceiling. Coming inside of her was merely indescribable. It felt as though nothing else in the world beyond the magic of that moment mattered, and it was everything I had ever wanted.

"Fuck," she cried and gasped, and only after tightening my hold around her did she manage to calm down. It took a little longer, though, for the trembling in her legs to calm down, but even though this affected her mobility, I had to admit that it made me feel quite satisfied.

Eventually, and since she could no longer move as was recommended for her safety, I sought a non-slippery place. I ensured she held onto me and grabbed the shower gel. I took charge of cleaning us both, and it was an interesting experience to say the least.

I had never been this way with a woman, I realized, as I rubbed the soap all over her body, and as she stared up at me with those mesmerizing eyes, I didn't even think I would ever be able to be this way with another woman as well. There was just something about her that made this seem so right and so perfect. I couldn't even explain it, and eventually, I stopped trying. We had real-life problems to attend to, but for the moment, I put everything out of my mind and focused on cleaning her as best as I could.

Chapter Twenty-Six
Madison

A
ll of this felt like a dream, but reality wasn't exactly giving way for us to have as much fun as we wanted, so I had to remind myself that it wasn't. It was difficult, however, when I stood before the gorgeous vanity of his bathroom with my hair wet and wrapped in a towel. He was toweling dry, standing completely naked behind me, and I couldn't keep my eyes away from him. He was so gorgeous with his wet hair and naked torso that I didn't know what to do with myself. I wanted to scream, and I wanted to cry, but somehow, I managed to hold back when I reminded myself that all of this was temporary. In a few days, we would be heading back to reality, and all the vultures in the office would occupy every second of his time. Perhaps, at the end of the day, he would even remember that we had done any of this here in Thailand. I hoped he didn't, and in a way, it made me want to take a picture for memorabilia, but he was too important a man for that, and I couldn't risk him becoming suspicious of me in any way. Right now, this moment felt as

though two imperfect souls had come together in the most perfect way, and I didn't want to ruin it. So, I seriously took as many mental snapshots as I could and stored them deep down in my heart.

"Do you have a dryer?" he asked. "I could use mine if you don't."

"Yours," I replied. "Definitely use yours."

He smiled as he glanced at me through the mirror, and I watched as he began to comb through his curls.

"You're used to using a comb, right?" he asked, and I nodded. "Yeah, how do you know?"

"My niece," he replied. "She has curly hair."

My eyes widened then because I didn't even know he had a niece.

"Oh," he watched me through the mirror and smirked at my surprise.

"I have an older sister, she's married. She lives in Dallas, and their birthdays are coming up, so you'll need to send them gifts. I have a dad, but my mom passed away a few years ago. He's not very social, plus he loves his ranch in Ohio, so he hangs out there with his buddies and rarely comes to New York. I think in all the time I've been in the city; he's only visited me maybe once."

"Oh," I said a bit surprised that he was telling me so much but grateful either way. I wondered then if I was to reciprocate, but I decided that that would probably be inappropriate. However, it was necessary that he tell me all of that since I was his secretary, and I needed to keep track of all the important people and events in his life.

"You sound like you have a lovely family," I replied.

"Interesting maybe, but lovely's doubtful." I was amused by this.

This made him laugh. "All families are like this."

"Right," I replied, nodding. "You're right."

We remained silent then, and I just eyed him, but suddenly his question woke me up.

"What about you?" he asked. "Do you have family in the city?"

I was immensely surprised that he was asking me this, and at the same time, I tried my best to control my excitement. Maybe this wasn't crossing the line; I mean, he was my boss, and we weren't enemies, so it was normal for us to exchange at least base-level information about each other and our families.

"I have both my parents," I told him. "They live in New Jersey. They used to live in the city for a long time, in Brooklyn. I was actually born in Queens, but ten years ago, they eventually got tired and wanted to move away just as I was entering college, but I refused to be a part of that. I don't know what it is, but I really love New York, even though living there requires huge amounts of money that don't make any sense, but I still love it a lot. It has its charm."

"Right," he replied. "I could have opened the company elsewhere, but I always wanted to be here, so as soon as I could, I moved from Ohio and came here for college as well."

"Did you ever consider living anywhere else?" I asked just as he turned off the dryer.

"No," he replied, as he wrapped the cord and set it down.

"You?" he asked, returning my smile.

"No," I replied, and he returned my smile.

"I think we can go to bed for now," he said. "They all seemed to have the situation under control, and if anything pops up again that is getting out of hand, they'll just reach us. We have a tasking and quite possibly long day tomorrow, so we could both get some rest. We've also been quite active over the past few hours."

Once again this made me blush, but then when I finally revealed my face once again, a heart-stopping kiss from him was waiting. Grabbing one of his towels, I made my way out of the room, promised to return it, and returned to mine. I was slightly disappointed because a part of me had hoped we would fall asleep together, but this definitely was crossing the line because I didn't see him agreeing to it. Even though previously he had brought me back to my bed, and so tonight, before I was overly politely asked to leave, I gathered my things and headed out of his room.

..

Chapter Twenty-Seven
Hunter

Golf wasn't my favorite sport at all. Over the years, however, I had been forced to not only learn how to play it but how to play it well as well. Due to the industry I was in, which consisted mostly of much older people, basketball wasn't exactly their sport of choice when they needed to have friendly meetings or matches like this one. Early that morning, we arrived at the clubhouse and met the officials along with the Swedish business manager and his team who were already waiting.

I was immediately upset to see him there, but he was an evil I couldn't get rid of just yet, so I tried my best to ignore him. After the initial greetings and some light breakfast, it was time to head out to the course. I had been preoccupied all morning with handling the situation in New York and entertaining my present guests, so I hadn't paid much attention to Madison.

It was hard now not to notice her. All the other men in the club did. She was in the usual golf skirt and T-shirt, with her hair up in a ponytail. To say that she looked gorgeous was nothing but an understatement, but I tried not to stare. I headed over to her then and wished that I could kiss her. In that moment, truly, it felt like I needed the kiss but all I could do was stare at her and sigh.

"Do you need something, Sir?" she replied.

"Are you coming along?" I asked, taking in the bag she had slung over her shoulder. I knew it contained everything she needed to work and communicate with the office. She was dressed for the course, but it was very apparent that she was aware that she was working and would have no time whatsoever for playing or leisurely shenanigans.

"Yes, Sir," she replied. "Y-you don't want me to?"

"It might get hotter later on," I replied, looking out across the lush green course.

"That's okay, I have sunscreen and my hat," she replied with a smile. And then I watched the smile spread across her face. "Do you have sunscreen, Sir? I didn't mean to bother you."

Before now, I had truly never been bothered that she called me Sir, and now, it didn't bother me, but it did something strange to me. Namely, it made me feel even hornier around her. I didn't get the kick of respect I was sure she intended by addressing me in this way. Instead, it felt as though she was role-playing and teasing me with every mention of the word.

This was such a foolish thought because I was her boss; however, the implications of this beyond just ensuring that she kept my life and schedule organized had never really occurred to me the way it did now.

"Yes I put on sunscreen and you can stay here," I replied. "If you want, of course. You're out of the sun, you're not overheated, and you can monitor the work on the desk over there."

"Oh," she said and nodded. I could see her face fall slightly, and as always, I was going to ignore it, but I couldn't. I grabbed her arm before she could go out of my sight.

"I'm not trying to drive you away, I just… I don't want to strain you necessarily. But if you think being on the course is what you prefer, then of course, come along."

She stared at me then, with a smile on her face. It was shy, and it made the corners of my mouth curve as well.

"I'd like to come along and stay in the golf cart. I worked at a golf course when I was much younger, and I enjoyed the sport. I haven't had the time or chance to return again, so I'd really like to relive the experience."

"It's settled then," I replied, and her smile this time, fully exposing her gorgeous white teeth, was blinding.

"Thank you, Sir," she replied, and we headed out together. I saw Felix, the Swedish man, watching us, and once again, I couldn't help but sigh. The officials called out to me, so I had to leave her to her own devices.

"Let me know if there's any update from the office," I said, and she nodded.

"Yes, Sir."

Chapter Twenty-Eight
Madison

It felt so weird calling him Sir. After all, the man had seen me in ways that even I hadn't seen myself. It felt now as though we were playing a game that only the two of us were aware of. It was exhilarating, to say the least, but it also made me feel so nervous. And then there was the way he touched me. I didn't even think he realized it, but when he spoke to me now, I noticed how he touched me. So intimately, so carefully. It truly made breathing difficult. And he stared into my eyes like he was trying to figure me out, to understand all that he could about me. Maybe I was the one reading too much into it, as always, but it was the way I felt.

Generally, I was happy about how things were progressing, about how we were relating to each other. It was much more than I had imagined things would be between us, ever, but I also deeply suspected that things were going so well because we were not in the city, which meant that I had a very short period of time to enjoy all of this, and none of that made me feel good in the slightest. Still, as I followed behind them, ready for whatever he needed, I admonished myself to forget about the past and future and to simply just live in the present.

Just then, however, Mr. Felix fell into step beside me, and just like that, my mood plummeted into the depths of hell.

"How are you doing on this fine day, Miss...?" he began, his tone falsely pleasant.

I glanced at him and managed a polite smile. He was important to this project, and no matter how I felt about him, I couldn't be outrightly rude. The events of that night replayed nearly verbatim in my mind, from the exchange at the entrance to our restaurant room to Hunter coming to my rescue. So, I was well aware that he had purposely forced me to drink, and equally aware that it had been with bad intentions, which he would have probably not hesitated to carry out if Hunter hadn't been available.

However, I found that I wasn't as angry at him as I should have been, because his malicious intentions had led to something that I could have never even dreamed could happen. So, in a way, I was supposed to be hating him, but he didn't need to know this. What he needed to know was that he needed to stay as far away from me as possible, and I truly wished that he would respect this and comply.

"What's your last name?" he asked, interrupting my thoughts.

I sighed, "Parish. My last name is Parish."

"Incredible name," he replied smoothly. "I've been trying to speak to you, but things have been a bit hectic, right? I hope you'll have some time for me today?"

He was no lackey. He was a very successful businessman, and although he was much older and less rich than Hunter, I was sure that he was very aware that I had been avoiding him and sometimes even downright ignoring him.

I truly couldn't help pretending, but this entire vacation and our time in Thailand was only just beginning, and I didn't want to have to bear his advances for the rest of it.

"I mean no disrespect by this, Sir, but I really hope that we can keep things strictly professional between us," I said, trying to be firm. "I know that you're working in collaboration with my boss, and I respect that and you, but I am not really comfortable with anything else beyond that."

At my words, he came to an immediate halt, and I had no choice but to stop as well.

"Aren't you being a little too cold?" he asked, his voice taking on a slightly offended tone.

"I mean, I watched the way you are with your boss, and you can't honestly tell me that things between you two are strictly professional. No one over the age of ten years is that naive, and as we can both clearly see, I am not under ten years of age."

He laughed at this joke, so satisfied with himself, and I wanted to punch him in the throat.

"Yes, Sir," I replied, my voice tinged with frustration. "I can very clearly see that you are not under ten years of age, and neither am I. So, I am aware of what happened that night and the intentions you had towards me."

At my words, his expression instantly soured. "Is that what your boss told you? That I had bad intentions towards you?"

Before I could respond, he continued speaking. "You believe him? You have to know that he wants you for himself, so why wouldn't he say the most heinous thing ever to you about me?"

I stared at him and wondered why I was even wasting my time conversing with him.

"Understood, Sir, but from now on, and in order to prevent any future misunderstandings, please let's limit all communication solely between you and Mr. Swift."

I walked faster to get ahead, but he grabbed my arm, and I was immediately alarmed, as was the rest of our party ahead, because my bag dropped to the floor.

"Oh, my God!" I gasped in horror, realizing my laptop and tablet were in there. These were my only means of contact with the office, and I couldn't let this asshole cause me to break them. He had no choice but to let me go at my reaction, and I hurriedly picked up the bag.

"Is everything alright, Madison?" I heard Hunter call out.

My attention went towards the golf course, and I sent a loud bellow in reply. "Everything's fine, Sir," I replied, although I didn't need to, as I knew that he didn't believe me. And he wasn't particularly happy with Mr. Felix being with me.

"I'll go on ahead," Mr. Felix finally said. "But I'm sure there are some misunderstandings between us, and I look forward to clarifying them in the future."

I absolutely did not look forward to clarifying anything in the future, but once again, I had to hold back for Hunter and his company's sake and for this deal. He didn't really focus on it, but I had heard stories throughout the office about their interest in expanding into this area. He, however, had never been on board, so I was incredibly happy now that he was exploring it. Therefore, I had to be as patient and as tolerant as possible to ensure that the rest of the week and meetings with partners went extremely smoothly.

Soon, I was on a golf cart along with two people I didn't know, whom I assumed were the assistants and staff of the other men present. We followed the golfing parties across the course as they got ready to start their nine-hole game. For a while, I paid attention to what they were saying as well and couldn't help but be amused.

They called it a friendly game, but each of the men present was playing to win. There was no money involved since there were government officials present, but I could see the excitement, dedication, and focus in all their eyes as they started swinging and hollering. They were all vastly different ages, with Hunter the youngest, and yet they all got along through their common spirit of competition and achievement. I shook my head because I was enjoying the drama, but through it all, there was one man that I couldn't look away from.

To me, the concept of being infatuated with anyone had always seemed somewhat laughable. But that was until I started working for Hunter. He was strict and a workaholic, insatiably ambitious, and he was all I'd ever wanted.

It brought to mind now, as I watched him excel even in a sport he didn't particularly like, what Emma had once said to me. "You know these kinds of men won't give you the traditional kind of love you want, right?"

By that, she had meant he would spend nights in the office rather than with me, and sometimes he'd be gone on trips for long stretches of time. I'd told her that if I even got the chance with him, I'd understand because I didn't want to stay at home either. I'd be busy as well, or perhaps we could even be busy together, just like now. I was in contact with New York, ensuring that everything stayed afloat so that he could concentrate on these moments fully, and it made me incredibly happy to support him.

Given that I had never quite been as magnanimous with my well wishes or time for anyone else, it was confirmation of just how deeply I felt for him. Another of Emma's digs, however, came to mind, and it was the fact that I felt all of this and more because of how well he paid me. She could always be trusted to turn even the sweetest of circumstances bitter, but back then, I had been inclined to agree with her mostly because what was the point in disagreeing when I knew he could never be with me?

It wasn't because I felt I wasn't good enough, but it was because of how I was forced to dress and present myself in those dreary clothes and unattractive appearance. How was he even to notice that I was a woman, much less be attractive?

Now, however, I had never felt more free with him, and I was no longer covering up and hiding my allure. But it made me think of New York even further, and as a result, it made me dread ever returning there.

Chapter Twenty-Nine
Hunter

No one zoned out as much as her. In one moment, she would be staring at me intently, and in the next, I would move from the spot I was standing in with the others, and she would still be staring, completely lost in her own thoughts. More often than needed, I headed back to the cart for a drink, and I savored each and every one. This time, however, I noted that she was getting hot, so I decided to stop for a moment and chat with her as she handed me a cold bottle of water.

"You want to head back to the hotel?" I asked, and she shook her head. "No, I need to be on top of updates, and I like it here."

This pleased me, so I nodded and returned the bottle to her.

"It is a beautiful course and country," I remarked, looking around at the greenery and scenery, and had to admit that it was quite stunning.

"Yeah," she replied. "I wish we never had to return to New York."

"You want to stay here forever?" I asked, and she nodded.

"Can we?"

"Let's talk about it after we're done here and return to the club for lunch," I said, and her smile widened even further. My heart skipped a beat because for a moment, I couldn't help but connect this moment right here and the way she looked at me to how I had always imagined the person I would fall in love with would look at me.

She'd ask for something, and I'd be sure it was a done deal, but of course, she would still need some persuading to agree. This, of course, was not even a possible deal, but with her, it was easy to imagine that everything was possible. I almost kissed her right then and there, but thankfully one of the men reached out to me, and I came to my senses. We both knew what had been about to happen, though, so she turned away, while I couldn't help but notice the slight flush of her cheeks. Whether it was due to the heat or that she was blushing, I couldn't tell. Maybe it was her makeup, but whatever it was, it made her look ethereal.

Soon enough, we completed the game, and even though it was very clear that I was the winner, we concluded that there was no winner. Still, I wasn't there to randomly play golf, so as we returned to the clubhouse for lunch, the thrill of the game gradually faded away, and we moved on to business conversations.

This was the most important part which needed all my attention, but it was hard to focus when she was so close by. She didn't even bother eating, as all she did was focus on listening and taking meeting notes, and throughout it all, I especially loved how our eyes kept meeting. It was as though she was so attentive to me that the moment she sensed that I was staring at her, she either lowered her gaze, averted her eyes, or found the courage to look right at me as well.

Eventually, though, it came to an end, and even though she couldn't sit with me, I pulled out my phone and sent a message.

"Get something to eat there; mango sticky rice is out of this world. Get it with the ice cream."

"I don't know," she replied. "Ice cream and rice sound a bit off to me. I'll get coconut chicken instead."

"I thought you said you're familiar with Thai food thanks to your friend?" I teased.

She smiled, "I am, but there are some things I have avoided, and they've been easy to avoid because they can sometimes be quite overpriced."

"Well, the food here is free, so eat."

"Yes, Sir," she replied, and when I glanced over at her table, she couldn't hide the smile on her face.

She got up then, and I watched as she called a waiter over and, after placing her order, headed over to the bar. I really wanted to speak to her, if for no other reason than to just be close to her, so I rose to my feet with the guise of ordering something stronger.

"McCallan," I asked the bartender as soon as I arrived, yet she didn't turn. She knew I was beside her; she could recognize my voice, and yet she didn't turn. So, I turned around and leaned against the counter as I took in the ambience of the area.

"Any news from New York yet?" I asked her.

"A couple of news channels wanted to report it, but the

Public Relations team has it under control. The breach has been found and intercepted, and right now, they are in the process of retrieving all relevant information and completely preventing this from ever happening again."

I went quiet then, as I thought of what to do to facilitate this as well, and it soon occurred to me that I didn't need to think too hard because soon enough, I would be returning to the city, and I would be able to meet with our CTO. I already had some ideas in mind.

"Find someone for me," I told her.

"Yes, Sir," she replied instantly, pulling out her phone to take notes.

"Dylan Fisher."

"Dylan Fisher?" she repeated.

"Yes. He's one of the best in the industry in cybersecurity. We can't recruit him because he has a thing against stable employment, but he will do some consultations for us."

"Yes, Sir," she replied and seemed to immediately get to work on this, but I stopped her.

"Have lunch first," I said. "We can continue afterward when we return to the hotel."

She nodded, and resisting the urge once again to kiss her, I moved away.

Chapter Thirty
Madison

The day was going so much better than I had anticipated. No major crises had come up yet, and it made me realize just how scared I was that we would have had to cut the entire trip short and return to New York.

Sighing and needing a little while to myself without any watchful eyes, I got onto the bar stool and took my seat. Just then, his whiskey was delivered, which made me relaxed that he hadn't even touched it.

I stared at the drink, and with no further choice, I took it over to him. He thanked me for it, and I decided to head over to the bathroom. With all this intense staring he was doing, I needed to be sure that I looked good.

Just then, however, a door from the men's bathroom swung open, and someone almost ran into me. I looked up, ready to apologize, but when I saw who it was, the words died on my tongue.

"We meet again," Felix said. "Is it just me, or is the

universe trying to bring us closer together, but you're avoiding it?"

I managed to smile but didn't bother saying a word because he was making reading him even more difficult for me. Smiling, I tried once again to move away from him, but he caught my hand.

"Not so fast," he said. "You're always so cold whenever we meet. I've apologized for that night. I've told you that it was just a misunderstanding."

I really didn't want to engage with him. There was no point whatsoever, but I had to do something to stop him from thinking that it was okay ever to come up to me.

"Really?" I asked. "You apologized? Because I haven't heard any apology from you."

The smile instantly left his face.

"I spoke to you earlier," he said. "I told you that I didn't have any bad intentions towards you."

"Saying it isn't enough," I replied. "But I feel like you did, so I'd really like it if, as a result, we keep our relationship and interactions solely professional."

"Have I been anything but?" he asked, and I tried to pull my hand out of his grasp, but he wouldn't let me go.

"This is what I mean," I said. "You can't do this."

"No, you absolutely can't," came the sudden voice, and my heart nearly stopped in my chest.

I turned to see Hunter before us, and his gaze was as sharp as daggers. He was glaring so angrily at Felix that I almost wanted to step in the way so that he wouldn't hurt him.

"It's alright, Sir," I said. "He was just trying to apologize for that night."

"Don't speak on my behalf," Hunter said.

"The fact that he gives you free rein to do whatever the hell you want around him because you're letting him fuck you doesn't mean that anyone else should." Felix replied.

My eyes widened in shock.

"W-what did you just say?"

He smiled.

"Isn't it obvious? You think that you two can hide the fact that you're fucking each other's brains out at night? I don't mean to be offensive, Mr. Swift, but I do think that despite the leeway you give to your secretary, she should learn to be respectful to your business partners. Speaking to me so rudely is unacceptable because I do have a company of my own and staff to manage, while she, on the other hand, is nothing but a meager secretary."

I was close to tears; however, I would truly have rather killed myself in that moment than to show how hurt and ashamed I felt. And so, I managed to work up a smile, wanting this moment to be over. Needing this humiliation to have never happened.

"I was just heading to the bathroom; I'll be out soon," I said, not to no one in particular, and continued on my way.

What I heard next, however, was the agonized shout of a man as he was punched so hard his body was slammed against the wall.

Something wet splashed over me, and I was so scared that I nearly screamed. For a split second, I was sure that it was Hunter, so I turned around, ready to intervene in the best way I knew how. But then I soon saw that it was Felix and that he was melting down the wall like wax. He held his face in his hand and couldn't stop yelling or bleeding for that matter.

"You broke my fucking nose!" he yelled. "You fucking bastard, you broke my nose."

Hunter, on the other hand, looked as though he hadn't even moved a single muscle. The only evidence was the fact that by his side, I could see him flexing his right hand.

"Avoid me for the rest of this conference," Hunter said. "I don't want to see you in any of the meetings we attend, and when people are greeting, I don't even want to see you in the vicinity, or you'll have to explain to them why I will be breaking your nose for the second time in the same week."

"You...you fucking asshole!" he yelled, but he didn't try to go after him. I was so petrified and shocked as I looked at both men because I couldn't even process what was happening and the consequences that would ensue. The consequences!

Hunter was going to lose this deal. It was a small one! It was his entrance into Asia. This was why he never wanted to have any relationships with the women he worked with. This was the reason why he always separated his personal life from his professional life. This was all my fucking fault. Now he was upset and, on my side, but it wouldn't be the case tomorrow or even a week from now.

"Sir," I immediately turned to him. "I think this is a misunderstanding. He was just trying to be friendly with me."

At my words, he gave me the most furious and angry look I had ever seen on his face. It seemed even worse than the way he had looked at Felix, and it was more than enough for me to keep my mouth shut.

A small crowd was gathering, and in their midst were two of the officials we had been having lunch with. I couldn't believe it. He left me there, and then he left the clubhouse. I couldn't follow. I couldn't be in the same car with him; I was sure he wasn't going to wait for me, so, I returned to grab my things and then left the clubhouse altogether.

I didn't want to go to the hotel at first, but then I realized and recalled that we weren't in the same room. Though it was side by side, he did have his own room, and I had mine, so I could stay there comfortably without being scared that I would run into him.

How the hell had things escalated so badly? I couldn't believe it. It took a while for me to get myself together, but soon enough, I was able to grab a taxi, and he took me back to the hotel.

When I arrived, the corridor was deadly quiet, as well as his room. There were no sounds coming from it.

I wondered if he had even returned to his room or if he was still somewhere within the hotel. It didn't matter. All that did was that I was hidden away where I couldn't run into him. After heading into the room, I locked the door, which was completely fruitless because I was sure the door connecting to his room was open. Yet I couldn't dare lock it because he was sure to hear it, and that in itself was another huge drop of blood in the well of contention that was now between us. I couldn't believe just half an hour earlier we had been all over each other, and now I was more or less hiding from him. Without even bothering to take off my clothes, I got into bed and tried to think of where exactly I had gone wrong.

I knew he was angry with me because of the way I had interfered, because of the way I had tried to cower and diffuse the situation. But what else had he expected me to do? Fan the flames? Felix, that asshole, was absolutely right. I was nothing but his secretary. And so, I had to act like one, but instead, I had caused such significant damage to his business operations.

Knowing him, I knew that was unforgivable. He never let anything, or anyone come in between his work, and I would be no exception whatsoever.

Sure, he was furious right now on my behalf, but would the same be the case later on? Would he even care? All he would see when he looked at me was the woman who had made him lose a huge deal. And that was something that Hunter would never find acceptable when he came back to his senses.

This, unfortunately, and despite how worried I was, was one of those things where there was no immediate solution. We both had to calm down, and we both had to come to our senses and resolve this logically. He, as well, had to recall that I was nothing to him but his secretary and the woman he slept with. He couldn't mess up his business relations for me, no matter what.

Sighing, I shut my eyes and tried to get to sleep. My current way of thinking was the truth, but it didn't change the fact that it was incredibly painful. But I was okay with approaching things this way because to me, he wasn't just my boss and the man I slept with. He was someone that I cared incredibly deeply about, and I didn't want, as a result, to negatively influence the thing that he cared deeply about.

Chapter Thirty-One
Hunter

"Hey!"

At the overly excited call, I pulled the phone away from my ear.

"Piper," I called, and I could hear the smile. I also heard the noise of kids running around and felt so exhausted. I always loved her family and of course my nieces, but I couldn't truly fathom how she was able to handle so much activity around her all the time.

"What's up?" she asked. "You're still in Thailand, right? Don't tell me you're back already. I told you to take this as a vacation for once. Geez, you need it!"

"I took it!" I told her. "I'm calling you because I took this as a vacation, and so I have the time. Get it?"

"Ah," she laughed. "You're right. You're right. How is it?"

I heard a male voice call from somewhere in the distance, and she promptly responded. "Hunter."

"Oh," came the response, and a second later, my brother-in-law's voice came on the line.

"Hunter!" he greeted. "The man! What's up? How's Thailand going?"

"It's good, it's great," I replied. "Beautiful country."

"Fucking gorgeous!" he exclaimed. "I backpacked across Asia after I graduated college."

This made me laugh because he was obviously about to dig his own grave.

"You mean the year you and my sister were broken up."

"Shhh," he said. "Don't mention that. I had fun, though. She thinks I was heartbroken and wallowing in a basement somewhere. I mean, I was, but I was wallowing in Thailand the best way that a guy should at that age, if you know what I mean."

I chuckled, but then he stopped.

"Wait, do you know what I mean?"

"Please give Piper the phone," I said, and he laughed.

"Talk to you later, bro."

"Alright, later," I said, and the phone was returned to her.

"I heard what you both were saying, and I'm just going to ignore it because we've been fighting all week, and I don't want another reason to kick him out of bed again for the third time this week. I'm beginning to think now that he annoys me on purpose just so he can spend the night in the basement in his fucking man cave."

"You sound like you're living the life, Piper," I said, and she immediately shot back.

"Unlike you with your one vacation in seven years, which is also a work trip as well. Shut up."

"Yes, ma'am," I replied, and the line briefly went silent.

"What's wrong?" she asked. "Ready to talk?"

"Why do you think something's wrong?" I asked as I turned and stared out the window at the gorgeous sunset.

"Because it's you, and if there's nothing wrong, you'll only be calling me if you are conflicted about something. It wouldn't be anything regarding work but something personal, so it means—"

"Oh my God! Is there something wrong with Dad?"

I was taken aback. I mean, everything she had said was right, but she hadn't even thought that this could possibly be about anyone else besides us. She immediately remembered her facility to remember.

"Hunter? Hunter?" she called worriedly at my silence.

"What's wrong? What's wrong with Dad? I spoke to him this morning."

"Then what is happening? Who are you having issues with?"

I was truly intrigued and amused.

"So apart from him, you didn't think I could be having personal issues with anyone else?"

"With how?" she asked. "Do you have any friends that aren't business partners? That automatically makes them business relationships, so why would you ever want to talk to me about them?"

I listened and shook my head.

"So it could be about a woman?"

"Why would it be about a woman?" she asked. "Purely out of curiosity."

At this, my face fell, and at her silence, I knew she was trying to provoke me until I turned red from fury.

"I'm sorry I called," I apologized. "I forgot just how completely unhelpful and aggravating you could be."

"Stop," she burst out laughing. "I'm sorry I'm teasing you; you know I'm playing with you. And now it's about a woman, I just didn't want to be too direct in case you changed your mind. You know how you are about personal issues. The fact that you're even discussing this means that you care about her, and I am so scared to ruin this."

"What are you talking about? Why would you ruin it?"

"You're opening up about romance, or you're involved in it even. If Dad heard this, he would burst into tears. My eyes are already wet."

Shaking my head once again, I went silent.

"Am I pushing it, right? Am I pushing you away by making this sound like a big deal? I'm so sorry. It's not a big deal. It's casual. Irrelevant."

"Piper, please stop talking," I said. "You're giving me a headache."

"Yes, Sir," she said, and finally, the line was silent.

"I'm not saying that I care about her, but... I am sleeping with her."

"That's good enough. Dad asked me yesterday if I wasn't sure you were gay. Phew."

"You two sure have a lot of time for gossip on your hands. He hasn't called me all week. Does he even know I'm in Thailand?"

"You always travel all over the place; he stopped keeping track all the time. We all did, actually. And he knows you're busy; you know he doesn't bother you until the weekend."

"Sure," I replied.

"Alright, before we get distracted, tell me what's wrong. I'm excited, by the way. Can you tell I'm excited?"

"Stop."

"Alright," she replied. "I just wiped my mouth shut; you can't see it."

"Um..." I didn't even know where to begin. I didn't even know why I was so mad at her. And that bastard, Felix.

"It wasn't her fault," I said. "I mean, I know it wasn't her fault. And she knows as well, but... I got mad at her."

"Okay," Piper said, no doubt finding it very hard to understand what I was saying or even talking about.

"She was being harassed by someone else."

"What?"

"Not fully harassed, just he was unrelenting in trying to get her attention, and she was obviously beginning to feel uncomfortable."

"And let me guess, you punched his lights out?"

She laughed, and I remained silent until she realized that that was exactly what had happened.

"Oh no," she said. "Hunter, you didn't."

"I broke his nose."

"Hunter!" she yelled. "Cool and all that, but Hunter! She must have been terrified."

"Not terrified, just... this is why I'm mad at her. She tried to defend him."

"What?"

"Not exactly defending him, she just tried to say there was a misunderstanding of some sort, but at that point, when she was so clearly uncomfortable by his advances, then why the hell would he even—"

I stopped then as the answer hit me like a bag of bricks.

"What?" Piper asked. "You just realized something, right?"

"Yeah," I replied and sighed. "I thought she was being too lenient and too nice by trying to come to his defense."

"And now?" Piper asked.

"Well, now I know that what she was trying to do was to help me."

"What do you mean? How was she helping you?" Piper asked.

"He's a business associate. We're currently exploring avenues in expanding into Asia, and this guy, in particular, has proved to be a helpful connection thus far."

"Ah--," she said. "But wait, she works with you? I thought you never did that? Something about clearly not mixing your personal and professional lives. Why did you change this?"

"I didn't change it."

"So why—"

"Ah--" she said, "You didn't change it, but... it's her. It's also the reason why you're calling me. Also, the reason why you lost your temper. Maybe on all of this, you're not even angry with her, especially now that you realize why she did it and that she was acting in your best interest."

"So you're saying the person I'm really angry with is myself?" I asked.

"Yes," she replied. "That is exactly what I am saying. You don't agree?"

It took me a while to decide on how I was going to respond to this, yet nothing felt suitable. Or more accurately, nothing seemed like it wouldn't bruise my ego.

"Hunter?" Piper called.

"I don't disagree," I said, and she went silent.

"Are you taking me for a fool here?" she asked dryly.

"No," I took the question seriously. "I see what's happening. And it wasn't what I intended from the start. I just... maybe this entire trip was a bad idea. All vacations are usually this way. What a fucking distraction!"

"Distractions aren't the worst things in the world, Hunter," she said. "You're human. These desires... the fact that you couldn't resist her... that's what makes you human. And moreover, you're not usually like this with most people or anyone else for that matter. Why ignore it? Why trivialize it?"

These questions I had absolutely no answer to.

Chapter Thirty-Two
Madison

There were so many perks to being with a billionaire. For instance, now we had just arrived at the tarmac and had a private plane waiting. His private plane.

We had flown into Bangkok on it, and back then, I had been too scared to take a picture. Worried more than anything of seeming uncultured. I had told myself that on this trip to Phuket, I would do it, but then here I was flying to Phuket with him a few days later, and I still couldn't take a photo.

He was ahead of me, acting like he had been all morning, as though I didn't exist. So, the least thing I imagined he would want was me taking a shot of his plane. I didn't want to aggravate him even further, and this time around, it wasn't even because I was worried I was going to get fired. At this point, I didn't even care if I got fired or not.

Perhaps it would be better if I did because if I had been expecting not to be affected by him after we had slept together and to be able to carry on as we had previously, no matter what happened, then I must have been deluded. Because I was sick to my stomach.

He wasn't rude to me, but I had never felt so invisible. Not even when he truly didn't notice my existence. But then at least he had spoken to me like I was his secretary. So far, he hadn't said a word.

Sighing, I stopped for a moment on the stairs and truly considered just quitting. Perhaps it would be best for me to just quit and return to the city. Perhaps that was what he wanted. Perhaps that was why he was icing me out.

"Miss Parish," the air hostess called from the entrance to the plane, and I looked up at her.

"We're leaving," she smiled. "Please come on board."

I looked at her and then glanced towards the windows. Met his gaze then, and it was only for a moment. Not because he looked away, but because I did. Because my heart jumped in my chest, and because I couldn't stand it.

Nodding, I continued heading up with my luggage in hand, and she took it from me. I went with her and was soon seated opposite him while she stored my hand luggage away. I put my seatbelt on, looked ahead at the captain's door, and the doors were shut.

He was going through his phone, but I couldn't dare exhibit the same nonchalance, so I remained still and gave all my mental and emotional energy into deciphering how I was going to resolve this.

Soon we took off, and she came over with refreshments. I picked up a can of tea while he, on the other hand, accepted the flute of champagne she offered.

I turned away then and thought, and as soon as she was out of the vicinity, I spoke.

"Sir..." I said. "This is your vacation. And it is the first one you'll be having in a very long while. I really don't want to put a dent on it, so... maybe when we arrive, I can go my own way for the next two days till we have to return?"

What followed after my words was complete silence, but I knew that he had looked up from his phone and was now watching me.

"Do you know why I was mad at you yesterday?" he asked.

"Yes, Sir," I replied without looking at him.

"Tell me then," he said. "Why was I mad at you?"

"You were mad because I had interfered. I was trying to defend... I was trying to lighten the situation even though I could very clearly see that you didn't want to make light of it at all."

Another stretch of silence followed, and I couldn't bear it anymore. So, I dared to look at him.

"I didn't want anything to interfere with your life, Sir," I said. "I'm meant to make your life easier and better, not make it even more complicated. That is my job and that is what I am dedicated to doing. And so, in that moment, I didn't react the way I did because I didn't feel wronged. I did it because he is a business associate, and I knew just how important this expansion could be for the company. I've been around the teams for months, and I cannot have missed their discussions on it. And so, considering all of that, I—"

"Why do you consider everyone else all the time?" he interrupted me. "Why don't you consider yourself?"

"It's not my job to consider myself," I repeated. "And... with all due respect, Sir, it's not yours either. With our...

relationship over the past few days, I understand that this might make you want to come to my defense when things like this happen, but—"

"I didn't come to your defense because I'm sleeping with you," he cut me off.

"I did that because you're my secretary, and your safety and well-being are my responsibility."

"Yes, Sir," I repeated. "And I agree with your words. I appreciate them deeply, but I wasn't explicitly in danger, and you cannot care for my welfare at the potential detriment of your business. You can only do this when our relationship... when our relationship is more than professional. And this is the one thing that it is not."

"It terrifies me that because of what happened yesterday, the officials wouldn't want to work with you anymore."

"They're not our only way into Asia, Madison," he said. "There are countless other opportunities."

I watched him, knowing this was true, but I didn't think if I repeated once again how I didn't want to interfere negatively in his life and work, he would probably not agree with me.

Saddened but at least grateful that he had spoken to me, I turned away and stared at the gorgeous vistas. I asked myself if I regretted sleeping with him, and I couldn't bring myself to say that I did. So far, it had been all and more than I could have ever imagined, and I wouldn't trade even a single moment for anything else. I knew from the start that it was bound to get complicated. We both knew, and so now it was. We had to truly decide how to move forward. I, for one, understood that if we moved forward as we were, more issues were going to arise, and I made my decision then.

"I think that, in light of things, Sir, it would be better if we could manage to revert back to a solely professional relationship. I hope this is something you can agree to, as I am sure that in the long run, it will be more beneficial to the both of us."

Another stretch of silence followed once again, but then his response came.

"Okay."

Something in my heart clenched so hard that it was as though someone had sent a knife through it. It was so painful that it stole my breath away, and in response, I was so incredibly angry at myself. I had been the one to ask for this, so what now was my problem? He had given me what I wanted. He was giving me what I wanted, so why did it hurt so much?

Unable to remain in the cabin because my throat was now completely clogged with emotion, I was certain that I would be crying in seconds. I got up and excused myself, ensuring to do it with a smile so that he would see and be completely convinced that it was a smile.

I headed down to the gallery and met the air hostess there, preparing our meal. She was so beautiful I was momentarily struck for a while. It was a perfect distraction because she smiled at me once again, and I smiled back. I headed into the bathroom then and shut the door.

I thought of what to do. I hadn't brought my phone, so it wasn't as though I could talk to anyone. All I had was myself and the silence, and I had to deal with it. I had to figure this out on my own. He had said *okay,* and so now we were solely boss and secretary again, so why the hell was I so fucking sad?

I shut my eyes and tried to calm my emotions, but soon enough, the tears started to flow from my eyes. They fell down my face, and I wondered if I had made the wrong decision.

Emma had told me to fight for what I wanted, and what I wanted was him, but it wasn't that simple. I couldn't convince myself that what I wanted was him, and I didn't want what was to him a momentary thrill to mess up his work and progress so much. Maybe I was overthinking all of this. He had said earlier that we should go with the flow, at least until we returned to New York, so had I been too impulsive by suggesting what I had to him? By insisting that we break off all activities between us that weren't solely related to work. I couldn't take it back now. I wasn't fickle, and I couldn't appear like that before him either, so I allowed myself to mourn the way I had wanted to, and then I wiped the tears off my face and got up.

After staring at myself in the mirror and ensuring that I looked as normal as possible, I reopened the door. There was very little I could do about my reddened eyes, but he wasn't going to be staring at me anyway, so what was the issue?

I returned to the cabin and saw that the air hostess was serving our food.

She was all over him, I realized. She was smiling, leaning forward, batting her lashes. From pain to anger was all I could feel then because why couldn't all these fucking women just do their jobs? I instantly felt better then about choosing our work, his work, over extracurricular thrills. So, I tried my best to ignore her, and soon she came over to me.

"Whatever is available is fine, thank you," I said.

She was a bit startled by this.

"Grilled Sea Bass with a mango and papaya salad, served alongside jasmine rice? Is this selection okay, or would you like to tweak it or choose something else?"

"It's fine," I replied, and she went on her way.

He began eating while I looked out the window. It was time for me to think about what the fuck I had done to occupy myself when we had flown over.

From what I could remember, he had been working as usual to conclude tasks from New York before we headed into Thailand, and he had to put his focus on all things happening there. And so, I kept myself busy as well, planning his itinerary, cross-checking reservations. I pulled out my laptop then and began to search for new things to include on his itinerary so he would be able to relax. I also searched for things for myself because this time around, we weren't sharing the same room. We had two different rooms, and when he was relaxing on the beach, I wanted other things to do. The only time we would be a bit closer in proximity to each other was late that evening when it was time for us to head over to the yacht. We would be on it all night until the next afternoon, and I had been so excited about it. But now, as things were going, I would probably not be able to show my face.

Sighing, I shut the laptop once again and put it away, and just then, my meal arrived.

She definitely didn't flirt with me, but I did notice that her button was now more open than it had been, and so now I could very clearly see her cleavage. I frowned so deeply at this that she had to stop to ask me what was wrong.

I looked at her and then at him and returned my attention to my food.

"Nothing, thank you."

I ate through the meal because I needed the emotional support, not because I could taste my food or anything. I still didn't want to consume any alcohol, but my inability to handle myself in the midst of it was how we had gotten into this predicament.

Soon enough, she returned to take away our plates, and then she came back with desserts and ice cream.

I rejected mine, he did as well, and soon enough, the cabin was quiet.

Chapter Thirty-Three
Hunter

I didn't think I had ever seen her sulk before. It would've been amusing if I wasn't furious with her at the distance she had established between us. I, of course, didn't agree with what she said, but I wasn't one to plead with anyone, and I expected her to take that back on her own accord. But I had forgotten just how stubborn she was, so even though this was very clearly hurting her, I completely expected her not to take it back till forever.

Sighing, I shook my head and put my laptop away.

"How is it that you're the one who suggested we be solely professional, yet you look like you've been trying to hold back tears for the past two hours?"

At my words, she turned to me.

"I... I haven't been holding back tears."

"You're lying to me again?" I asked.

"You expect me to say that I have even if I have? Isn't that a bit unrealistic? I'm not lying to you; I just don't have to be completely transparent with you. I don't owe you that unless it solely concerns your work."

She had yelled a little, and to say it startled me was an understatement. My brows raised as I watched her, and when she turned to me, I could see the fear in her eyes. I could also see the tears that gathered.

"I'm sorry, I didn't mean to... I'm sorry. I'm just -"

"Come here," I said, and the tears fell from her eyes.

She was such a fucking baby, and I couldn't believe just how much I loved this side of her. She was so bloody honest, so bloody transparent. Once again, I was beginning to understand why I had felt so comfortable with her without even realizing it. Now it all made sense to me and made me understand that I wasn't in any way going to honor her suggestions.

"Come here," I repeated, and she shook her head as her hand lifted to wipe the moisture off her face.

"That's an order," I said, and a few seconds later, she rose to obey because she couldn't defy this.

She headed towards me, and to my surprise, she held my gaze. She didn't look away but tried to look as unaffected as possible, but everything gave her away.

"Sit astride me," I said, and her eyes widened.

"Sir?"

"Astride me," I replied. "That too is an order."

She watched me, and then she did as I had asked.

She was back to dressing as unimpressive as could possibly be, so there was nothing difficult about this. She had on baggy, dark, ill-fitting pants and a hideous blue dress shirt. Knowing just how sick her body was underneath this dreary outfit, I almost cried when she had come out from her quarters earlier this morning and met me at the elevator. In a way, and given how nice she was at dressing, I was convinced I knew how standoffish she was. And so, the way she had acted since then, and everything she had said, none of it was surprising to me.

And I realized how, as I watched her, I myself had also unconsciously decided how I was going to respond. I was going to wait to call bullshit on her feigning that she had a steel heart and wait for her to break.

"I had thought you'd at least be able to hold yourself together till we get to the hotel, and I couldn't see you, but you couldn't even keep it together for the flight?"

At my words, her eyes widened, and then she tried to get off, but it was too late. My arms banded around her, and I ensured that she stayed in place.

"Let me go, Sir," she said, and she smiled.

"I won't. I don't want to. You, on the other hand, seem to be looking for every opportunity, even remotely possible, to let me go."

She stopped then and looked at me, and tears rolled down her eyes again.

"I'm so sorry, I'm not usually emotional. I don't know what the hell is wrong with me; I just-"

"You like me," I said, and I could feel her entire body turn to stone.

"Sir?"

"Am I wrong?" I asked. "You like me, and you care about me. You also care about my business because I care about it, ¡and you didn't want to bring any harm to it. And because of this, you're willing to deny yourself. Am I wrong?"

She watched me, and then she lowered her head. I leaned forward and whispered into her ears.

"If you were the one, and you had someone in your life

who acted this way toward you... then, coupled with the fact that the sex between you two is unbelievable, would you let go so easily?"

She leaned forward and rested her forehead against mine.

"Stop... please."

I held her even tighter, and she had no choice but to stare into my eyes.

"Do you really want me to stop?" I asked.

"You know I won't force. Since you've already expressed what you want, I'll respect it. But for the sake of giving things a second consideration, would you rather find a solution with me?"

She watched me, and then she nodded.

"I admit that my reaction yesterday was quite over the top. But I don't regret it though. If it were anyone else, I cannot say that I would have been as annoyed or affected, but because it was you, I was more sensitive than I usually am. However, I am not going to apologize for that either."

She watched me.

"I told you earlier that we shouldn't control our time together during these ten days. Afterwards, after we return to New York, we can deal with whatever the consequences are. But for now... can we just not think for once? About repercussions and about the future? Which means that if I get pissed off that he keeps harassing you despite the very clear warnings to stay away from you, then I will punch him in the nose once again, and you cannot get scared or worried. As I told you, no one person can ever be powerful enough to negatively affect my business or hinder my way. This is a trivial concern on your part."

She nodded, and I could only hope she was taking in all that I was saying.

"So... what do you say?" I asked. "We go back to truly being on vacation. Without any restrictions?"

She considered this, and then she leaned forward and kissed me. The plane wasn't that huge, so I was certain that whatever we did could easily be discovered by the air hostesses; there was no room for us, at least, so we couldn't go anywhere else. Madison, however, seemed not to care.

Her hands went to the buttons of her blouse, and then she began to unbutton them. I realized then that there was one more thing that I wanted to say.

"Also," I said, "From now on, don't dress that way anymore. I'm not a man without self-control, and we've already established that you're more than just a female I truly don't mind advances from, so there's no need to cover up in order to help me resist temptation because as of now and between us, that is impossible. And I know what you taste like, and whenever I have the appetite for this and for you within however many days or hours, then I need you to make yourself available to me. Unless of course you don't want to."

She nodded just as she finished with the buttons, and then she was pulling the fabric off her shoulders.

Chapter Thirty-Four
Madison

I had no idea what I was doing. I had no idea what was coming over me, but what I did know was that I wanted him right now and I didn't care who was watching. In fact, as I stared into his eyes, my heart burning with affection for unbelievably saying all the right things, I had to admit that it thrilled me that she would be in the galley and that she would hear.

But I didn't care. I was, however, concerned that he would.

"We don't have to go too far," I said as I slanted my head and kissed him. Given all the contention so far, my tears, my heart, and my despair, this kiss had to be the sweetest thing that I had ever tasted.

He didn't hold back, and I treasured him even more for it.

"This is my plane," he said. "We can go as far as you want."

"Golden fucking words."

Smiling, I stared into his eyes, and as the time seemed to

stop, it truly felt like I was in heaven. It also helped immensely that when I looked out toward the window, all I could see around us were the clouds.

With his arm wrapped around me, he began to kiss down my neck, savoring every inch of my skin, and I gave myself wholly to him.

He said we had the rest of the trip, and since I had already thrown a monumental tantrum and needed things with him, I was sure that I was going to be cautious before making the same mistake twice. Hence, all I could see was a very smooth and decadent remaining six days.

He grabbed my breasts in that almost violent yet stimulating way of his. There was something about the way he held them that made butterflies flood my stomach. It was just so carnal, so possessive, and as a result, I couldn't keep myself from grinding on him even if I wanted to.

There was too much of a barrier between us. Too many clothes, but I could still feel his hardness between my legs rubbing on my clit. The friction was exquisite, his smell intoxicating, and his warmth so goddamn sweet I couldn't help but moan.

He pressed a button then, and I was somewhat startled. Soon, however, as the frosted glass slid shut all around us, I realized there was actually a provision for privacy. As I looked around in surprise and then returned my attention to him, he explained.

"I got the plane for business, so I didn't imagine I'd need the private room. This, though, was a last-minute provision included for extremely private meetings."

"This is business, Sir," I said, and as I reached behind

me, then my bra came unhooked. "And an extremely private meeting."

"I love your smart mouth," he said. "You know this, right?"

My heart skipped several beats in response, and this was incredibly dangerous. He could say things like this to me, but I understood his intention.

And so, recalling my admonition to myself not to over-think, I accepted his mention of the word and stored it deep in my heart like a treasure. His mouth moved to my breasts then, and as the sheer pleasure coursed down to my core at his kisses on my nipples, every stray and unnecessary thought was instantly wiped out of my head.

"Too many barriers," he eventually said, and I completely agreed.

I rose to my feet when he finally let me go, and he watched, his chest heaving as my hands went to the button of my slacks. I unbuttoned them, and underneath was one of Emma's sexiest lingerie. She would be so incredibly proud that I wore them, and that they were now live in action, but at the time earlier that morning when I had slipped them on, she was the farthest thing from my mind. It was just that I wanted to feel desirable, even as, due to my fight with Hunter, I had felt as though there would never be any use or need for that again. He had let me in in a way that I was very well aware that he let little to no one in, and I had turned it into a fight.

"Well, not anymore," I said to myself as I thanked my past self for choosing to wear this absolutely sinful piece.

I put a note in my mind to thank Emma for it the next time I was on the phone with her, and it took everything inside of me not to resist taking a picture of him as well as he took in the sight with unbridled appreciation.

"Is this something I should know about you?" he asked as he coolly headed into the string that held the fabric to my waist.

"You dress in sexy underwear when you're mad or having a hard time. I hope this is true because I expect to intervene from now on."

Once again, my heart squeezed and hurt because he was speaking as though we had more than this. As though we had a future together. I knew him enough to know just how much he hated deception and manipulation, so he was saying all these things because perhaps he saw some sort of future between us when we returned to Manhattan. It was probably not going to be a full-blown relationship, but it did make me feel as though he had some kind of plan that was indeed exciting.

There was so much to look forward to. I quickly stepped out of the pants, and they puddled on the floor and I sink down to my knees. His hand instantly went to his belt to unbuckle it, and by the time I reached him, I instantly took over. In no time, his gorgeous, solid cock was exposed, and my mouth began to water. In the light of day, I could see every inch of it, and my heart fluttered in amazement. It was fucking beautiful—pink flushed and so aroused, veins strained against the sides. I took my time and licked up and down the gorgeous length, committing every inch of it to memory. I understood now that all of this was a dream, this exquisite, beautiful kind, but it was bound to end, and I didn't mind. It was already better than anything else I ever had, and as a result, rather than bemoan the short time-frame, I was going to give myself to every single moment with complete abandon just like this, and just like now.

"Look at your eyes," he said. "They're sparkling. You love my cock this much?"

"You have no idea," I replied, parting my lips and wrapping my mouth around his throbbing head. I loved his taste in a way that I couldn't describe. It was uniquely his, and I couldn't get enough of it. A few sucks, and he was already leaking desire into my mouth. I licked him further downwards to his base, and once I began to pull his balls into my mouth, I knew I was unraveling him.

At first, he remained calm, but when I began to jack him off in tandem with sucking his balls, I understood that I was overwhelming him. He didn't hold back as he threw his head back against the seat and moaned. He was louder than I had ever heard him, and I understood that there was no holding back with me, at least. I relished his reaction.

"I understand," I said as I sucked him even harder. I straightened then, and he leaned forward to kiss me. It was so carnal, so sinful, and when he pulled away and smiled, I knew he was thoroughly enjoying himself.

"Keep going," he said, leaning back against the chair, and he didn't have to ask me twice.

"Yes, Sir," I said, and continued.

He hardened first as I milked him, and it wasn't long before both of my hands joined in the sweet assault. Finding that rhythm and pressure that drove him wild was always a thrill. With one hand wrapped like a vice around the base and the other moving in tandem with my mouth up and down his length, I blew him until he couldn't remain still.

Having a man who was so in control with everything

else in his life completely lose it as a result of my hands and mouth was indescribable. My jaw hurt, but I didn't stop, and soon enough, I was rewarded with his release.

Grabbing my hair, he loosened the band, and just like that, it was flowing over my face.

"Beautiful," he breathed, but as I glanced up at him, I deeply suspected that he wasn't exactly seeing me. Perhaps a blurry visage was more appropriate because his eyes were too glazed over with pleasure.

After kissing me on the top of my head, he leaned against the chair, and in the next moment, he was spurting harder, and I almost choked on his cum. I didn't want to waste any drop of it, so I kept his dick in my mouth and sucked as hard as I could until he couldn't take anymore.

He was breathing so hard at the end of it that he couldn't catch his breath.

It took a while for him to recover, and by the time he did, I was now seated astride on his lap. I watched him as I pushed his hair out of his eyes, but he still couldn't look at me as he tried to get himself under control. I kissed him once again and dove into the whirlwind of emotions that made him ready to go again.

"You're going to be the death of me," he said as we broke slightly apart for a moment. I smiled as I continued to grind against him, and then I grabbed him, unwilling to wait any longer.

He reached his hand underneath me to stroke my clit, and I threw my head back, enjoying it just the way that I wanted. I knew that she could hear us, and I couldn't believe just how turned on I was.

But I was enjoying him unfathomably, and I was glad

that she would hear and know, so hopefully, she would know how to back away.

One of his fingers slipped inside of me, and then another, and I began to ride it. Biting down on my bottom lip, I savored his touch until he kissed me once again and let go. I understood then that he had gotten the feel that he wanted and had handed the reins back to me.

Beyond wet, I slipped the dark lace to the side and hoisted myself up, positioning him at my entrance. Watching him, I did the same to him as I lowered down on his length, and once again, he shut his eyes. I moaned as he entered me because I wouldn't ever get used to how big he was.

I could see it clearly in real life, but there were no words to describe how decadently he fit inside of me. I was stretched so sweetly and filled so thoroughly that I couldn't help but collapse against him, needing to process this, needing to know how to handle this.

I couldn't stay long without moving, even though I didn't want it to end. But once again, the admonition to live in the moment came to mind, and the enjoyment of this current moment, in particular, was so sweet. My heart wanted to fly out of my chest, perhaps because we had fought and reconnected, but I felt so damn close to him in a way that I never had before and couldn't believe was possible. Our hearts beat as one as he held me, and as I fucked him in and out, I moved my hips, pulling out just until his tip was at my entrance and then slamming back down onto him.

Eventually, I rose completely and sat on the couch with my knees underneath and by his sides. I guided him back to my entrance and moaned loudly. I began to ride him then, and he nearly lost it. I could see the veins throbbing by his temples, down his neck, and feel the sting of his hard grip as he reached behind to grab my ass. He was every bit as intoxicated by this moment as I was, and we both didn't want it to end. My pace increased, and so did his thrusts, trying to make this as hard and impactful for me as possible.

"Oh," he moaned. "Fuck," he swore as he continued to mold my ass. It felt so good. He felt so good, and so did I. I leaned forward to kiss him, finding a way to grind myself. My legs were literally no longer on the ground, and neither was my sense in my body. It felt as though it was somewhere on the clouds, floating by, lounging, and sipping on a daiquiri, having the time of my life. I wasn't jealous because nothing could compare to this feeling right now. The feel of his dick hit me at just the right spot over and over again as I fucked into it, chasing the unbelievable sweetness and thrill. Eventually, though, neither of us could keep up. I was trembling all over while he was clenching hard and cursing.

I couldn't really appreciate it due to the intensity of the situation, but a corner of my brain didn't miss the novelty of it at all.

He cursed in real life, especially when one of his employees momentarily pissed him off, but only there. I could still recall the first time I had heard it. He rarely got angry, despite how strict he was with his work, but when he did, he was scarier than the devil.

"Fuck, I adored this man," my heart couldn't help but sing as I wrapped my hands around him in desperation.

I cried out as I came, pleasure rampaging through my body like a storm. I could feel the hard clench of his abdomen as well as his collapse against me as he began to come as well. His entire body spurted and tensed yet I didn't stop riding him. I couldn't stop even if a gun was held to my head. Pleasure had completely taken over both of us and reduced us to nothing less than animals. Unable to control ourselves, unable to catch our breath. Eventually though, and thankfully when it was announced that we would soon be landing, I had no choice but to regain my senses.

Sure, the privacy screen was helpful, but I was sure that couldn't remain as it was as we descended, so I was forced to open my eyes and that was when I found that he was watching me as well. He brushed my hair out of my face so affectionately that I was almost sure he was falling in love with me, and if this was a stretch, he looked at me as though he was seeing me for the very first time.

"I have to say," he said. "I am incredibly glad you came along on this trip. I cannot believe I would have taken it alone."

This made me smile, unfortunately, however, I didn't have much time for much else as I got up and collapsed onto the seat beside him. I was so exhausted I almost dared to fall asleep but, in his arms, solely in his arms.

"Hello, Sir," we heard the air hostess call.

"Yeah," he replied as he unhurriedly began to redo his belt buckle.

"We'll be landing soon so you have to put your seatbelt on. And take the screen down if you don't mind. My apologies for the interruption."

"No need," he said as he zipped up his pants.

I was too lazy to handle myself and bolder than ever.

"Sir," I gave him a look after he was done, and he laughed because he knew exactly what it was. He grabbed my pants and pulled them onto his lap so that he could help me get dressed as well. I felt so pampered and so special but none of it compared to when he spread his seatbelt between us and then extended the seatbelt around both of us.

"Ready to land in Phuket?" he asked into my ear as he nibbled on my earlobe.

"I am," I replied and turned around to kiss him.

Chapter Thirty-Five
Hunter

T hings were intensifying and escalating between us. Fast. I knew it and she knew it as well. She, however, was under the impression that I was opposed to things truly getting serious between us. But I wasn't, at all.

Up till now, I hadn't met anyone I was even remotely interested in going far with, but as I watched her descend the plane and immediately greet the driver on my behalf to ensure that everything for our drive to the resort was put in place, I couldn't stop the warmth I had for her from intensifying in my heart.

I headed over to the waiting car and took my seat in the back. Then I shut my eyes and tried to imagine if I had ever felt this way with anyone else before. So safe, so enthralled, so confident.

Soon, as she got in as well and her scent washed over me, I realized that I hadn't at all. And so, I couldn't stop myself from opening my eyes and watching her.

She smiled at me, but I could tell just how shy she had

become. We rode in silence, and I shut my eyes again, trying to get some sleep. The previous night I had barely been able to get any, and it had astounded me because never in my life had I lost sleep over any woman. She was opening up a part of me that I didn't even know I had, and I wasn't going to shy away from it. My suspicion, though, was that she would, and so even though all I wanted was to hold her hand, I refrained.

There was something, though, I couldn't stand, and this I only discovered when we arrived at the resort, and she brought our keys over.

"Different rooms?" I asked, and she nodded, amused.

"Of course. We weren't sleeping together when I made the reservations. In fact, we weren't even sleeping together up till just a few days ago."

"But now we are," I said and stared at her.

She could read my mind. She had to be able to, or else I was going to turn vengefully.

"Yeah, Sir," she said, barely able to control her laughter, and then she turned around and returned to the front desk. It took a while, but I had emails to catch up on, and waited for her return.

"The best room," she held up the key card. "For the both of us."

Rather than take the key from her like she had expected, I leaned forward and kissed her. In a way, it felt like we were on our honeymoon. I never thought I would think of the term regarding me, but here we were all of a sudden, and I planned to enjoy every bit of it.

We were right by the beach, and it was breathtaking. It was a secluded beach. When I saw the huge infinity pool in our room, I decided that that was what I wanted to test out first. Instantly, as I set the bags down, I turned to her.

"Fancy a swim?" I asked.

"Do you know how to swim?"

"Um... yes, I do, but I think we should shower first."

"Why?" I asked. "It's just us."

I didn't give her a chance to protest. I didn't even give her the chance to take her clothes off. I lifted her onto my shoulders, and she squealed in excitement.

"Do you want something to eat?" I asked, and she shook her head.

"Champagne, and something sweet," I suggested.

"Put me down so I can make this happen, Sir," she said, but I shook my head.

I didn't set her down, though.

"These next two days till we have to go back to Bangkok, you're not my secretary, agreed?"

She stared at me, and then she nodded.

"Agreed."

I put her down then and returned to the room. I found the necessary numbers, and a few minutes later had some savory and sweet desserts, along with champagne, headed up to us.

It was getting late, but I loved the ambiance of the entire villa. It was full of activity, but I didn't quite want to go anywhere just yet. From what she had told me, she had a yacht docked somewhere waiting for us, but I wanted to enjoy the room with her first, so I headed over to the pool.

I found that she had completely stripped down and was in it. I could see her clothes discarded by the corner, and that she was in nothing more than her underwear.

That, in my opinion, was too much clothing, so when I stripped down, I made sure to strip all the way down.

The moment I was naked, her mouth fell open, and instantly she looked behind her to be sure that no one else could see us. Our lodging was quite private, but still, there was very little barrier between us and the ocean beyond and the rest of the world. I didn't care. I got into the pool.

I had a pool in my apartment back in New York, but I had been so occupied over the past few years that I couldn't even recall the last time I had used it leisurely. Most times I went to the gym in the office, took a shower, and headed straight to my office. This was the most relaxed I had felt in so long, and the fact that I was spending it with her was more good fortune than I could process. And so, as she came over to me, and I could feel that she too had completely discarded her clothes, I crushed her body to me and kissed her.

"Good fortune," I said, and she was slightly startled.

"What?" she asked.

"Nothing," I said and kissed her again. She melted completely into me.

Chapter Thirty-Six
Madison

"So you two have been doing nothing but having sex all day?" Emma asked.

I laughed at this because I wished it was true. It wasn't true, but then I started to wonder why it wasn't.

"Hey!" she called, and I came back to the present. I was combing through my hair and just about to turn on the dryer. I glanced towards the locked door, then and thought.

"What's going through your mind?" she asked.

"I don't know, I'm just wondering why we haven't been having sex all day, but it feels like heaven so far."

"You had sex on the plane and then in the pool!" she exclaimed, and I laughed at this.

"We didn't have sex in the pool; we just fooled around, and you wouldn't believe, but we raced a few laps to see who would be fastest."

"Let me guess, he let you win," she rolled her eyes, and I shook my head.

"No, he didn't. He beat me every time, and then I got

tired, and we just basked in the sun then fell asleep. We're going to have lunch now, that's why I'm getting ready."

"Wow, you really are having a blast," she said, "while I, on the other hand, have to find a new manufacturer."

"Why? What happened?" I asked as I massaged the oil into my hair. "I thought you were already set since last month."

"Well, he suddenly brought up some excuses about the materials being more difficult to acquire than he had expected, and so he's had to increase my minimum order quantity."

I sighed as I listened to her and then lowered down to stare at her.

"All of this talk of your work is making me want to start baking again."

"What?" she asked, shocked. "Are you serious? Didn't you quit because you were burnt out?"

"Yeah, but I think I want to try again. I keep thinking of it, and I never stop doing it. I just think I was trying to do too much at the same time. This time around, I think I might want to focus on just one specialty. Maybe cheese-cakes? I suddenly want a cheesecake. Anyway, back to you, I'm good at sourcing out things. Want me to find something and do some research for you? You seem like you need some help and sleep."

"I'd love that," she said, "but there's too much you don't understand about it."

"That's not a problem; I'll go through your conversation history,"

Her mouth fell open.

"You're joking," she said.

I shook my head.

"No, it's my job to read other people's minds and make them as understood as possible."

"It's eight months of communication," she warned me.

"Don't worry, I'm particularly free these days, so I'll start slowly, and that way I'll understand what you need."

Her eyes softened as she stared at me, and I shook my head.

"Go to bed," I said. "I'll give you an update tomorrow."

"Thank you so much, Maddy," she sniffed, and the call came to an end.

I picked up the dryer then and got to work with my hair, and a few minutes later, I was done. I wished we could spend the rest of the evening just sleeping, but I was too excited despite being exhausted and didn't want to waste any moment of the two days we had here.

Everything felt so new and so exciting, even the resort itself. And so, as I got out, I gave my attention fully to the panoramic views of the Andaman Sea.

I quickly took several pictures from where I stood, and then I went in search of Hunter. I soon found him in the sitting area already lounging and waiting.

"Lunch will be here soon," he said, and I couldn't help but head over to join him. He was shirtless, and it was a sight to behold.

His tattoos were gorgeous, his skin clean and glistening, and his hair slightly blowing in the late afternoon breeze.

"You fit so perfectly into this lifestyle," I said as I brushed his hair out of his eyes, and he laughed.

"What kind of lifestyle?" he asked. "Idle?"

"Leisurely," I replied. "You look like a surfer who's never been out in the sun, or heat for that matter."

He smiled and doubled over, and I moved even closer to him.

"I love everything I'm hearing. Too bad I'm a boring entrepreneur who deals in renewable energy and spends all his day in an office."

"Too bad," I sighed, and he leaned forward to kiss me. Just then, there was a knock on the door, and instantly, he got up.

"I'm starving to death, and that knock indicates that our meal is here. I'll be right back."

"Alright," I replied, feeling a bit weird that he was the one going to answer the door as it was my job. However, once done again, I tried to admonish myself that there was no need to hold on to ideals that went against the current focus of my life for this afternoon, which was to sleep, relax, and take in every single moment without any troublesome hints for further obligations.

Soon, the restaurant staff arrived with our lunch, which was a selection of grilled Andaman lobster, Phuket-style blue crab curry, massaman lamb curry, steamed sea bass in lime sauce, and so on.

I immediately dug in, and we both enjoyed our food as we stared out towards the ocean.

I watched him silently and decided that I hated to share a bit of what I had been talking to Emma about earlier.

"Did you read my resume before you accepted me for the job of being your secretary?" I asked.

"Your resume?" he repeated. "No, I didn't."

I wasn't surprised at this, but in a way, I still was.

"Then how were you sure that you would be okay with me working for you?" I asked. "Back then, Human Resources more or less put the fear of God into me that I was to use my expertise in renewable energy to impress you because you would be scouring through every inch of my CV."

"I did give it a glance," he replied. "But ultimately, I'm not even sure how you got hired. You know how my schedule is. One moment I'm reading something, and the next, I'm called away urgently. Perhaps Derek just decided then that you were qualified when he couldn't get me to finish reading enough to give a judgment."

This amused me. "Remind me to give him a hug when we return," I said under my breath, and he laughed.

"I don't need to be reminded," he said. "I'll give him a hug for the both of us, especially because I know it'll give him a stroke."

"I was so worried because I was sure that you would notice that rather than look for a job straight out of college in the renewable energy field, I instead opened a cupcake bakery in Brooklyn." His eyes widened at this.

"Really?"

"What happened?" he asked. "Why did you close the store?"

"It started as a little hobby in my apartment, and then when orders started increasing, I decided to open up a little shop. But I was in there working all the time, and when I projected my life twenty years in advance, all I could see was me still baking in that store, and it truly wasn't what I wanted. I loved baking, but it was much more fun when I was just doing it for myself and for loved ones."

"I'm learning a lot about you, and I'm loving it," he said, and I smiled.

"I say all this to say that I'm going to bake you something later tonight. I'm thinking a cheesecake. Do you like cheesecake?"

"I love cheesecake," he repeated. "And I can't wait. In fact, I'll join you and see how you work."

I couldn't believe his words, and he seemed amused at my shock.

"What?" he shrugged. "You see how I work every day, so I guess it's time to see how you work, at least with regards to baking."

I leaned forward then to kiss him, and then continued in detail.

"I have to get some supplies in town. So, do you want to come along?" I asked.

"When I asked you about how you would like to spend this part of the vacation back in New York, you said solely eating. You didn't want to move. You just wanted to sleep for the entire two days?"

"Really?" he asked, and I nodded.

"Well, I don't mind staying in bed," he said. "And I trust you to make what I want even more desirable because I get to spend the time with you."

I couldn't help but blush, but at the same time, I felt so thrilled because all of this felt too good.

"Live in the moment," I told myself and looked at him.

"So you wouldn't mind coming with me to town before the sun sets?" I asked, and he nodded.

"I'll be happy to. We've both napped, and we're not going on the yacht tonight, are we?"

"No, tomorrow morning," I replied, and he nodded.

"Alright then, finish up your very late lunch, and we'll be on our way."

Chapter Thirty-Seven
Hunter

"Where are we going?" I asked as I glanced down at the sandals on my feet. I was wearing a shirt at least, but for some reason, it felt wrong. I looked at myself in the mirror, but all that changed when she came into view. She had on the most gorgeous flowing white dress all the way to her feet and a pair of flip flops.

I had only ever seen her looking dreary in her oversized work clothes or looking breathtaking in a formal dress, but not... she looked like an angel. Absolutely gorgeous, free.

I couldn't stop staring at her.

"What?" she asked, suddenly self-conscious as she hurried over to the floor-length mirror before me. She all but pushed me out of the way and then she stared at herself. I could see the appreciation in her eyes, and I couldn't help but shake my head. I did, however, want to cancel the outing and go back to be with her.

"Should we order in?" I asked. "They should have cheesecake somewhere there, right?"

She turned to me with a sullen expression, and I immediately regretted putting it out there.

"I'm just saying that because right now I want to be naked with you. I want to be here, lounging until we're incredibly well-rested and intentionally having mind blowing sex till we both pass out."

Her cheeks instantly flushed red, and my heart nearly couldn't take the gorgeous color across her cheeks.

"No," she refused. "I want to make cheesecake. We have all night to test that theory, and if we have cheesecake, we might just be able to take a break in the middle and then keep going."

I laughed at this because we both knew it was impossible, but right now, between us, there was no use whatsoever for reality.

"Alright, let's go," I replied as we walked out of the room.

I put my arm around her shoulder, and I loved how it fit perfectly there given how much taller than her I was.

"We're headed to the Cherngtalay Local Market," she replied as she pulled out her phone. "I would have loved to walk, but it will take too long, and I didn't think you'd be up for it, so I have a car ready."

I'm up for it if you are, but do you know the way?"

"No," I replied, "because cell service here is too unstable, so let's just go with the driver."

"Alright," I replied, and true to her arrangements, we met the man waiting for both of us outside of the resort. We got into his car, and soon we were on our way. It was a very vibrant market, I couldn't help but note, as we arrived.

All around, there were stalls with fresh fruits and

produce, as well as stalls selling local crafts and textiles. This caught my eye in particular, as well as the spices and handicrafts.

It had been so long since I had gone to a market of any sort that I almost couldn't believe how much enjoyment I was getting out of just being here with her.

I followed her where she went, and soon enough, we stopped by a stall with smoke coming out of it. It looked like some grilled meat called moo ping.

"I want some of these," I said, and when I reached my hand into my pocket, I realized that I didn't have any money whatsoever.

I had never felt so lost and unprepared before, and as I looked at her in shock, she burst into laughter.

"I've been handling a lot of things for you for a while," she said, and I was taken aback.

"Jesus, you're invaluable. What would I do without you? Remind me to give you a raise when we return."

At this, her eyes softened, but then sensing she might feel uncomfortable with this, I immediately took it back.

"I'm kidding," I said, "I wouldn't want you to feel as though our personal relationship is the reason for it."

She, however, was surprisingly and particularly shameless in this regard.

"I don't think anything," she said. "I have absolutely no problems with that. In fact, I think I deserve it, and if you wish, I'll be willing to prepare a hundred-page PowerPoint presentation explaining why I am utmost positive that I had worked for and deserved a raise."

"Given the way you rode me on the plane, I can tell you that you don't need a hundred pages. You just need to do it again at a faster pace later tonight, and you're halfway to being approved."

She gasped out loud as she indicated to the stall seller to package a couple of pieces for us.

"I agree, and I guess I'm going to have to fuel up then because I will be working harder than ever, I can assure you."

I couldn't help it then; I kissed her once again, and she was startled. She looked around, and then she hit me on my chest. It was a soft hit, it was affectionate, and it made my heart flutter in a way that it hadn't in years.

"Your pork skewer," I said, and she accepted two pieces.

She turned to the vendor then, and after paying, we continued on. We watched and bargained for fruits while she found the ingredients she needed for her cheesecake.

"So far, I haven't been able to find cream cheese and graham crackers," she said, and I watched the disappointed look on her face.

"We might have to go to more international stores for that," I said.

"Yeah," she replied, but it's getting late, and I have a very important pay raise interview to prepare for and ace.

I smiled at this and gave a different suggestion.

"How about you just ask the resort staff to deliver it to you? I'm sure they have it and are more than willing to, for a price of course."

"Wonderful idea," she said, and then she turned to look into my eyes. I wondered why, but I soon got my answer when her hands settled on my shoulders, and then she lifted herself to the tips of her toes. She kissed me on the cheek, and then, extremely shy, she lowered down and looked away.

"Ooh, a salad!" she announced louder than was needed. "I've always wanted to try those."

She continued on her way, and I couldn't help but shake my head.

Chapter Thirty-Eight

Madison

The kitchen in our room was the most gorgeous kitchen I had ever been in, fully equipped with everything I needed in shining steel and gleaming marble. As the sun set, casting its glow over the kitchen, it felt like heaven. I got to work with a tune in my heart, and when I looked up searching for him, I saw him walking across the deck on the phone as he checked up on New York.

In a way, all of this felt surreal, and I guessed it was, so I was going to enjoy it to the fullest. But then, as I prepared the crusts of the cheesecake with the crackers, I couldn't help but feel slightly sad. We claimed we were simply platonic and having fun, but my heart was beginning to believe that less and less, especially with the way we were with each other at the market. We were so affectionate, teasing and playing with each other, sharing pork skewers and finishing each other's cold salad. I was so happy; it was to the hint of delusions.

Sighing, I continued with my baking and pressed the

crust into the baking dish. Afterwards, I got started on the filling with the cream cheese and retrieved the limes that we had purchased. All in all, it was quite quick for me to get the cake made, and then it was in the oven. He wandered in just then, and I didn't even realize that he was staring at me because I was waiting by the oven and scrolling through my phone to go through Emma's assignments. I was scrolling through her conversations with her suppliers so I could know how to help her find someone else and the requirements that were needed. However, I was so sure of this, but the way things were going right now between myself and Hunter, it was as though we would only be able to focus on this when we returned to Bangkok. Still, and when he was completely distracted, I promised myself that I would slowly chip away at her work.

"Speaking to family?" he asked, and I looked up then. He was finished with his phone so, I quickly checked the cake and found that it would be done soon, then turned to walk towards him.

Just as I arrived, however, he suddenly picked me up and set me down on the counter. My heart jumped once again with excitement, but before I could even think of getting down, he was already kissing me out of my mind. I submitted completely to it, and by the time I pulled away, I had completely forgotten about my cake in the oven.

"So..." he said. "How about your pay increase interview?" he asked, and I quickly pushed him away before I got completely distracted.

"Cheesecake first," I said. "I put a lot of effort into it."

I headed over to the oven and retrieved it, then set it on the table. It looked absolutely wonderful, and when I turned to him, I could see that he was impressed as well. I cut a piece for us, grabbed two forks, and right then, standing in the kitchen, we both devoured that first piece. He instantly reached for a second, and once again, we shared it on the same plate, standing.

"Okay, we need to put a pause on the cheesecake. I have an interview before I completely change my mind," he said, and my heart jumped.

"Yes, Sir," I replied, and just as I set my fork down, he lifted me clear off the ground and carried me off to bed. I squealed in excitement as he tossed me onto it, and then he began to strip.

Grabbing the edges of my dress, I pulled it over my head, and in no time, I was completely naked. He pounced on top of me, and as his entire naked body pressed against mine, I understood that I was in heaven. He was hard and warm everywhere, and the sweetness of his lips and touch inside of me was incomparable.

That night, I lost my mind several times, and by the time we were returning back to Bangkok the day afterwards, I was still dreaming about it.

Chapter Thirty-Nine
Madison

"Challenges and Opportunities in Southeast Asia's Renewable Energy Landscape"

"What?"

I glanced at the message and sent my response to Emma.

"This is the topic he's giving the lecture on."

"Wow, that sounds quite boring."

"It is," I replied with a smile as I reviewed my report.

"Shouldn't you be up there on stage helping him navigate through his notes?" she asked. "And even if you didn't have to, wouldn't you just like to be close to him, hehe?"

This made me smile, and I couldn't help but shake my head because no matter how much I tried to ignore her, I couldn't stop myself from talking to her.

"He's fine. He told me not to bother; he knows how to use a clicker. He wasn't given this company; he built it himself, and he's had to present quite a number of slides on his own over the years to investors from all over the world."

"Interesting," she said while I returned to work.

I had to send the updated report on the breach and everything that had happened along the way to the entire team. It was due the previous night, and my plan had to finally get out of bed with Hunter and find a desk to work at, but several times I had tried to get up and his arm around my body pressed me right back down to the mattress. Just thinking about it now and watching him up on stage made butterflies fill my stomach.

When we were like this together, it was so hard for me to remember that he was my boss. But I couldn't forget. Forgetting was detrimental to my job, so I sighed and continued my work.

"Have you found a dress yet?" Emma's message popped up on my screen once again.

I looked at the message and thought about it. It had been on my mind ever since I had reversed the schedule that morning and realized that we had an event to wrap up the conference in a few days; it was going to be incredibly fancy, and I had been looking forward to it, especially after seeing just how excited and affected he had been by me dressing up the first time.

I replied then.

"No, I tried scouring the internet for something this morning, but then I'd have to try it on and return it if I didn't like it, and I haven't really seen anything that's good. Plus, I sincerely doubt anything of theirs will get past my hips, and I don't have a sewing machine to adjust anything or know my way around getting one here.

"Wow," she said.

"What?" I replied.

"If these were his problems, I am pretty sure you'd find

a way to solve them. But because it's yours, of course, you didn't want to put in that much effort."

This was true, and it instantly made me feel bad.

"Thanks a lot," I replied, and sent a bunch of naughty smiley faces.

"My point is that you shouldn't relent just because you have the man. I mean... this is a different environment. You're across the world and far away from the reality of New York. This gala, I feel, is the last time for him to truly understand what he's missing by not being with you officially. Sorry, not the last time, but your last chance to show him that you're a dream, and in my very humble opinion, you shouldn't waste it. If you impressed him earlier on, then this is the time to blow him out of the park with how beautiful you are."

"He sees me every day," I replied. "I'm pretty sure he knows what I look like."

"Exactly," she said. "So you have to be someone else. Someone more alluring, unbelievable. You have to look like the dream he never thought he could have."

"I don't know exactly if I'm the dream he never thought he could have."

"Then you better be," she said. "You better be, and I'm the friend you have but don't deserve, so I went ahead and found you a dress."

I was about to shut the chat off completely so that I could focus on my work, but at her words, my eyes nearly popped out of their sockets.

"What?

"Strappy, elegant, jet black with the most gorgeous ash

gradients. I was keeping it for myself for when I launched the brand."

"Send me a picture," I said, and a few seconds later the image popped up.

I gasped.

"Right? You bought this and you didn't tell me?"

"It was going to be a surprise; that's how special it was to me."

"So let it remain so, don't give it to me. You'll be launching your brand soon."

"No," she said. "I'm letting it go, and I won't be launching soon. That damn manufacturer sent me back to square one. But it's okay. I'll find another dress. A better dress. But this time around, you're the one who has to take drastic action and win, so I'm shipping it to you. It should arrive there in two days."

"Oh my God!" My heart flooded with excitement and warmth. "I don't know how to thank you."

"I know," she replied.

"I have some of your clothes here so I'll use those for a little adjustment. Send the address of the hotel you're staying at and contact information."

I typed it all in immediately and sent them off.

"Done," I said, and this time around the chat came to an end. I closed it and couldn't believe how happy I felt. The last few hours and days had been put into this word, and as I recalled that we were back in Bangkok, which meant that the trip was slowly coming to an end, I couldn't help but feel sad. But as I gazed at the dress once again, I found renewed hope because I definitely still had some cards up my sleeves. And if I didn't, then at least on the last night, it would be unforgettable. At least I hoped it would.

A loud round of applause erupted, dampening the hushed hall. I looked up, and I could see that he was done with his speech. It had lasted more than forty-five minutes, and I knew by now that he didn't quite enjoy it, so I was glad for him that he could return to his seat.

He told me the previous night in bed that sometimes during his talks, he had fought with just falling asleep right there, and at first, I couldn't believe him. That was until I recalled the time I had fallen asleep standing in a club with deafening music and people packed together and rubbing on each other like sardines, yet I had fallen asleep. I believed him then.

I searched for his gaze, and I couldn't believe I expected him to search for me and look for me.

I wasn't too far away, and just before he returned to his seat, he found my eyes and sent me the sweetest, most subtle smile.

I lowered my head then, unable to help but blush. I hoped no one saw it, yet at the same time, I hoped everyone did. I hoped the whole world did and knew that I was having the time of my life.

Sighing, I reviewed the report once again and wondered why I hadn't sent it yet, and that was when I recalled that it was taking forever to upload. The file was too heavy, but the internet here was abysmal. But it needed to get to New York, and I was slowly growing frustrated.

Sighing, I decided then to try sending it via email rather than uploading it to our server. Maybe that would be better.

I found the emails of relevant addresses and added

them all to the send-to list. Afterward, I wrote a quick note, attached the document, and the email was sent off in minutes. Afterwards, I put my laptop away and couldn't wait for our lunch break. We had decided to have it in one of the most critically acclaimed restaurants in the city. We were going for authentic Thai dishes this time around and not fusion foods, since our time here was coming to an end, and we couldn't leave without properly exploring the country's cuisines.

Chapter Forty
Hunter

I was more than ready to take my seat after the presentation. Public speaking wasn't hard for me, but I always felt a huge sense of relief afterward and couldn't quite enjoy it no matter how hard I tried. I did wish, though, that she was beside me, but the way they did their conference arrangements here was different. Instead of my party, I was surrounded by other officials and guest speakers in order to facilitate networking opportunities.

Just then, there was a message on my phone, and looking for a reason to be distracted as the next speaker started his own presentation, I glanced down to see whom it was from. I had expected it to be from her, but when I saw instead that it was from our CTO, I wondered why.

"Sir, have you seen the report just sent out by Miss Parish?" she asked.

This was a strange question, and I wondered why she was inquiring about it. I forwarded the message to Madison and returned my focus to the speaker. She replied a few minutes later.

"The report is completed, Sir," she said, and I nodded. A few seconds later, another message came.

"Sir, there's been a mistake made. I can't seem to reach Miss Parish. Please let her know that she needs to speak to the IT department urgently because a ghastly error has been made."

I was instantly alarmed because she never just used the term "ghastly" casually. Unless the building was on fire, and the building was never on fire.

"What's happening?" I asked, hating that rather than call her to handle this over the phone, I was stuck texting.

"She included some external email recipients accidentally in the email she sent out, and now all the wrong people are aware of the breach that we've been working so hard to solve and cover up. IT is trying to hack into Levi's company's email now to see if we can retract it before he can do anything with it or even see it. He hasn't contacted us yet, so I hope he's completely oblivious. I'm so sorry to ask this, but I hope she can respond to me."

Shocked at all I was hearing, I turned around and met her gaze. At my frown, she instantly understood that something was wrong, so she lowered her head, and a few minutes later, she sent me a message.

"Is there something wrong, Sir?" she asked. "Do you need something?"

"Why can't New York reach you??" I asked.

"I, uh... I forgot to charge my phone last night, so I'm trying to conserve the battery until after the conference or until I can find a charger."

"You made a mistake," I sent my response back. I was quite irritated, although I tried to calm myself.

"A mistake?"

"Yes! Somehow, Levi Boone from the City Post got the comprehensive report on the breach update you just sent out. That is a disaster. If we didn't want to be in the news in a few hours, then we better find a way right now to ensure that he didn't see either email, and if he did, then you have to make him forget that he saw it."

After typing this, I glanced back, and just as I had expected, I saw that her face had turned completely white. She didn't look at me any further. Instead, she rose to her feet with her entire frame crouched down and all but ran out of the hall.

I shook my head because, in order to resolve this, she was going to have a terrible day. Maybe Boone truly hadn't seen it yet, but hacking into a major publication server so suddenly was incredibly dangerous, and if we were caught, it was going to be all the worse and more newsworthy.

Such a silly mistake she made. I understood it was because the email list of the actual parties she was supposed to send the report to must have been abysmal. But it was so easy not to check. So easy to confuse one name for the other. But she was never this careless before, so I couldn't help but feel confused.

I had truly wanted all of this to be over without incident and had felt so lucky that it had been a tech case. But I should have seen this pile of shit coming my way, and now my foot was in it.

Furious, I put the phone away and for the sake of appearances tried my best to keep my attention on the speaker.

Chapter Forty-One
Madison

"You have fucking lost your mind!"

I held the phone against my ear and couldn't help but tremble all over.

"You sent the email to Levi Boone?" she yelled into the phone. "You fucking sent it to Levi Boone?"

I couldn't believe what was happening. For a second, it felt as though I had suddenly been plunged into a nightmare, and for a long minute, I wondered if perhaps none of this was real. Maybe I had simply fallen asleep in my seat, and I was having a nightmare. Incompetence was a recurring nightmare for me, and I had worked my ass off to ensure it never happened. But now...

"Madison!" she yelled.

"I'm here," I replied.

"'I'm here'? That's all you can say? The entire IT team is trying to hack into their servers right now. Do you understand that we could get sued for this, and that's just the beginning? If this gets out, our stocks are going to be buried."

"Yes, Ma'am," I replied, and she went silent. Then she cut the phone.

I pulled the phone down from my ear as I stared out at the magnificent view, wondering how in fuck's name I could have made this kind of mistake.

I couldn't believe it.

"Of course, I knew the answer. I had been distracted. Talking to Emma about the dress, thinking of my boss seeing me in it. The boss I had now monumentally disappointed and was about to cost millions of dollars either in a lawsuit or as a result of loss from investors."

I shook my head then and couldn't stop the tears from rolling down from my eyes.

Somehow, a part of me had known that this was going to happen. A part of me had known that his reaction was valid and that my distraction was sooner or later going to cost us. Going to cost him. And now I was fucking stuck in Thailand with no way to resolve this. All I could do was remain on the internet and on Twitter, constantly refreshing the asshole's page to see if he had posted anything about it on Twitter. That's where it would spread like wildfire. It was fast, it was personal, and he wasn't going to hesitate one bit. I even fucking had him in my mail lists because of all the attempts to contact Hunter for a fight or the other over the years.

He was incredibly salty about all we did and our success, especially because from the very beginning, Hunter had refused to feed him any information. I had just sent our report to our mortal enemy and wanted to shoot myself in the mouth. How could I have made such a mistake?

"How could I have made such a mistake?" I asked myself, over and over again.

Lowering my head and just staying there was commotion behind me. I almost fainted. The sessions for the morning had come to an end. This meant that Hunter would be coming out soon as well, and then I'd have to face him.

There was a talk panel later that afternoon after lunch, and he had to participate in it, but how was he to do any of this in peace when his company was once again in crisis in New York?

Sighing, I turned around and hoped for the best.

I headed back into the hall as most of the crowd had dispersed and found him talking to a few of the conference guests. As always, he was surrounded by acquaintances, but for a moment, in the midst of it all, he paused and looked over at the door at me.

His gaze lingered for a very long moment, and then he turned away to continue with his discussions.

Soon, however, much shorter than ever, he excused himself and headed over to me. As he walked over, looking majestic and expressionless, I wanted to run. Just run so far that I would never have to face him again, but I couldn't do that. So, I waited and watched him until eventually, he stopped before me. He looked at my face, and in that moment, I truly wondered what he saw and how he felt. Regret was probably at the top of his list; he probably knew that I had been distracted because I would never otherwise have made such a stupid mistake.

But I had, and now we needed to work.

"Is the car ready?" he asked, and I nodded.

"Yes, Sir," I replied.

He turned away without a word, and I trailed behind him as we headed down to the lobby of the building.

"Let's try to get something under control before lunch is over. And if we can't by then, then I need you to reach out to the conference organizers within the next hour to tell them that I might be late, and then I need you to write this moment to speak to the people and tell them to get ready because we might be leaving for New York later tonight."

"Yes, Sir," I replied and wrung my hands so hard behind me that I nearly peeled my skin off.

Chapter Forty-Two
Hunter

She looked like a puppy that had been kicked. Sad, forlorn, rejected. I knew she wasn't feigning it to get compassion, but that hit was the fiasco that she understood she had messed up and was completely powerless to fix it.

It had happened so suddenly, I almost imagined they had made a mistake. From the outset, it seemed so simple. We'd sent an email to the wrong person, but with the breach that we were still trying to contain, the repercussions were all I could think about, and it was the kind that would take the company months to recover from.

I glanced at her as we rode back to the hotel and saw her staring out the window. Our plan had been to head out to a restaurant for lunch. I'd told her that my intention was to try the local cuisine before we left, because all the experience I had of Thailand was fusion foods. However, that wasn't the whole truth. I had wanted it to be a date, our first date, and now it was completely ruined. I wanted to tell her that this was my true intention, but I had grown nervous because a part of me was waiting for this shoe to drop. It wasn't that she was incompetent, but that I understood that when distraction was introduced into a professional relationship, especially one as intense as ours, mistakes were bound to happen. And mistakes I truly couldn't stand.

Sighing, I returned my attention to my phone and asked for updates.

"So far, everything was silent. There was no sudden publication, no posts on Twitter. Perhaps everything would work out and it would be fine."

"They still haven't been able to hack in," my CTO replied, and I couldn't help but sigh.

We soon returned to the hotel, and without a word, we went our separate ways.

"Order lunch," I said to her, and she nodded just as she opened her door.

"I wasn't icing her out, even though I was upset. I wanted to be warm about this, but until it had passed, I really didn't know how to be. And a part of me, perhaps, was trying to use this to come to my senses.

Going over the past few days we had spent together in Phuket, I could feel my entire brain chemistry shifting. I couldn't stop thinking about her, couldn't stop wanting to be around her. It was wonderful, but at the same time, the doubt that plagued me that I was off my game, that I was doing the wrong thing, continued to plague me. This discipline had brought me this far, and I didn't want to take it for granted. So, I decided then that I would remain calm and see how the day played out.

The second I arrived back in the room and got started on damage control mode, I got on a call with the PR teams, and we got ready to handle the upcoming disaster. This was her job. She was supposed to be facilitating this, and the fact that I couldn't even call her over to my room to yell at her for just tucking her head between her legs, and disappearing was part of the problem, so I decided to just give her some peace and continue on my own.

"We're gathering everyone and getting ready in case this turns into a shit storm, Sir," the reporter I received informed me. Soon the call ended, and then there was a knock on the door.

My entire body tensed at this. Whether it was because I hoped it was her or that I hoped it wasn't, I couldn't make up my mind.

Whatever it was, I had to respond, and so I opened the door. A cart was rolled in, and I saw that who knocked was the hotel staff.

However, she was nowhere to be found. Since we had gotten together, we had shared and looked forward to every meal together, but apparently, now it was no longer the case. I watched as the restaurant staff arranged the food before me, and I picked up my utensils. However, just a few bites in, and I couldn't believe how tasteless it all seemed. I couldn't stand this any further, so I decided that rather than stay upset, I could think clearly for what seemed like the first time since this vacation began. I decided to once again trust my heart and loosen up. Whatever happened would be solved, so there was no reason to ice her out and let her wallow.

I made up my plan but decided at the last moment to hiss under my breath. I headed toward the door connecting our two rooms and knocked on the door.

For the first few seconds, she didn't respond, which made me wonder if perhaps she had left the room. Just as I was about to turn the handle, however, the door was opened.

"Lunch is here," I said as the door opened and revealed her saddened face.

"I, uh... I have mine, Sir," she said.

"Where is it?" I asked.

"Uh... I looked behind, and she headed over to her bed side table. She picked up a sandwich, and I stared at it.

"Come to my room," I said. "There's enough food for two."

I didn't leave any space for negotiation, so I turned and returned to my chair. She complied, and soon enough, she was seated on the chair opposite me.

"There's more than enough here," I said, and she picked up her utensils.

I knew she wouldn't argue because as she was staying to avoid any unnecessary attention on herself given how sensitive the moment was, insisting that she wasn't hungry would have done the exact opposite of that.

We ate silently together, and I couldn't believe how tense things were between us now when just the previous day we had been enjoying ourselves in Phuket like newlyweds. This was life, and we needed to be able to deal with it. I was here, and it didn't take long for me to realize and understand that she wasn't just my secretary to me any longer. This was what I had fought for from day one, but now, as I took in her gorgeous demeanor and contrite expression, I wondered why I had pushed for that. I loved my work, but... this person... she was special. She was just as special, and I couldn't stand the fact that she was tormented by this.

"Everyone makes mistakes," I told her. "Next time, you'll know to be extra careful with the email. I know because most communication within the company is internal, you forgot to exercise a bit more caution with manually inputting the addresses, but that's okay. We'll be fine, and you'll do better."

She didn't respond, and when she lifted her gaze to mine, I didn't need to be a genius to know that she was fighting tears off with all her heart and soul.

She looked like she wanted to say something, but in the end, she decided against it. Instead, she nodded and started eating. I watched for a moment and decided to focus on my own meal.

It was the most silent we had ever been with each other, even from the first time she had arrived at the company. In the first few days, if I recall correctly, she hadn't said a single word besides when and what was needed. I recalled having a conversation back then with the Human Resource manager about her because unlike earlier secretaries who had occupied the position, I had immediately been dissatisfied.

With her, however, I had almost barely noticed her presence. She had done her work, minded her business, and life had gone smoothly.

I looked at her now and truly couldn't believe the change because it was most definitely not feeling that way. Now I could no longer ignore her existence in my life. She was a part of the very fabric of my existence, and I truly didn't want to be careless with that.

I set my food down then completely dissatisfied with her.

"Can you check if we can move the lunch reservation we previously had to dinner?" I asked.

She looked up, then slightly surprised at my words.

"What if - we're not going back to New York?" she asked.

"Who knows?" I replied. "Maybe we're all just overreacting, and maybe everything will be perfectly fine, and we'll be able to conclude our time here eventfully."

At my words, she nodded, but before we could say anything else, my phone began to ring.

I had his phone number saved, and the moment I saw that he was the one calling, my stomach instantly turned. I had truly lost belief in what I had just told Madison. That we were overreacting and that this wouldn't be bad. That we could come through smoothly. But with this call now, I understood that the shit storm was about to start.

Sighing, I picked up the call and rose to my feet.

I wanted to leave the room during the call so that she wouldn't be worried, but I understood then that by doing so, I would be proving my point about how much her having so intertwined with both my personal and professional lives was a distraction. I no longer wanted to separate it, and so I was going to do my very best to integrate them both.

"Mr. Boone," I greeted.

He laughed out loud into the receiver, and I truly considered flinging the phone out of the window. There was no way he wouldn't gloat. There was no way he wouldn't have a blast with this. Over the years, I hadn't refrained from humiliating him as much as I could, and so now, of course, he was going to milk this error for all that it was worth.

"Mr. Swift," he greeted. "For the first time in what feels like years, I had a very good dream last night, and this morning when I woke up, I didn't know whether to be afraid or grateful. Was it a good sign or a bad sign?"

"It's been on my mind all day, and then just a few minutes ago, I received a call from our IT department saying that they had sensed a hacking attempt from your company and have been trying to fight it off for the past few minutes. A hacking attempt? From you? I was stunned, to say the least. I mean, what could you possibly be trying to hack into our servers for? We're just an online newspaper. Plus, there was the fact that your guys called me, so you didn't even know if you were trying to call me, and this was just, how to say it, a romantic approach? Then someone suggested I could check my email because maybe you sent something to me and were trying to retrieve it. I mean, as a news outlet, we've had quite a number of damning information against very important people that they've tried their hardest to retrieve from us, all to no avail, I might add. I really don't know why you billionaires keep trying to quash a bug. And I am, for the record, by the way, a big bug."

He went silent, and I nearly threw the phone aside just so I could massage my temples.

"I wouldn't be calling you if they had."

"What about the other attempt?" I asked.

"Smart," he laughed.

"Well, that I can do very little about, but it's all speculation now, isn't it? And if anything, what it gives you is street credibility that you have the talent and guts to do this. So, I don't think it's too much of a problem."

At this, I went silent, and so did he.

"So..." he said. "Should I expect a fat wad of cash, Sir?"

"Come to my office," I repeated. "We'll talk then."

"Blackmail material? I think not. That's my condition, and rather than blackmail, you can consider it as collateral to ensure you don't fuck me over, since, as you know, that is your specialty."

"Sir... I would love to truly, but are you even in the country? I've been hearing of your escapades so far. You're in Thailand at that conference to the East. My ability doesn't need for another three days. I know because I was supposed to be there, but yet again, I had to face queries from my editor because you billionaires just can't leave me alone."

"I'll be back soon. Contact my secretary. Set a meeting time. And do it quick before this thing gets out of hand."

"Yes, Sir," he replied, "and I truly hope you'll be able to manage it back soon before this whole thing goes south. For instance, in twenty-four hours, it will definitely have gone south, and I can't let my milk go bad now, can I? I might turn into a very big, loud, and angry baby who cannot shut the fuck up."

I didn't bother responding to this. I needed to end the call because I was sure I was going to kill him. Truthfully, this was the most difficult part of this entire nonsense. I hated losing, and I hated feeling as though someone had one over on me. However, this was now the case, and I couldn't help but be fucking pissed.

I put the phone away then and lifted my gaze to hers.

"Did you hear?" I asked, and she nodded.

"I'll wait for him to contact me."

"He'll probably reply to your email or send you a message," I replied.

"Handle the time as well as the flight. We should be out of here later tonight or early tomorrow morning."

"Yes, Sir," she replied.

I couldn't remain in the room any longer, so I headed out and shut the door behind me.

Chapter Forty-Three
Madison

I didn't know what to do with myself. He left the room and I truly wished with all my heart that he hadn't. It was his room, and I was the one that was supposed to leave, but before I could even get my mouth to work, he was already leaving.

Sighing, I headed into my room and sat on my bed. Well, everything was canceled. Every motherfucking thing. I wanted to just curl up in a ball and fall asleep forever, but I couldn't mess up any longer, so I started to make the needed calls in preparation for our departure.

First, I called the pilot again to confirm our departure time, and then I began to arrange with the flight attendant to ensure that she would be available.

After that was settled, I moved on to the conference organizers. We had already informed them that we wouldn't be able to make it for the panel later today, but there was a host of other absences that I had to explain to them. They were for sure going to be pissed, and I couldn't imagine just how much further this would annoy Hunter.

I thought about it then and wondered if perhaps I should suggest to him that we bring Mr. Boone to Thailand instead to resolve this. Since there wasn't going to be a fight and he wanted to make sure that things went away as quietly as possible.

This was a risky suggestion, but I couldn't truly think of any other solutions, so I put on my shoes once again and headed down.

I could call him to ask where he was, but I truly didn't want to bother him, and I was sure he hadn't gone far. Just to be sure, though, I called our driver on my way down, and he assured me that he hadn't been called yet, which meant that Hunter was still in the hotel. It was beyond huge, so I couldn't walk around just looking for him.

I thought then of all the places he could have headed to, and only the restaurant and bar came to mind. Or perhaps the gym? Maybe he went for a swim? Those places seemed more likely, so I headed to them immediately.

I couldn't, however, find him, so I only had one last option left, which was the bar. I was sure I was wasting my time, though, because he usually didn't drink at all.

However, when I arrived there, I found him seated at the counter. I stopped in my tracks and could feel my heart twist inside of my chest. He was drinking. There was a tumbler of what looked to be scotch before him, but that was not all that he was indulging in. Right beside him was a woman. She was wearing the shortest of dresses and was all legs. She was talking to him, flipping her hair over her shoulder, smiling, and he was watching her. I turned around then. Suddenly, I couldn't breathe, and suddenly, I couldn't think.

I instantly slaked away and was nearly sprinting to head over to the elevator. When I arrived, however, I wondered why the fuck I was running.

Alright, he was talking to a woman. So? He wasn't allowed to talk to a woman ever again? I tried to take a deep breath to calm myself. Maybe it was nothing. I still had to do my job, and this time around, I had to fucking do it well.

And for that, I couldn't not go to him. I had to go over there, and I had to ensure that right in front of her, right in front of the both of them, I had to be able to do my job flawlessly and without emotion.

So, I straightened my back, built my courage, and returned to the bar.

I couldn't help but count my steps as I approached because I had to focus all my attention on them. My legs were trembling, and it was driving me fucking nuts. Still, I was able to head to him, and at my appearance, he looked up. I could see his frown, most probably from a mix of seeing me and being startled that I had suddenly appeared before him.

I didn't bother with a polite smile and got straight to the point.

"Sir, I was wondering if we could instead invite Mr. Boone over here," I said. "I know you usually don't like to break your commitments, and I'm trying my best to minimize the annoyance and frustration that this will cause you. Is this something you would consider?"

He listened to me silently, and then he picked up his glass.

He took a long sip, and to my surprise, he drained the cup.

The woman was still beside him, smiling and listening, and it pissed me off to no end.

"You haven't apologized," he said, and my heart stopped.

"I know you're sorry. Your remorse and contrition are oozing out of your pores, but you haven't apologized. Verbally."

At this, I was sinfully too close to tears, but still, I managed to keep myself together, and I truly couldn't believe or understand how I was able to do that.

"Yes, Sir," I replied, and briefly lowered my gaze so I could stabilize my tone. With renewed determination, I returned my eyes to his and apologized.

"I'm truly sorry for this, Sir. I'm going to try my best to make up for it from now until we reach New York and resolve it all."

"Your effort, New York," the girl beside him squealed and leaned even closer to him, all breasts and all. "I love New York. I've always wanted to visit. Since you're going back there, then maybe you take me with you?"

I couldn't listen to any more of this for even a second longer. I turned around and returned to my room. It was as I returned, however, that I understood that I had messed up once again.

because I hadn't even gotten his response on my suggestion about flying Boone over here. As I arrived at the bank of elevators, I wanted to pull my hair out and scream.

I had to go back. I had to find a way to go back so that this could be resolved. However, I soon found that I couldn't. Sighing, I headed into the elevators and returned to my room.

I wanted to call Emma because I needed some relief, however, I fought this. I didn't need any relief, I decided. I needed to feel this pain so that it would never happen again. So that my brain could be reset. And if I called her now, she was going to give me solutions that could very well be viable but would no doubt lead to me quitting my job and continuing on with my life.

I couldn't afford it. Now more for personal reasons than professional, but it was all the same to me. So, I decided then to suck it up, head to my desk, and keep in contact with all parts of the machine back in New York to ensure that there were no further hiccups and mistakes.

A few hours later, I had communicated our sudden leave with the conference organizers and arranged for our departure. All that was left was for his bags to be packed, as we had about five hours before we left. It would be in the morning, and it was the earliest we had been able to arrange it, but it was passable.

Now all I had to do was inform him. I stood before the door connecting our two rooms and couldn't believe how intimate we had been with each other there. Work had stripped every bit of that away, and it truly made me wonder once again if it had all been in my head. I understood his current behavior now, understood that he had withdrawn from me. I deserved that. However, rather than ask off, I could pack his bags. What I wanted to ask was if he would ever draw back close to me again.

I tried my best to push this hope out of my mind. I tried to convince myself that it didn't matter and that I didn't really want it, but I couldn't. I could, however, definitely shut up about it, and so I zipped my mouth closed and focused solely on getting ready to leave.

I knocked on his door, but he didn't respond. It was late now, nearing midnight, so I wondered if he was asleep. He couldn't be because then I'd have to wake him when it was too close to the flight. And I couldn't call him either, in case that startled him awake. Plus, as I looked underneath the door, I could see that his lights were still on. I didn't want to lose this chance, so I pulled down the handle and walked in.

Chapter Forty-Four
Hunter

I was in the shower when I heard the scream. When I reached to shut off the faucet, I found that it was accompanied by almost delirious laughter. I was so confused as I had no clue whatsoever what was going on. It was most definitely a woman's voice. Once that was sure, and since there was solely one woman who would react that way around me, I immediately got out and wrapped a towel around my naked body. I was wet all over, but checking if she was okay was more important. As I reached my bedroom, however, it's safe to say that I was confused by the scene that I saw was an understatement.

There was a woman in my bed. Usually, this wouldn't be an issue. In fact, it would have been especially welcome since for the past few days there had been a woman in my bed. However, this time around, I almost didn't recognize the woman currently making herself very comfortable in my bed. She was naked, this much I could assume from the covers she held high up on her chest, and she was smiling like a complete moron. And to my right was my secretary, who was frozen in the middle of the room. I turned to her and found that she wasn't even looking at me. I was surprised and wondered why she wasn't getting this woman out of there. When she, however, turned around and left the room without a word, I was even more confused. But that was to be dealt with later, so I turned to the intruder on my bed.

"I got your keys earlier," she said to me. "It was the best gift, thank you."

"What?" I asked, and I became more irritated as her gaze roamed down my body. And then she let the blankets go, and I could see indeed that she was completely naked. I sighed then, glad that I was leaving, otherwise, this was the worst possible mood I could be in to even tolerate this nonsense.

"What the hell are you doing here?" I asked.

"You were in such a bad mood," she replied. "I wanted to surprise you. To cheer you up."

I stared at her and truly wondered how and when she had gotten in here. Was this something that usually happened in Thailand? She followed me, which meant that my things were in danger. Perhaps she had come here to steal from me. At the change in my demeanor, she immediately understood that something was wrong.

I wanted to call out to Madison, to call the cops and get this woman out of my room. I remained calm as I headed over to the safe and opened it just to confirm everything was still intact. I checked, found my passport and valuables, and then I shut it back and turned to her.

"I don't know what your game is," I said. "But I'm pretty sure I didn't give you the key to my room. Maybe this is some ploy or scheme you arranged with the hotel staff to exploit the rich businessmen that come here, but do I fucking look like I'm horny to you? Get the fuck out of my room. Because if there's nothing missing, I'm going to let this go, but if you don't leave within the next ten seconds, I'm going to ensure you're arrested for theft and sexual predation!"

At my words, the smile disappeared from her face. It was almost as though she thought I was joking, but then a few seconds later, she understood that I meant every single word.

"I'm sorry," she cried as she jumped out of bed and hurriedly began to gather her things. "I'm sorry, Sir, I'm sorry. I thought... I thought wrong." She was naked as she gathered her shoes, dress, and purse, and then she was running out into the hallway. For a little while, and at the manic way she had left, I was almost amused, but then my gaze went to the adjoining door, and I became upset all over again. Why the fuck had she just walked out? Hadn't she understood the gravity of the situation? Why hadn't she thrown the woman out and immediately called the cops? I headed to her door then, intending to give her a piece of my mind. Truly, I had been holding back all day, and it had frustrated me because if it were any other employee, they would have both lost their job and been sued all in one for endangering my company the way her mistake had. However, it was her, so I had forced myself to exercise the kind of leniency that I didn't even know I was capable of.

I didn't have to knock, but I was going to just so that she could understand how fucking pissed I was with her. I geared up for it to be as loud as possible because I just couldn't understand why she had reacted so nonchalantly and to even not been alarmed at all. However, just then it hit me. She wasn't just my secretary. And even if she was... she would have reacted the same way. The woman had been naked in my bed while I was in the shower! She couldn't fucking read my mind and know that I was just as startled to see her there as she was. I paused then with my hand against the door and realized, "Fuck." I cursed and took a step backwards. Her reaction then made sense to me.

Of course, she was shocked and upset. She probably thought that I had betrayed her and cheated on her. I mean, we weren't exactly a couple, but I assumed to both of us it was an unspoken rule that until we were officially done with the other, that neither could sleep with anyone else. I understood this and accepted this, so I turned around and returned to the bathroom to complete my shower.

She was right in getting upset, but I didn't exactly care to comfort her right now with everything that was happening, so I tried to put the entire issue out of my head. Usually, she would come in to help me pack and to ensure that nothing was left behind. It was her job, but lately, these things that could be passed off as her job were beginning to feel more domestic than anything else, and we'd been having a blast. In a way, it was almost as though we'd been playing dress-up and I'd been enjoying every moment of it. But now it was no longer the case and so everything seemed to just be a bitter reminder of how close we'd been when we were more personal with each other, and how efficient she'd been when our relationship was solely professional.

These complications I had expected. If something went wrong, all that was happening now was bound to happen, so

I refused to feel distraught or surprised about it. Instead, I focused on liaising with the New York office in order to prepare for whatever shit was coming our way. We were prepared with the memos and information to send out to shareholders just in case the news got into the wrong hands and was suddenly publicized, but of course, this was the worst-case scenario.

Soon, we arrived at the airport and got on the plane. As I finished my last call before the flight, I couldn't help but wonder why I hadn't put worst-case scenarios in place as well when it came to our relationship. Of course, I had expected mistakes to happen in this as well and for shit to hit the fan, but I hadn't been prepared for it. I had thought it would take a little more time. That we would have time. However, this wasn't the case at all, and I couldn't help but feel incredibly sour about it. Sighing, I shut my eyes and ignored her while she sat as usual in the seat she always sat in and shut her eyes. She was going to feign she was asleep for the rest of the flight just so I wouldn't talk to her. I was almost tempted to watch her but, in the end, I decided to just leave her alone. We needed this time apart so we could reassess. After this, I vowed to myself that if we were to continue this, then I had to put preparations in place to ensure that our relationship didn't take these kinds of dangerous hits. If I was going to go on with her, then I had to readjust my priorities. It could no longer be business first. It had to be her.

This was my worry and fear, but it wasn't that I wasn't open to it because some things were undeniably more important. I just had never allowed it before for mere distractions. I had always wanted for whoever drew that kind of prioritization from me to be someone I was immensely serious about. And now, as I thought of her and felt her presence around me, even if it was detached, I couldn't help but admit that I felt warm. I felt comfortable and I felt at home. I had always been anxious and preferred my own company from the days of my youth, till now. But with her... I felt myself, I felt safe, and I felt good. I nodded to myself as my decision was made. But for now, however, we were both going to stew, and when it was time to talk, hopefully we would have thought long and hard about the things we wanted to say and would be able to communicate it clearly to each other.

Chapter Forty-Five
Madison

"I'm going to quit. I'm typing my resignation letter right now."

"Hm... why have I heard that one before?" Emma asked.

At first, I ignored her, but I needed someone to blame so I kept responding.

"This is all your fault, you know?"

She sent me choked emojis.

"How the hell is it my fault? What are you talking about?"

"You distracted me. You were talking about the dress, and I was excited, and I mistook his email for someone else's, and now I'm in fucking trouble. Now his company's in trouble." I trailed off for a little while, and I couldn't help but feel bad.

"That's unfair," she said, and I nodded.

"I know, I'm sorry. I just... it was my fault, but you contributed."

"Accepted. Now, how are we going to fix this? And you better stop thinking about resigning."

"He..." My mind went to what I had seen on his bed, and I still couldn't believe it. I was so hurt, it felt like my heart was being crushed from the inside out. However, I couldn't delve into my emotions about this. I glanced at him and saw that his eyes were closed. He seemed so peaceful while I was struggling to keep my eyes dry. I wanted to hurt him so much I couldn't think.

"He hasn't spoken to me," I said to her. "And he..."

"I'm sorry, once again."

"He what?" she asked. "You keep saying that and then stopping. He didn't... he wasn't violent toward you, right? Maddie?"

"At this point, I wished he was violent towards me. I could have stupidly been able to forgive him. It wouldn't hurt this much."

"He didn't do something worse?" she asked. "What couldn't possibly be worse?"

I didn't respond to this and continued on with my resignation letter, but soon enough, she understood and sent a brief message.

"Please don't tell me another woman is involved."

"Yup," I replied.

"Fuck!" she swore. "Fuck!"

"Why would he do that? I mean, nothing has happened yet. Perhaps all of this will die down now. Maybe there'll be no damage even? How could he do that?"

"They met at the bar," I said. "Spoke for hours, and then she ended up in his bed. I feel so stupid, I want to jump out of this plane right now. Of course, we had gotten together. Of course, we had sex. I was available, and I had all but thrown myself at him. That was the same thing said and done except she wasn't just his fucking secretary with an incredibly good job on the line. I feel so stupid, I don't know what to do with myself. I didn't even know how to face him."

She went silent, and this made me feel even worse.

"I'm pathetic, aren't I?" I asked. "I should have known better, right? He's a fucking billionaire. He's a workaholic. I should have known better."

"Does he usually just fall into random women's beds?" she asked.

"What?" I replied.

"You know him best, don't you?"

I thought about her response and didn't know how to process it.

"You're not pathetic," she said. "Because you know him. You forget that you know him. You didn't just start sleeping with him. There were no barriers to knowing him before you two got together, and this was why you are so in love with him. So, I'm asking, is he the kind to just see a woman at a bar and take her back to his hotel room?"

I considered her questions, and once again, I felt hopeful because when I thought about it, he wasn't the kind to do that. But what did I actually know about him? Sure, I had been his secretary with no boundaries to him since I needed to know all that I could to make his life as easy as possible. However, ... I didn't know what he did outside of the office and when my working hours were over. Come to think of it, I realized now that it was insane for me to assume that a man like him didn't have a personal life. Of course, he did. He didn't have to flaunt it. And he had his own time to himself despite the fact that it felt as though he was always in the office. But that wasn't the case at all. Sighing, I decided then to stop thinking about him, to stop thinking about any of this.

"He drank at the bar," I told her. "He drank at the bar, and even if he's not usually the guy to do things like this, I wouldn't be surprised if he did because he drank at the bar, and... maybe he was doing this as well to send a message to me. To remind me that there was no commitment between us and so there was no need for me to expect him to be lenient with me. Actually, and now that we're talking about whether I know him or not, I should tell you that the fact that he hasn't fired me yet because of this is incredibly out of character for him. He's fired people for much less. Much, much less. So rather than force him to have even more torment for how to handle this in order to save my feelings, then it's best for me to quit."

"Alright," she said, and my heart sank.

I closed the chat app then and focused on my resignation letter. Was I looking for someone to talk me out of this? I knew that I didn't want to but... why wasn't I willing to fight either?

I read it one last time and opened up my email. If I sent it now, he would see it when he woke up. However, if I didn't, then I would be waiting for him to fire me after all this was done. I didn't know which I wanted or preferred. Either way, I was going to be kicked out, I guess I just had to choose now if I wanted to make it easy for him. And in the end and shutting my eyes, I sent the email and shut my laptop. It was so uncomfortable and painful because he was only a few feet away from me. What I didn't realize, however, was that he wasn't already asleep. He hadn't dozed off as the notification came on his phone. Instantly, I shut my eyes and turned away in complete disbelief that he was still awake. I understood though. It was probably hard for him to fall asleep.

"Focus," I cursed under my breath. Now I would have to call him. I wanted and wished with all my heart that I could check how he had read it. However, I couldn't do it. I couldn't risk meeting his eyes... I would break down from the hurt. And so, I kept my eyes shut until finally, I fell asleep.

Chapter Forty-Six
Hunter

I was immensely glad to be back in New York. I had enjoyed my time in Thailand for the most part, but there was something about being back here that made me feel so much calmer. I felt as though I was back in control and better equipped to handle whatever difficulties came my way. Right now, though, it seemed as though they were piling up. From the issues with the company to that leech Levi Boone, and then, of course, to the email I had received on the plane from the woman I knew now I was in love with.

If she didn't act this way, try to escape every time things got hard, it would probably have taken me even longer to understand just how intensely I felt about her. Because if it was anyone else that toyed with my emotions and was successfully able to, I wouldn't have hesitated to get rid of her a long time ago. But the more she pushed away, the calmer I remained, I realized. Because I knew what she wanted wasn't what she wanted, and it's definitely not what I wanted either. So, all I had to do now was to be patient. In my struggles to win in business, I had accumulated quite a lot of experience, and one of the most important ones was the fact that I had to carefully judge how to handle things in steps and in order of priority, otherwise, I was going to mess up. And so, I understood that hers had to be the last. We both needed time, her more than anything else, and so I didn't address the email.

We were both wide awake, and I knew she was aware that I had seen it, but I deleted it completely from my mind. I knew she was hurting, but she knew better. At least I hoped she knew better, but in case she had forgotten who I was and why her assumption that I had slept with that woman was insane, I was going to give her the time to come to her senses.

My driver was waiting for me at the tarmac, and as soon as I got in, I headed straight to the office. She sat in the front while I sorted through emails and communicated with the team about my arrival. I had tried to fall asleep on the plane, but after that damned email she had sent to me, I had been unable to. I was still able to remain calm though because so many times, I had felt as though everything was falling apart around me, and thus far, only my ability to remain calm had kept me sane, so this time around, I was going to employ reason as well.

At the office, my executives were waiting for me at reception.

"Sir," they greeted, however, their eyes were only briefly on me before they turned to the secretary behind me. I glanced at her as well and realized that their eyes were too eager. I was reminded there that they weren't aware of my personal relationship with her, which meant that they were going to smoke her. Human Resources was probably going to fire her.

Sighing, I waited until we arrived at the elevators, and then I turned towards her.

"I think I left my phone in the car, can you please help me and go check for it?" I asked. She seemed a bit startled at this, but as she looked at the other executives beside me and understood that whether the phone was there or not, she would be avoiding being stuck in an elevator with them, she immediately turned around and nearly ran away. We got in, and the elevator remained quiet, and then, then I said what I wanted to.

"Don't attack her, don't scold her. She's my secretary, I'll handle it. Just focus on damage control."

The elevator was silent for a while, but eventually and one by one, they responded.

"Yes, Sir."

"My Human Resource manager Derek, and my CTO however, came into the office with me. Though they at least allowed me to enjoy my office for a moment. I looked at the clean and familiar space and shut my eyes. I was so incredibly happy to be back. After a few moments, I turned around and leaned against the desk. Knowing that Derek's complaint would be the easiest to solve, I turned my attention to him.

"Go," I said, and he smiled at me.

"She needs to go."

"No," I replied. "Next."

I turned to our CTO, however, before she could speak, Derek cut in.

"Sir, I can't have her foolishness spreading as company

culture. When you mess up to this magnitude, you get kicked out immediately. This is the way I run the staff, and you've never interfered till now. I don't want to be lenient with her no matter the reasons."

I looked at him and couldn't believe the pushback I was receiving.

"You're really pissed, aren't you?" I asked.

"It's such a basic mistake. She's been so good the past few months. Was it Thailand that messed with her head? I'm so bloody disappointed. To think of what this could cost us. I haven't been able to sleep in the past twenty-four hours."

I looked at him and truly didn't know what to say. I could see how upset he was, and he was one of my original employees, so in this matter, I had to be delicate and also for Madison's sake. If I handled this wrongly and with force, she might not get fired since I wouldn't let them, but she wouldn't ever be able to enjoy herself in the company anymore, so in the end, everything would be a mess.

Sighing, I nodded and held up my hand.

"I understand how you feel and what you need to do, but you need to understand that we need to be calm. Let's wait till the dust settles, and then we can call her in and have a discussion."

He stared at me, unable to defy me since I had responded this way. I could see the surprise on their faces since usually I wouldn't care, and they could do whatever they wanted, and boot out any employee they wanted to that hadn't been personally approved by me.

Sighing, I returned to my desk, motioned to the chair before me, and my CTO took her seat.

"When is the meeting scheduled with Levi?" I asked.

And then she pulled out her phone.

"I'll ask Madison. Why isn't she here yet?"

I was the one who scheduled the meeting, and it will be in about three hours.

"Alright, you arrived right on time."

Chapter Forty-Seven
Madison

I had never been so nervous to be at my desk before. Not even on the first day I had started working there. Given all the rumors about how almost no secretary had been able to keep working with him, I had a lot of things to be nervous about. Today, however, it feels as though I am floating on air. There was nothing certain. The future was so foggy I was seconds away from a panic attack. I didn't know whether to feel hopeful or regretful. I was just lost, and it was the absolute worst feeling ever. Still, I managed to keep calm and just wait.

Thankfully, none of my other colleagues were coming by as the entire office was much too tense, but they were blowing up my phone, asking for explanations, offering their condolences. Apparently, while I had even nursed a tiny bit of possibility that I wouldn't be fired for this, it was obvious to everyone else that it was a foregone conclusion. Apparently, the Human Resources manager, Derek, had already yelled and announced it, so all that was left now was to make things official. I was out of a job, but I had already resigned, so there was nothing to feel too sad about, right?

I looked around at this gorgeous office. I had been stunned the first time I had come in here. Everything was so modern and luxurious, yet so simple, just like the man himself. I was truly going to miss it all. Having a crush on him made coming to work an unbelievably exciting affair, despite how dreary whatever tasks we were working on were.

Shaking my head, I wondered if I should go grab a box from one of the storage rooms to put my things in, but I understood that it would cause unnecessary stir as everyone was watching and waiting. So, I decided to just have my things arranged and ready to go. It wasn't that I was eager to leave, but that I was trying my best to be ready, trying my best to accept this, so that it would sink in, and the sadness could quickly pass.

Suddenly, the door to his office was pulled open, and instantly I jumped to my feet. Unfortunately, however, I completely forgot about all the stationery I had on my lap. I had been emptying them from a box I had long forgotten about, and now they were all over the floor. It was so noisy I couldn't even look to see who had come in because I couldn't believe what had happened. My prayer was that it wouldn't be Hunter, but when I eventually turned my head and saw that it was the two other executives apart from Hunter, who I was sure would have fired me in Thailand if they could, I almost wished it was him. He would understand that I got scatterbrained when I became anxious, he had somewhat found it endearing before, so maybe now he wouldn't look as irritated and disgusted with me as these two currently did.

Derek gave me a look of disbelief, and then, shaking his head, he walked out of the door. He didn't even say a word to me, and he was the first person I had been introduced to in the company. He had fucking hired me.

"Hey," the CTO greeted, and I forgot about gathering my things on the floor.

"Ma'am," I replied, and she smiled.

"You're -" she stared into my eyes. "Was everything alright in Thailand? You seem quite scatterbrained as of late and distracted."

I thought back to all the unbelievable sex I had been having in Thailand, the drunken nights, the drunken propositions, and smacked business associates, and baking.

"Hm," was all I could say in response, but she became even more curious as she cocked her head.

"Everything was fine," I replied. "It was relaxing."

"I guess you became a little bit too relaxed."

"Yeah," I replied and lowered my head.

"I'm sorry I yelled at you on the phone. I was a bit shocked and distraught, plus there was a lot already happening here. I mean, there was a lot happening there, so I really didn't have to deal with this new shit."

I lowered my head once again and nodded.

"I know. I understand. I'm sorry."

Her gaze went down my outfit, and I didn't need anyone to tell me that she had indeed noted something peculiar. I wasn't dressed as neatly as before. It was still the same dress shirts, but they weren't buttoned all the way, a tiny hint of my cleavage could be seen. I had slight makeup on, and my hair was curled.

"You two -" she started. "He approved of you spreading your wings a little in the way you dress? I mean, not that he ever restricts you -" she said as she tried to look around, and truly, I was more amused than offended.

"I'm not recording to gather evidence for a wrongful termination lawsuit, and he doesn't require it. In fact, it was Derek that insisted so as to make his job easier and so he didn't have to change secretaries."

"You're right. You're right," she said.

"But you two did become friendlier though, right? I mean, even though he doesn't want to fire you even though he's fired people on the spot for less? Much, much less?"

At her words, I couldn't help but feel warmth all over my body.

"Call me when Levi Boone's here," she tapped on my desk and continued on her way.

I, however, barely even heard her. He didn't want to fire me? But I had already resigned. However, as this thought came to mind, and soon enough she was on her way, I immediately leaped to the floor to begin to retrieve my stationery and other crap, and a few minutes later, my inter-company phone began to ring.

I knew he was the one; he was the only one that used this line, and I couldn't help but stare at it.

"You've already resigned," I told myself. So why was it so hard to face him? Why was I so anxious, nervous, and afraid? It made no sense. I made no sense. The phone began to ring again, and this time around, I wasted no time whatsoever in picking it up.

"Sir?" I answered, however, he briefly went silent. I waited.

"I thought you'd left," he said.

"No, Sir," I replied. "I'm here."

"Come to my office," he said, and I nodded.

"Yes, Sir."

I set the phone down and headed over. I knocked on the door even though I knew there was no need. He was expecting me. Still, I knocked, and then I walked in. Earlier, even though I hadn't been trying to make him fall in love with me exactly, I had always been able to look him in the eyes, I wasn't timid, and I wanted him to at least know that I existed beyond being just his secretary. This time, however, and despite how hard I tried, I couldn't meet his eyes. Instead, I stared at the space behind his head. It was the view of the city, and it was so gorgeous. It had felt like forever since I had last seen it, when instead, it had actually only been a few days. Between then and now, it felt like a lifetime.

"Madison," he called, and I automatically turned to face him. I realized then just how exhausted he seemed. Everything had been so relaxed, and I had seen him laugh and enjoy himself, but now he seemed as stiff and strained as he always was. What was interesting, though, was that I was almost sure he preferred being this way. Preferred being at his seat of power and in control.

I smiled then for absolutely no reason, but as his expression remained the same, I wiped it off my face. He watched me as I stood before his desk, and this time around, I looked at him. There was nothing to fear anymore, I admitted. It was the end, and I had loved almost every moment of it. I would always be grateful to him for being so lenient with me. He was a great boss.

"I saw your email," he said. "I saw it on the plane."

All I could do at this was nod.

"You mean it?" he asked. "You really want to resign?"

"I messed up," I said. "Monumentally. You would fire others in an instant. I... I need you to know that I don't consider myself above reproach for any reasons whatsoever."

As I said these words, I once again remembered the woman I had found in his bed, and I felt even more silly. Of course, I wasn't above reproach. How the hell did I think I was to him?

"You're right," he replied, and then he rose to his feet. "You aren't above reproach. He walked around his desk, and then he sat at the edge of his desk and faced me.

"If you really want to leave, then I won't stop you. But I'd like it if you stayed. If you don't want to, then you can pack up your things right now and leave."

All of his words felt like shards going straight into my heart.

"I'll wait," I replied. "I mean, after sending in my resig-nation, I'm allowed two weeks before my replacement is found and they're properly trained."

"Is that the rule?" he asked, and I nodded.

"So, you'll be here for an extra two weeks?"

"Yes, Sir," I replied, and just then, I realized why I had probably done this. If I were to get fired now, by either him or the other executives who want nothing but to see me with my head hanging out the building, I wouldn't get that extra two weeks with him. I was a little amazed at my subconscious mind, but till this moment, it didn't even recall it.

"Yes, Sir," I replied. "I have two more weeks."

He stared at me, and I wondered if he realized this as well.

"No," he replied. "If you want to leave, then now is the best time to."

I was shocked, and so cold, I wanted to button up my blouse.

"I -..." I started, but I couldn't for the life of me come up with a single thing to say. My entire body, mind, and soul were protesting at his insistence for me to leave immediately. He couldn't do that. I didn't want him to do that.

"I..." I began. However, there was no valid excuse I could give to him. He owns the company. Sure, he might not have set the rule, but he was the only one who could decide whether to enforce it or discard it.

"Why did you join this company?" he asked. "You told me you joined after you quit baking. Why this company? Why green tech? Why renewable technology?"

"I completed my masters in it because," I replied. "I wanted to go on to be an environmental lawyer but... uh... I used that money and started the bakery. And when I needed a change, I thought I could explore this route. I actually applied for the legal department so I could be a paralegal first. I thought I'd be able to learn the ropes that way and get my foot in the door. And through that, and since the salary was good, I'd be able to scrape enough up to put me through law school."

"So how did you end up as my secretary?"

"It was a last-minute application sent in," I replied and

couldn't help my sigh. "I, uh, saw the salary after I had applied for being a paralegal and found that it was comparable. Higher even. So, since my end goal was to earn money anyway, I applied as well. And this was the job I got called in for. I wasn't qualified, definitely. I didn't have much experience, but Derek... when he hired me, he told me it was urgent because, you know..."

"I had just fired the last person that was in the position and needed someone immediately."

"Yes, Sir," I replied.

"He didn't expect that you would be able to tolerate me for this long."

"Well, you've been close to perfect all along," he said. "So... amongst other reasons... I want to keep you on. But you didn't seem to want to stay on. At the slightest trouble, you want to run far away. Why? That's what I need to understand. Otherwise, you can't... I won't want you here any longer."

"I've told you," I replied. "I respect who you are and what you do, and I understand it. I never wanted to be a liability, and I never wanted you to turn a blind eye because of... because of me. In fact, because of... I hold myself to a higher standard. I didn't want you to be lenient with me. I should do better, I know better."

"You're also human, and you make mistakes," he said. "You don't even want to extend grace to yourself when you make mistakes?"

"The others didn't have grace extended to them," I replied.

"You don't know that," he said. "You weren't there. They made several mistakes. To you and external parties, it might have seemed small, but it wasn't to me. Or perhaps these mistakes gave me an insight into their person that made me understand that they weren't suitable for the role. The gravity of their offense was not only what determined that they're fired. So far, you haven't been that way. You've done everything almost perfectly; your attention to detail is unparalleled. So, you made one mistake... a monumental one. It's worth firing you over, but I don't want to. So, are you staying or not?"

I listened to his words and felt tears gathering in my eyes, however, I couldn't let them fall. I'd rather die.

"I... I turned away from him. "Can I have the two weeks to truly consider this, Sir?"

"No," he replied. "I want your answer now. If you don't have it, then, I'd prefer you pack up your things and leave."

I stared at him in shock. No matter how hard I tried to respond, I couldn't.

"There's an alternative," he said and rose to his feet. I was more than eager to hear it.

"You could get transferred to another department," he said. "You want to work in legal? Then you could get transferred there. No matter what, you're a valuable asset and I don't want to lose you. This you can take your time to think about, but in the matter of being my secretary, it's now or never."

He turned around then and returned to his desk. I watched as he settled in and still didn't know what to say to him. Both positions were so incredibly attractive, but as I watched him, I realized that I didn't want either of them. What I wanted was him. I wanted his undivided attention, his care, his love... his commitment. What I wanted the most was him, and if I became either his secretary or a paralegal in his firm, the chance of having him was little to non-existent. Work would always stand in the way. Work would always come first.

I looked at him then and responded.

"Can I please have until the end of the day, Sir?" I asked. "I would like to see how things play out with Levi Boone."

"If it doesn't explode in our faces, will you reconsider your resignation?" he asked.

I didn't respond to this.

"You have to make this decision now because I won't allow you to make it then. I need you to be resolute and steady and to be willing to fight for the thing that matters the most to you. The fact that you didn't seem willing makes me doubtful about what matters to you and what doesn't."

I heard what he was saying, and I understood. So, I nodded in response.

I didn't think my nod answered any of his questions, but he seemed too exhausted to pursue any of it, so he turned his attention to his computer.

"You can have until the end of the day."

"Thank you, Sir," I said as I walked out of the office.

Chapter Forty-Eight
Madison

"I'm out of money."

"What?"

I was so incredibly distracted and concerned by what was going on in Hunter's office that more woes were the last thing I wanted to have to deal with today. However, at her words, I couldn't help but stare at her message in concern.

"What do you mean by you're out of money?"

"My savings have been depleted!" she cried. "I either have to choose to go ahead with manufacturing the first collection, samples at that, or if I should say reset."

I stared down at her words and couldn't help but feel immensely sorry for her. That was as she was stating the truth though because she was known for exaggeration.

"Why didn't you move out of your place and come stay with me?"

"Sacrifice and all."

"My space is also a loft," she replied. "Industrial loft. It serves as the company's office and studio as well."

"Well, you can't afford it now, but it doesn't mean you won't be able to."

"I can't lose this place, Maddy," she said. "You know how much of a miracle it was when I found it."

"Sure," I replied, expecting the other shoe to drop.

"You know I want to ask for your help, but you're not making it easy for me at all with the way you're responding."

She was right, and I immediately felt remorseful.

"I'm sorry. This whole thing with Hunter is crazy and everyone is tense, but none more than me. I didn't know what they concluded in the office, and now that asshole has left and Hunter is in there in silence. Executives have gone by, and then they've left. They couldn't just go in because he hadn't yet called anyone, but everyone's fucking exhausted and anxious."

"Especially you," she said, and I nodded.

"Especially me. Anyway, let's not make this all about me? What favor are you trying to ask me for? Just spit it out?"

"I need you to invest in my company," she said. "We can be equal partners. I can't do it alone anyway, plus the administration side of running the business is so fucking boring and tedious. All I want to do is wake up, design, and sew. So, do you think this is something you can handle?"

I stared at her words, and for a while, I was almost convinced she was joking. And then I was sure she was mistaken.

"You... you want to be partners?"

"Yes!" she said. "I'm getting too burnt out... I need someone to be crazy with me, plus you've been involved with this since the beginning, and we could be millionaires.

Plus, now that you're having issues with your current company, maybe this is the chance you need. Maybe this is a good thing? I mean, I know we've not made any money yet, but we will soon, as soon as we have our samples and can get our fashion show off the ground."

"Right," I replied.

"Please tell me you're thinking about it?" she asked.

I glanced at Hunter's door and told her the truth.

"I am," I replied. "And I can't believe it. Currently, I'm having a serious identity crisis. I want to leave the company, but then I can't; I need the money. Plus, what else would I do? However..."

"My offer is exciting, right?" she squealed in excitement.

"Interesting," I responded. "Not exciting; there's no money involved. But..."

"But what?" as she asked. "Ask any questions, and I'll be more than willing to answer them."

"What if I run out of money too? I mean, I have some savings, but it's not much; maybe it can last us three months."

"That's enough to get us off the ground," she said.

"No, we need at least a year's salary to get us off the ground," I corrected. I sighed and could hear the defeat in her tone.

"Alright," she replied. "I know it is not without hardships or risks, but if any part of you wants to consider it, I'll be very, very excited to have you on board."

This made me smile.

"Alright Miss Cullen," I replied. "I'll think about it and get back to you."

"Thank you so much, Maddy, I love you," she sniffed.

"I'm not making any promises," I said.

"I know, I know, I know. You're just considering, and for the record, no matter what you decide, I will accept it a hundred percent."

"Alright," I said, and then I put the phone away. It was dark now. A couple of hours had passed with him remaining in the office, and with executives coming by, but not being allowed to speak to him. From what I had gathered, they had been working, but his instructions were brief and direct to them, with none to me.

I had never felt worse or even more restless. I wanted to know what the conclusions from the meeting were. What had it cost him or what was it going to cost him? He gave me till the end of the day. Was I still allowed to be here? However, the end had come, and I still didn't have a definite answer to any of the options I was considering.

I had no choice now; I had to go over to him, and we needed to come to a conclusion before I lost my fucking mind.

Chapter Forty-Nine
Hunter

I heard the knock on the door and knew exactly who it was. I was just finishing up with my work for the day, catching up on all the issues that had been left waiting for me over the past few days. And of course, there were the updates from the media storm.

Our legal team had been completely confused with the instructions I had given them not to meddle with anything. There was no point. The second he had walked out of the office, I had made my decisions and gotten on with my life.

There would be no further response from the company, and none of the executives thought I was in my right mind, but I didn't mind.

"Come in," I answered, knowing exactly who it would be.

She headed in, and I could sense how nervous and exhausted she was. I truly wished that she would go home, but I knew that she wouldn't, and given the ultimatum that I had given her to give me a response before this day had ended, I understood why she would be reluctant.

I shut my laptop, then grabbed my coat and rose to my feet.

"Have you made your decision?" I asked.

She stared at me; however, she didn't respond. Not until I was close to her and almost ready to leave myself.

"I, uh... I want to know what he asked for."

I watched her, considered her request, and then I nodded.

"He wants shares. Rather than car payments. He wants a chunk of the cake, and I'd rather not do that. If he wants to buy it, he could. I can't stop that, but to give him that, I'd rather cut my arm off."

"Oh," she said, and I nodded.

"I'm leaving. You should head home too."

I headed toward the door; however, she soon stopped me.

"I... I have shares. You could give him mine."

I stopped in my tracks and turned around to face her.

"What?"

"A few months ago, I got some shares in the company. It's not much, but rather than you give any to him, you could give him mine."

"You bought shares in the company?" I asked.

"Yeah," she replied.

"Why?"

She smiled, and it made my heart flutter.

"What do you mean why? I believe in you. I mean, I believe in your company and what you do."

I stared at her, and then I sighed.

"Come with me. Let's have dinner together."

Her eyes widened in shock.

"Really?"

I didn't bother responding.

She followed me, and pretty soon we were riding down the elevator side by side. A couple of employees were still loitering around, so I exchanged greetings on my way out, but eventually, we were in the privacy of my car and headed towards Oxygen Bar and Lounge.

It wasn't my favorite restaurant, but it was a bit far away, so I didn't go as frequently as I wanted to. However, I felt much lighter, and I knew that for the day to be somewhat of a success, I needed to resolve my issues with her as well. I knew she was nervous, however, I remained silent until we arrived and were seated.

The waiter came to take our order, and while waiting, we started off with some scones and a bottle of red wine.

She took a sip and began to talk about her company shares while I watched her.

"What's the catch?" I asked.

However, she seemed confused by my question.

"What do you mean?"

"What's the catch to me using your shares to satisfy him?"

"Um..." she instantly sat up. "Nothing," she said. "Absolutely nothing. It was my fault, and I don't want you to bear the costs at all."

I watched her and shook my head.

"You do realize that you're not acting like an employee, don't you?"

"What do you mean?" she asked.

"Sometimes you act like you're in love with me."

She stared at me, and then she lowered her head. I

couldn't believe I was doing this, but with her, I couldn't be indirect, and this was the same generally across the board. What was the point? It was a waste of time.

"Are you?" I asked. "Are you in love with me?"

She lifted her gaze to mine and held it, however, she didn't respond.

I smiled. I hadn't exactly been expecting her to reply.

"Let me ask you something you should be able to respond to then. The woman in the hotel? You think I slept with her, right? Is that why you resigned? Is that why you're no longer comfortable or confident about us?"

She continued to watch me.

"Don't lie to me," I said. "I know you want to act like you don't care and that you're unaffected by it, but don't lie to me."

She took another sip of her wine, and then she set the glass down.

"I... I know that I have no right to you personally. Officially or any way. But... seeing her hurt me deeply. I know that I messed up, and I know that you're technically allowed to date whoever you want but seeing that greatly decreased my desire to be around you. I respect you and what you do, but... I think it would be better for me to move on."

This annoys me so much that I could barely contain it.

"Once again," I told her. "You assumed."

She watched me, surprised.

"What do you mean?"

"Based on all you know about me, you really thought I had picked her up at the bar and brought her to my room to sleep with her while you were in the next room?"

She seemed completely confused at what I was saying.

"I'm asking you a question," I said. "You really think I did that?"

"She was in your bed," she replied.

"Did you see me fucking her?"

"So... she came in, but you two didn't go all the way?"

"I have no idea how she got in my room. I didn't invite her; I didn't know her... I barely even spoke to her. I was just as shocked as you were to see her in my bed."

She stared at me, her eyes still wide, and I shook my head.

"I guess now you have to convince yourself that you believe me, but trust me, if you don't know anything about this, you should know that I have no reason to lie."

"I know that," she replied softly.

"Then why didn't you just ask me?" I asked. "Why feel hurt and lash out all on your own? Why conclude that it's best to leave on your own?"

Her eyes filled with tears as she smiled.

"You're allowed to sleep with anyone you want. We weren't... We weren't official. You're my boss."

"You wanted us to be official?" I asked.

She didn't respond.

"You're assertive with everything else except when it comes to this, and when it comes to us. Why?" I asked.

She replied, "Because you're my boss."

"That's all I've thought of you as from the very begin-ning. It's been less than a week since the whole thing has been flipped on its head. I thought... I thought we'd have time to kind of find our groove. You know, maybe get closer, maybe even get tired of each other. By then, I'd probably be begging you to transfer me to another department."

"I can do that now," I said. "Is that what you want?"

"Doing that, I don't think it's within the company," she replied. "From what I've heard, everyone wants to fire me. And it just got worse today."

"These things happen. It'll die down. You should see the kinds of mistakes the other departments make."

"I'm your secretary. I do see them," she smiled. "I... to be honest, I don't know what the right decision is to make now. Continue to stay on or get transferred. I did get a third option today, and I think I might want to take some time to consider it."

"What's the third option?" I asked.

"Starting a lingerie company with a friend of mine." I listened to her, and then I nodded.

"Interesting,"

This made her smile.

"You think it's a good idea?"

"Why would I think that?" I replied, and just then, our food arrived. We focused a little bit on eating, and then I lifted my gaze to hers once again.

"You have an interest in lingerie?" I asked.

"Not exactly, but my friend is in love with it. She quit her job as a lawyer to handle it, but she's getting burnt out and broke because while she loves the creative side, she really hates the business side. I've learned so much from you over the past few months. Maybe I can take it on. Out of all my options, this makes me the most excited."

"And... I'm telling you this not as your secretary or employee."

This amazes me.

"Why are you telling me this then?" I asked.

"I'm pretending right now that I'm on a date with you," she said. "Since I don't know if I'll ever get to actually be on one with you. So, I'm telling you this so that I can remember us together and have the date we never had in Thailand."

"You're saying goodbye?" I asked.

She looked at me and then she shook her head.

"Life is long. New York is really small. Maybe it's not goodbye?"

I thought about her words there and then. I stopped and put my fork down. She looked at me.

"I'm going to tell you things now that I haven't told anyone else, so listen and do with it what you want."

"Alright," she replied.

"I never wanted to stop our relationship when we returned to New York. I wanted to keep going with you because of the way I feel about you... the way I feel when I'm with you... I really haven't ever felt that way with anyone else before."

"So if you do choose to no longer be my secretary and to go into business with your friend, then I'm happy for you to explore that. And of course, I'll be willing to lend my support however you might need it."

"Okay," she said. "I appreciate that."

She returned to her meal, and I did the same. I was very well aware that I still hadn't said exactly what I wanted to. I would leave this up to her.

Chapter Fifty
Madison

"So... are you guys dating or are you not dating?" Emma asked as she arrived in the apartment and collapsed on the couch.

"I have no fucking idea," I replied.

"Did he kiss you goodnight?"

"No, we shook hands," I replied, and her jaw dropped in shock.

"I know," I nodded. "I know. I think I'm going to lose my fucking mind."

"Maybe he's just giving you some space to come to terms with the changes you're making now so that you can be sure of what you really want."

I thought of her response and nodded.

"He told me that he wanted me to be assertive about the things I wanted."

"Was he referring to himself as well?"

"Maybe, but the thing is..." I turned to her. "I am assertive about the things that I want. Just not when it comes to him. At least not yet."

"If not now, then when?"

"I don't know," I replied. "But I'm going to take a bit of time to figure it out, and maybe eventually... I'll get the answers that I need."

Just then, the doorbell rang, and I watched as she headed over to the door.

"Pizza's here," she said excitedly and collected the box from the delivery guy.

"Keep the change," she said, and when he turned around, I had the most disappointed face for her.

"Keep the change?" I asked. "Really? Keep the change?"

"What?" she asked.

"It was like seven dollars."

"This is how you're already out of money. If you're this broke now and you're still telling him to keep the change, then I can imagine how much you've lost already from not negotiating properly and telling people to keep the change."

I rose to my feet and went over to the computer on the table.

"Let me see your records. All the payments and orders you've made so far for fabric purchases and samples."

She came over to the desk then, looking sheepish as well, even as I logged into her laptop.

"Where are the records?" I asked.

"On the website," she replied as she opened the box.

"What website?"

"The website where I made the orders. They keep them there."

"You don't have them organized? You don't have an excel sheet? How did you even choose the manufacturers?

Did you pick the best with the greatest quality, or did you pick the first one you saw, which was also probably the most expensive?"

"I'm not an idiot," she said as she took her seat, and I looked up then.

"I'm sorry. I didn't mean that you were," I said, and she took a bite.

"Pizza," she tore out a piece and handed it over to me.

So... I pressed on with my question as she took the bite.

"Where are the records? The invoices? The price quotes?"

She kept chewing without any response, and I was forced then to look at her.

"Let me guess, they're all on the website?"

"I would have arranged them, I just... I was trying to figure out the designs. Those were more important."

I stared at her, and then I nodded.

"Alright... alright. That's your forte. Admin tasks are not your forte, but that's why I'm here. I'll organize them. Did you at least put them in a folder? Your downloads folder has all sorts of screenshots and files, nothing is named."

I looked at her once again, and she looked away.

"Emma?" I yelled.

"I started six months ago. There's nothing I have done that gets between these six months. I'll get started on arranging them now and will have everything in folders for you within the next two hours."

"You should get some rest. You've been through hell these past two days. You just got back from Thailand... you should get some rest."

"No, I'm going to start with the invoices and research," I

said and immediately brought out my own laptop and got to work.

After a few more minutes, she asked me again, "You really sure you don't want to rest?"

"Nope, I need to go through everything I've done so far so that before tomorrow morning, I can know if I've made the biggest mistake of my life by agreeing to join you on this and possibly breaking up with the love of my life rather than just simply transferring to another department."

"Yes," she said, and I gave her a stern look.

"I'm sorry," she said sheepishly. "It's a mess, but I swear to you that you will most definitely not regret it."

Chapter Fifty-One
Hunter

"Good morning, Sir."

It was absolutely normal for me to be woken up every morning by 6:45 AM with her texts. In this way, which also contained a breakdown of the day's tasks, I would get up and have the time to head to the gym before heading into the office. She had always adjusted this from the beginning when I had expressed a passion that I would like to find the time to head to the gym more. And these were the little things that had made her invaluable to me.

I sighed as I stared at her desk because I most definitely had a very tough day ahead and I couldn't help but feel somewhat nervous about it because she wouldn't be there to filter all the bullshit away. I truly couldn't believe that she was no longer my secretary.

"Is it okay that I'm messaging you this way? I didn't want to be rude. And so early too. I'm sorry, I just wanted to catch you before you headed into the office."

I picked up my phone and replied.

"You don't have to call me Sir anymore or be so polite. I'm not your boss anymore."

"Oh, alright," she added a smiley.

"What is it?" I assumed.

"I'm really worried about just quitting. There are a lot of systems that I had put in place that you're used to, and even though I know I will be easy to replace, I would really like to work with my replacement even if it's remotely for a little while so that you don't feel the change."

This was exactly what I wanted as well. More preferably, I would have liked if she had never left, but there was something about her decision that showed how much I didn't truly like it but brought me a kind of peace that I couldn't explain. I truly was fine with it.

Still, I gave this a little bit more thought and decided to set my pride aside.

"I'll approve it," I said. "You can contact Derek and you two can facilitate it."

"Actually... I would like it if this was just between us. I didn't really want to liaise with your staff. As you said, you're no longer my boss, so consider this as a favor being done from one friend to another?"

I saw her message and for a moment I wondered if she was actually the one that I was texting so early in the morning. I checked her phone number to confirm she was the one and wondered how I felt about this approach. Eventually, as I threw the cover aside, I decided that I liked it.

"Alright. We should meet then," I said. "We can have lunch and talk about how this will work. I'll bring whoever my new secretary is."

"I'd love this, Sir, thank you," she said, and I couldn't help but be amused.

"Sir?"

"I mean Hunter. I'd like that, Hunter."

"Alright. See you at lunch, Madison," I replied and set the phone down.

I thought over the entire exchange even as I headed to the gym to get a quick workout in. About an hour later, as I was heading back to my apartment to shower, I decided that I liked this. The day ahead was going to be bloody, but thanks to her, I felt a bit better. I headed in then and was made aware that all the executives had come in early, as I had announced and informed them. I had no interest whatsoever in succumbing to Levi's blackmail demands, so they would have a field day consoling shareholders and generally handling whatever wind the news of the data breach blew our way.

I was ready, and as soon as I headed in and found the male secretary waiting to replace Madison, I was both sad and relieved at the same time. After informing him of the lunch, which I wasn't going to miss no matter what, I sat at my desk and immediately got started with work. My phone rang several times with Levi trying to reach me in complete disbelief that I hadn't succumbed. It made me feel even better, and so when later in the afternoon, the report was published, I brushed it off and joined the rest of the staff in damage control mode.

The worst of it was handled by lunchtime and I was just in time.

Before I left, however, I received a text message from her.

"It will be okay if you cannot make our lunch. I know you're upset, having a hard day."

I knew just how worried and remorseful she would feel, and it made me want to see her even more. So, I brushed away her concern.

"I'm fine, see you soon," I said, and the call came to an end.

Chapter Fifty-Two
Madison

"You need to sleep more," Emma hounded me. "You should have slept more."

I ignored her as I put on my makeup and focused on getting it right. After being out of practice for so long and yet trying to look as pretty as possible, I found myself using more swipes than needed. Eventually, I was done and turned around to see her leaning against the door frame with her arms folded across her chest.

"What am I supposed to see?" she asked. "Your face looks the same as always."

I gave her a look and hurried out of the bathroom because I was running late, and she followed.

"I didn't mean to be mean; I'm just saying if you want to blow him away, especially now that you are no longer his secretary and therefore don't have any of those crazy restrictions, then you should do more."

"This is my style," I said as I found the dress and blazer I wanted to wear. "Soft and pink. Plus, because of the mistake, his company's being pummeled from every angle today. The fact that he's even agreeing to meet with me is a miracle. I didn't even think he would respond when I sent him the message this morning. I was exhausted from all the work, and I couldn't stop thinking about him."

Sighing, I turned around to face the mirror, and she tsk-tsked.

"Would you stop that?" I complained.

"You're not helping at all. I'm just saying, who knows if you two will see each other after this again. You should wear a dress. That pink dress, remember?"

"The naked dress?" I asked, and she smiled.

"It matches perfectly with your makeup, and it's not the naked dress. Plus, it'll be perfect with your hair, which thank God, you're leaving wild and curly rather than tucked away into that hideous bun as always."

"What would I wear for shoes?" I asked. "I need to be comfortable."

"Fuck comfort, you're going to meet the love of your life. One afternoon, one lunch. Wear white stripy sandals. Not too high but gorgeous. Or maybe pink. You can take any of mine; we're the same size."

I considered what she was saying but still felt reluctant. Today was not a good day for him, and I didn't want to look as though I was having a blast. The blazer and loafers were sensible and appropriate, plus I was going there to work.

"You could give an excuse that you had a meeting across town for a new studio or something, and that's why you came dressed up. You could apologize even."

"That sounds pathetic," I said, and she was barely

unable to hold back her smile. I ignored her and headed to the door. At the last moment, I stopped in my tracks and stared ahead at nothing.

"What is it?" she asked. "Please tell me you're going to listen to me?"

Groaning, I turned around and hurried back into the apartment.

"Get me the dress," I said and quickly changed my purse. Soon enough, I was dressed in the pink floral ensemble, and I had never felt more feminine during lunch hours on a weekday afternoon.

"Gorgeous," Emma said, and I ignored her because I no longer had the time to allow her to gloat. I did blow a kiss to her on my way out, though, when I saw just how breathtaking I looked. I didn't intend to try too hard, and I could only hope that I didn't look like I was.

I took a taxi so I wouldn't get there late. At this point, I didn't even mind that I wouldn't eat; I just needed him to be somewhat happy to see me. It had barely been a day, and I was already reaching out for him.

Shaking my head, I checked my messages again and prayed that he wouldn't cancel. I checked online again for updated news about his company, and matters seemed to be improving. They had been prepared for it, and so the shareholders had been alerted ahead of time.

It made me feel sad that he even had to take this shit in the first place and that it was my fault. With that being said, I knew the first thing that I was going to say to him the moment I saw him.

I arrived on time, so I was able to choose the seat that

would afford the best view of him from the entrance. He was on time as always, and by his side was his new secretary.

I was so relieved that it wasn't a woman. It was selfish to want that, but it made me so incredibly happy and eager to see him.

The secretary shook my hand as soon as they arrived, and then I turned my attention to him. He had been stopped on his way by a couple much more elderly. They were probably business acquaintances, though I wasn't familiar with them. He greeted them briefly, and then he began to head my way.

He looked so gorgeous it nearly brought tears to my eyes. Today he was in complete black, and I knew it was a sensitive and serious day for him. It was usually his practice to wear all black from head to toe when he thoroughly needs to intimidate, and I could only hope that it wasn't me that was his victim because I knew from other experiences that I wouldn't survive it. With him, as handsome as he looked, I was already finding it extremely difficult to breathe.

I rose to my feet as he arrived and held out my hand for a handshake. But he took one look at it, dismissed it, and leaned closer towards me. I had no choice then but to completely accept the hug and to bask in it.

All at once, I was hit with the reminder of him. His scent, his warmth, and how gorgeous he looked. I almost couldn't pull away from him, and when I eventually did, I couldn't look away.

"Fancy seeing you so soon after your departure," he said, and I truly didn't know what to say.

We took our seats, and he kept his gaze on me.

"I'm Madison," I introduced myself to his new male secretary, James, and he introduced himself as well.

"I brought him along so you two could meet officially and remain in contact as needed."

"Yes, Sir," James nodded, and I did the same.

"You don't have to stay for lunch," he said, and the secretary took a little while to understand what he was saying. Eventually, though, it was clear, so after collecting my phone number and email and discussing how I had arranged and moved his schedule around after our return from Thailand, he rose to his feet.

"I think it would be best if I return to the office, Sir," he said, and I had absolutely no qualms about it. Neither did Hunter because soon, we were alone with each other.

He watched me as we ate, and I realized that for the first time, he truly didn't seem like my boss. It made me feel quite unrestrained. Seated at this table at this moment was just a man and a woman, and my clit wouldn't stop throbbing between my thighs.

"So, how was—"

"Have you started—"

We paused at the sudden outburst, and then we smiled at each other.

"You go first," he said, and I nodded.

"It feels so wrong being here with you knowing what the company's going through today. It also seems so wrong that you seem fine. I know inside you're upset, and I know this will set you back and—"

"No need to apologize again," he cut me off. "You're already doing your best to show how remorseful you are, and from time to time, I will make requests as well that you more or less have to fulfill because you're incredibly sorry."

I watched him, and I felt my heart swell with so much warmth it felt like it would burst out of my chest.

"You're consoling me. You know this, right?"

He watched me, and then I added,

"By starting with ensuring always that my secretaries become as competent as you were."

"Most definitely," I replied. "And?"

"That's a start. As more things come up, I will call on your services for free, and you will perform."

"I'll always be ready, Sir, at your beck and call."

His gaze narrowed, tamed in that salty gorgeous way that made me think of all the sex we'd had in Thailand. Raw, messy, sweet.

"Damn," I had to start to fan myself because seeing him and being dressed like this was all I could think about.

"How's your new job?" he asked. "Or perhaps I should say company? Are you just helping her turn it around as an employee, or is this a split endeavor?"

"We spent the majority of last night in discussions of how to proceed, and we've decided that an absolute arrangement will be better. I'll own fifty percent, and she'll own fifty percent as well."

"Good," he replied. "That's good. Partners are always beneficial, but no matter how friendly you are now, trust me when I say things can and will get messy along the line. So regardless of your relationship with her, you need to set down very clear boundaries and responsibilities from the onset."

He was giving me business advice, and I nearly couldn't

believe it. Still, I listened attentively, appreciating every single moment of it. My foot brushed against his leg underneath the table. It had been accidental, but on the brief pause in his speech, I knew that he had felt it as well.

Smiling, he picked up his glass of wine, and I couldn't stop watching him.

"I know you used to go boxing sometimes, even in the middle of the day when you really wanted to take your mind off things," I said, and I couldn't believe the words that were coming out of my mouth. "Back then, I had always wanted to suggest an alternative sport to you."

"An alternative sport?" he asked. "Why didn't you mention it back then?"

I looked at him, and everything inside screamed to hold back. This is... was my boss. Was your boss, I tried to remind myself.

"Your car," I said. "Any chance we can have five minutes to be alone?" I asked, this time, however, I was unable to look at him. "The glasses are tinted, the insides are spacious."

And just like that, he understood exactly what I was saying.

"The driver's waiting at the curb, but he can go down to the underground garage and make himself scarce. Ten minutes, you say?" he asked.

"Maybe more," I replied. "It really depends on how much sweating you need."

"Oh, I think you're the one that needs this exercise because I'm not going to be exerting much effort anyway. You're the one that'll be doing more of the riding."

"Still up for it?"

I nodded, unable to wipe the smile off my face.

"When exercising, you just need your heart to go faster for you to experience either kind of relief we're chasing here," I said, and then laughed.

"In that case, I am extremely certain that this... sport is just what I need."

Chapter Fifty-Three
Hunter

I'd never quite fucked in a car before.

The unavoidable discomfort because of how tall I am didn't particularly appeal to me, but as she lifted up her gorgeous dress and sat astride me, I couldn't believe just how excited I was.

"I thought we needed time away from each other?" I said as she leaned down to kiss me, and she had to stop midway to contain her amusement.

"We do need time away from each other," she replied, and then she kissed me. It had been just a short while ago since we had kissed, however, as her tongue slid into my mouth, I understood why despite the fact I was having the worst day ever, I had still found the time to come meet her. I understood that all I wanted to babble about was the new partnership she was involved in, and there was one more thing.

I pulled away from the kiss and stared into her gorgeous eyes.

"I don't know what's going to happen in the future

between us," I said. "But I do know that if you have to become my secretary again, I don't ever want to see you dressed in those life-sucking dreary clothes."

She cocked her head, smiling.

"You like what I'm wearing right now?" she asked. "Is this your way of telling me that I look absolutely gorgeous?"

"You look breathtaking," I replied.

"The pink... the curls... the heels... the smile... I feel like working with me has kept you in a box, and I truly can't wait to see how you fly now."

"Hmm," she said, her eyes roving over my face as she played with my hair. She was so affectionate with her touch and in the way she watched me. How had I not noticed this all these months? I was unobservant and obtuse, but it truly amazed me how much more I had missed over the months and years while I had been paying very little attention to anything other than myself.

"Well, now that you're seeing this, it's nice to know that you're looking forward to seeing more of me."

This amused me as I kissed her again.

"I'm looking forward to seeing a whole lot more of you."

She seemed a bit stunned as she stared at me, and then she shook her head to clear it.

"What is it?" I asked.

"I just... I thought I would be doing a lot of apologizing during this lunch and feeling remorseful and extremely sorry."

"You should feel all those things," I said, and I meant it. However, I truly couldn't keep the smile off my face. She, however, was able to immediately wipe off hers.

"I do feel all of those things, I swear, but the way you're

smiling, the way you're looking at me now, and treating me is making it very difficult."

"I know," I said. "Consider this as part of your punishment. Emotional torture."

"The worst kind," she said, and I couldn't miss the sadness in her eyes or tone for that matter.

"You've really been working me since the beginning of the year, and I had to keep it all in."

"Sometimes I was sure I was going to lose my mind," she said, and I held her even more tightly.

We'd come here to fuck, but there was something about the dark, cramped space. The heat seemed intensified, the intimacy, the closeness. I could see, hear, and taste more of her than I was sure I could anywhere else.

"Alright," she tapped me against the chest as she circled her arms around me. "Before I forget, I made some plans for your meeting today. I was going to ensure that I stayed in contact with your secretary so that I could at least have reasons to speak to you for hours, but it isn't just for fun. You've grown one of the most successful businesses in the country from scratch, and I have learned so much from you. But I have you on speed dial, and I needed to know that you didn't want that to change. For instance, now I think we're going to need investors, and I'm not asking for your money, absolutely not, but I am asking that I be able to come to you with inquiries about business decisions."

"Your knowledge is extensive, and... I just... your ego, and I can't let you go."

"Ah," I said. "So you're just here for my brain and not my body?"

"I'm here for the whole thing," she replied. "Every single piece. Your brain, your heart, and your body."

I nodded; however, she couldn't look away from me. Her eyes filled with tears, and then she cradled my face in her hands.

"I'm in love with you, Hunter Swift," she said. "With all my heart."

I smiled because as I said the words back to her, I understood in my heart that they were the most true and special words that I had ever said out loud to anyone in my life.

"And I'm in love with you too, Madison Parish." I replied.

At my words, she seemed shocked, and then she leaned forward once again to kiss. It went on forever, but by the time we pulled away again, all I could think about was the fact that it had been too short. Much too short.

"So... we're officially together now?" she asked, and I nodded in kind.

"We are."

"Wow, if only I had known?"

"If only you had known what?" I asked.

"To book that trip to Thailand, fall on my ass in the bathroom, and more or less force you into having sex with me. I'm usually so organized and have everything scheduled, but this particular one I dropped. I should have known to orchestrate it a long time ago."

I laughed at this, but I couldn't wait anymore. I couldn't chat anymore, and so I made quick work of her panties, and when I reached for her sex and saw the nearly missing hole within, I had to raise my eyebrows at her in question.

"It's one of our lingerie samples," she replied. "We

haven't had any extra time for research and development, so I'll have to test out the product."

"Business manager and model," I asked, and her shoulders dropped in exhaustion.

"Yes," she sighed, and I shook my head.

"You haven't even started, but don't worry, it's going to be a hell of a ride."

Epilogue
Madison

"This can't be happening. I can't believe this is happening."

I stare down at the model puking her guts out on the floor, and I couldn't believe what was happening either.

One of the assistants held up her hair and patted her back, while I turned around and went over to one of the dressing tables to find her a bottle of water. When I returned and handed it over, Emma was still panicking.

"The show has started," Emma whimpered. "They're going to call them out any moment. Hey, didn't we get a spare model? Why the fuck did we have to hire one that hadn't even had the good sense to not get drunk the night before her show?"

"Oh, I get it," her tone sharpens. "We're not a famous brand, right? So, you couldn't even have the decency to respect our time and our show. After all, it's just some stupid fucking gig for the money, right?"

At this point, if she got any louder, I was sure they were going to be able to hear her over the loud music and already ebbing Steel Dan making introductions.

"Come with me," I took her hand and pulled her to the stage with me, right in a corner where we could peek and not be seen.

"This isn't just some stupid show, is it? It's going to be televised, and every single seat is packed."

She stared out at it while I looked exactly in the direction of the seat I had prepared for Hunter. I soon found him, and maybe it was dim light, but he looked so impossibly handsome that I couldn't believe it.

"People care, and people are here," I told her. "This is a big deal, and we expected this. We'll fix it."

She went silent for a while as she looked out at the crowd, and then she turned to me.

"This is your fault. You know this, right?"

"How is it my fault?" I argued.

"You were the one who forced me into doing this show. I wanted this to launch quietly, and then Hunter had to butt in."

"He has the experience. He wanted us to hit the ground running and get as much exposure as we can possibly get."

"Well, we're definitely going to hit the ground for sure. This is ridiculous, for God's sake. We rented out a place; we have catering! Maddie!"

"We also have exposure."

"And no model! The piece she is showcasing is the final piece. You have to have a certain body type to showcase that. I'm shaped like a brick. You think I can do it?"

I narrowed my eyes at her and then turned around to look at the other girls.

"Maybe one of the early girls can take her place after they're done with theirs."

"And one of the final walks?" she asked.

"When they're all side by side for the photographer. What are we going to do then?"

"We'll figure it out. We still have about five minutes more," I replied.

I tried to pull her back with me, but just as we arrived, she stepped back and gave me a creepy look.

"What?" I asked as I looked around, trying to figure out what to do and how I could resolve this.

"You have the body type for the final piece," she said. At first, I didn't hear because her words... these kind of words just didn't compute, but then eventually, they hit me, and I turned to her in shock.

"Are you out of your mind?"

"This is for our business," she pleaded. "Our dream. You've put all your savings into this, and so have I. Even Hunter has invested."

"Because you made me force him to," I grumbled, and she nodded.

"Exactly. You want to waste his money? You want to go back with your tail between your legs and ask for your old secretary job back?"

I considered this and shrugged.

"He'll be happy to have me back."

"Of course," she snapped. "But I'll be homeless! I'll be forced to become a fucking lawyer again. Don't be selfish.

Get in that lingerie now and walk down the runway. It's like every other normal day."

"I don't dress half-naked and strut in heels on every other normal day," I protested.

And she shut her eyes.

"You're our only chance. We don't have time for this. You have to do this right now. We're out of time for you to consider. Your makeup needs to be done, and we need to make last-minute adjustments."

"Carlos!" she yelled out, and the makeup artist we had hired came over.

"See her face, hurry. Three minutes. She wears the final lingerie."

He too was surprised but never one to ask questions for chats more than he needs to with how little we were paying him, he took instructions, and I was pumped down onto a chair.

I couldn't believe this was happening, but it was my business, and I didn't have a choice.

I wanted to call Hunter, to come over to talk some sense into me, but he didn't seem to be responding, and so I had no choice but to wait and somehow pull this through.

"Fuck."

Hunter

"I can't believe you're at a fashion show," my sister Piper said. "I can't believe you're in love with a lingerie designer."

There were a lot of things she couldn't believe that I myself couldn't believe as well, but none of that was important. What was was the box in my pocket and what I was planning to do later that day. And of course, the program schedule and when exactly she would be coming out along with Emma to close out the show. Piper leaned closer to me then and nudged me.

"You're awfully quiet," she said, and I knew then that I had to tell her. I had to tell someone.

"I want to give her more exposure, that's why I suggested this show to them."

"It's a great idea. I love it. The show is gorgeous, the cameras are clicking. Wonderful start."

"Yeah, but that's not the only reason. I mean, that's not the only way I want to give her exposure."

"How else?" she asked, and once again, I didn't respond.

"Hunter," she called. "You're usually not antsy, but you've been antsy for a while now. Your usually calm persona is off, and I know it. But now I'm not sure if you're just being silent as usual or if you really can't respond to me because you're anxious about something. And that scares me immediately because you're never anxious. So, can you just-"

"It's starting," I said, and she turned away.

We focused all our attention on the stage, and the music started. One by one, the models came out, strutting their pieces, and I focused my attention on listening to Piper ooh and aahh by my side.

"God, they're gorgeous," she said. "I mean... I don't have the body for them, but damn, I want one just to look at it. Freaking gorgeous. Hunter, you have one-"

She turned to me, and she didn't stop because my face was overcome with shock.

"What happened there, are you okay?" she asked.

I nudged my head towards the stage, and there she was. Looking unbelievable.

I was shocked and awed all at once, but there she was in one of the pieces. I wanted to shield the eyes of the whole world from her body, but at the same time, I needed everyone to know that she was mine.

She looked so beautiful, so confident, even though I knew her well enough to know that she would have never wanted to do this. There was probably an emergency.

Shocked, I pulled out my phone, and there it was. Fifteen missed calls. Multiple text messages.

"Fuck," I swore.

"Fuck indeed. She's gorgeous. Jesus, how much luckier can you get?"

"Right," then I put the phone away and instead grabbed something else from my pocket. It was a black velvet box, and in it was a diamond ring that probably cost more than the building we were in.

"How much luckier do you think I can get?" I asked.

Piper turned to me, startled at my question.

"What do you mean?" she asked.

"If I... if I ask her to marry me..., do you think she will say yes?"

Piper went completely silent, but it didn't matter because my gaze was solely on the love of my life.

She stood with the other models, and then it was time to introduce the designers, and she came forward along with Emma. Someone seemed to be hurrying over from backstage then with a jacket of some sort, and I moved. I didn't second guess myself. I moved and got onto the stage, and to say it caused a ruckus was an understatement. Everyone was curious and excited, but she... only she was pissed off.

"You are so fired from being our adviser," she said. "So, so fired. I tried to reach you."

She said all this under her breath with gritted teeth too that the cameras wouldn't pick it up, but it was more endearing than frightening.

"I'm sorry," I asked. "I kind of had my mind completely occupied."

"By what?" she nearly yelled this one out.

"This is for publicity's sake," I said. "What I'm about to do now. I mean, it's not entirely so, but I want to support you all the time in whatever way I can. I'll probably do this again, but for now... I want to do it now where the whole world can see, hopefully, they will witness our engagement, and as a result, talk as well about all the happenings at your show where you just launched yours and Emma's lingerie line."

She went into shock as she listened to me, and then I shrugged off my jacket. I wrapped it around her, and then I lowered onto one knee. Tears filled her eyes in disbelief, and then there's another commotion interruption.

"There are so many things I want to say," I began as I pulled out the ring. "And a lot of them I've already said throughout these past few months. Being with you makes me feel like I've known you forever, but now I truly want to ensure that this becomes a reality and that this will not change."

"Madison Leslie Parish, I love you with all my heart, and so I am hoping that you will say yes as I ask you to spend the rest of your life with me."

I opened up the box then, and the room seemed to explode. Flashes went off from every angle. Of us... of the ring... of the lingerie that was being launched.

She stood, unable to speak. I slipped the ring onto her finger, and she pulled me up.

"Yes," she whispered into my mouth as she kissed me.

"With all of my heart... yes."

The End

Coming Next...
NOT YOURS YET

Chapter One
Liam

Harriet Rain, my future sister-in-law's best friend, is smoking hot. We've met a few times and we flirt and joke together and there's always that sexual vibe swirling between us that something could happen. But it's just too damn cliché to hook up with the Maid of Honor. Then the wedding day comes. The bride is beautiful, of course, but when I see Harriet walking down the aisle, that's the moment I know that I'm gonna become that cliché. And more...

I am going to marry that girl.

I don't know where the thought or the conviction comes from, but I know in my heart and soul it's true. I can't take my eyes off her as she walks slowly toward the altar where I stand beside my brother, Cullen.

Her blonde hair is clipped in place, half up and half

down, the down part tumbling in curls to just past her shoulders. She is wearing a pretty pink silk dress that brushes the floor and makes her hips look so grabbable and her breasts absolute perfection. Her cheeks are flushed, partly I think in embarrassment as every eye in the room is watching her walk down the aisle, and perhaps with excitement to see her best friend get married.

As though she feels my eyes on her, she looks up and meets my gaze. Her eyes are a beautiful pale green color and the earthy tones of the eye makeup she wears really bring out the sparkle in them. She's still looking me in the eye when she bites her bottom lip, dips her eyes, and gives a half smile. That shy, almost demure, expression does something to me, and I feel my cock stirring in my boxers. I force myself to look away from Harriet before the whole congregation knows exactly how I feel when I look at her.

Behind Harriet, the two other bridesmaids have begun to walk down the aisle too. Their dresses are the same style as Harriet's, but theirs are a few shades darker. I prefer Harriet's dress but let's face it, the woman would look good in a trash bag so it's most likely not really a fair comparison.

Finally, Max, short for Maxine, appears on her mom's arm. Her mom is giving her away as her father isn't a part of her life. When Cullen first told me that was the plan, I thought it might look a little bit strange, but it doesn't. It looks perfect. Everything looks perfect. Max's dress is a fairy tale ball gown of white tulle adorned with diamantes making her sparkle as she walks. My brother glances at me and we grin at each other.

"I told you she'd show up," I whisper.

"Yup, you were right. She's breathtaking," Cullen replies.

Harriet reaches the altar area first and goes to stand behind the empty space that Max will fill in a moment. The other bridesmaids join her and then Max and her mom reach us last. Cullen steps forward to receive Max's hand and then the bridal party and the groomsmen, me included, move away from the altar and take our places in the front pew to watch the vows get exchanged.

Max and Cullen decided to skip the part where the officiant asks who gives the bride away and all of that because Max's mom didn't really want to do it because she knew she would end up in tears and unable to speak. I must admit I kind of like it not being there. It's not the olden days when women were possessions. I think it's not so much a case of someone giving the bride away anymore, but that most brides want someone to walk with them down the aisle to help with their nerves.

Cullen and Max are both all smiles and most of the congregation are too except for Max's mom who is already tearing up before the vows have even started. Yes, she was right. She would have sobbed through anything she had to say about giving her daughter away.

The officiant smiles out over the congregation and the last-minute whispering and shuffling dies down as everyone focuses on the front of the church. The officiant begins by welcoming everyone to the wedding and then he talks about the meaning of love, and he reads a poem about ever-lasting love.

During the poem, I look around subtly and I can't help but watch Harriet. Her full attention is on the bride and groom and the officiant, and she has a soft smile on her lips. She looks beautiful and I want to be the one to make her smile like that. I can't help but wonder if that's the same smile she will have on her face after I make her climax. I can't start thinking like that, not here for fuck's sake, and the tingling in my cock confirms this.

I force myself to look away from her and concentrate on the wedding. It is my kid brother getting married and he's only going to do this once, or at least he'd better only do this once because Max is a keeper. The least I can do is pay attention. Harriet will still be here after the ceremony, and if I play my cards right, she will be around for a long, long time.

We have reached the point in the wedding ceremony where the officiant has asked if there are any objections to the wedding and the silence is deafening as he pauses to wait for any responses. If someone really did though, I don't know who would be scarier to deal with Cullen, Max, or Max's mom. My money is on Max's mom if anyone attempts to ruin her baby's wedding.

Cullen glances at me and catches my eye and I smile and give a tiny shake of my head. I've been winding him up for weeks leading up to the wedding, telling him I am going to object but of course, I'm not. Apart from anything, I don't have a death wish and Max might call her mom off, but only so that she could kill me herself if I made a scene at her wedding.

"It's always good when that part is over," the officiant says with a soft laugh which gets a quiet laugh in return. "It's all smooth sailing from here. Now, let's get you two married."

A short piece of music plays, and the officiant shuffles his papers and reads out a prayer, then the music ends and he smiles at the happy couple.

"Cullen, repeat after me. I call upon these people here present," the officiant starts and then he pauses, and Cullen repeats his words. The officiant goes on. "To witness that I, Cullen James Monroe..."

"To witness that I, Cullen James Monroe," Cullen repeats.

"Do take you, Lucy Maxine Granger," the officiant goes on and again Cullen repeats his words. "To be my lawful wedded wife."

Max cringes at the mention of her full name and Cullen grins at her. She can't help but grin back at him and then it's her turn to repeat the officiant's words and she beams the whole time. The officiant moves on to the vows and Cullen and Max are still beaming at each other all the way through them.

Cullen repeats all of the vows and then it's Max's turn.

"I, Lucy, take you Cullen to be my husband," the officiant starts, and Max repeats the statement. "To have and to hold from this day forward."

"To have and to hold from this day forward," Max repeats, her voice trembling with emotion.

He takes them through the for better or worse, richer and poorer, sickness and health thing.

"Until death parts us," the officiant says.

"Until death parts us," Max repeats and I'm sure I see a look of relief on her face that she got through all her part there without stuttering or stumbling over her words.

The officiant then talks a little bit about God and how

the couple has made their vows with God as their witness. I kind of zone out a bit at that point. I'm not big on religion.

"And now the exchanging of the rings," the officiant says, and I make sure to tune back in because this is my part. The officiant looks over at me and smiles. "Liam, the ring please."

I stand up and get the ring from the inside pocket of my suit jacket. I'm kind of relieved to be able to hand it over and not have to keep patting my pocket and making sure it's still there every five minutes. I walk up to the altar and hand the ring to Cullen. I pat his arm, and he beams happily at me. Then I take my seat once more as Cullen takes Max's hand in his.

"Place the ring on Lucy's finger and say your chosen vow," the officiant says.

"I give you this ring as a symbol of my love for you. All that I am and all that I have is yours for now and forever," Cullen says.

I hear a few sniffles from behind me and Max has tears in her eyes too as Cullen slips the ring onto her finger.

The officiant waits until the ring is on and then he smiles up at Harriet.

"Harriet, the ring please," he says.

Harriet pulls the ring from her small purse, gets up, and goes and hands it to Max. The two women smile at each other, both of them with tears shining in their eyes and then Harriet walks back away, and yes, I watch her ass as she walks. She sits back down, and the ceremony continues. The officiant gives Max the same instructions as the ones he gave Cullen.

"I give you this ring as a symbol of my love for you,"

Max says, holding the ring on Cullen's finger. "I am yours, always."

She pushes the ring onto Cullen's finger and they both turn to the officiant who smiles again.

"With the power vested in me by God, I now pronounce you husband and wife," he says. "You may seal your vows today with a kiss."

Cullen and Max don't need to be told twice and they wrap their arms around each other and kiss as the whole congregation whoops and cheers and claps. I look over at Harriet and I'm both surprised and pleased to catch her looking at me. She doesn't look away as I expect her to.

Instead, she smiles innocently at me, and I smile innocently back at her.

God, I want that woman.

Chapter Two
Liam

Once Cullen and Max have signed the register and Harriet and I have added our signatures as witnesses of the marriage under theirs, we have some photographs taken inside of the church and then we leave, Harriet with her hand in my arm. Her touch makes my skin tingle and I have to keep reminding myself that she's only linking my arm because it's the plan – the best man and the maid of honor walking out of the wedding ceremony together is pretty standard.

We leave the church and go for more photographs and then we finally reach the hotel where the reception is taking place. The drinks from the bar are already flowing and people are milling about talking and laughing together. The room falls quiet when the bride and groom are announced and Cullen and Max walk into silence followed by a cheer so loud that I see Max physically jump. The next hour or so passes by in a blur of food and greetings and chatting and then it's time for my speech. I get up, take the microphone, and smile out at the guests.

"Firstly, I'd like to thank you all on behalf of my brother and his new wife for coming today and for all the presents and cards. But especially the presents," I start, which gets a laugh. "Wait. Did I mention the presents?" Another laugh and I start to relax into my speech. "Most importantly, I'd like to thank Max for putting up with my brother. Cullen, you've got a good one here. Don't you ever let her go."

"I don't intend to," Cullen replies, and he wraps his arm around Max's shoulders, pulling her in, and kisses her on the cheek. She happily lets him.

"I get asked a lot if I'm jealous of my little brother and the truth is, of course I am. I mean look at his bride. Who wouldn't be a tad jealous? But I think they actually mean am I jealous because Cullen got married before me. And here's the thing. Anyone who knows me well would laugh at the idea of that because getting married and settling down has never really been on my radar, much to my mom's dismay," I say. Another ripple of laughter goes through the room and my mom rolls her eyes but she's laughing too.

I pause for a moment and then I make a decision that feels right, and I start to talk again.

"You know, I had this whole speech planned out where I would talk about how good Cullen and Max are together and how they are the sort of couple that have a love that dreams are made of and that they are the sort of couple that teenagers would refer to as end game. But here's the truth – you all are friends or family of the happy couple, and you know all of that. So instead, I'm going to make this short and simply raise a glass to Cullen and Max," I say.

I raise my glass and everyone in the room stands up and follows suit.

"To Cullen and Max," they echo.

I sit down and everyone else does too. Amongst the rustling of clothes and the squeaking of the chair legs people take their seats once more, Max looks at me and grins.

"Thank you," she mouths, and I grin back and give her a thumbs up. I know what that's about. Before the wedding I was winding her up, telling her all about the various things I was going to say or do during my speech, things that I knew would have embarrassed her. I had no intention of doing it, and deep down, I think she knew that too, it was just funny keeping her thinking that I might have been going to do it.

After a moment, it's Harriet's turn to make her speech and she stands up to a light smattering of applause. She smiles and launches into a lovely speech about her friendship with Max and how as her best friend, she has always wanted the best for Max and now she has it. To be honest, as much as I try to focus on the words Harriet is saying, instead, I find myself focusing on her mouth, the way it moves when she talks, and the full redness of her lips. And what it would feel like to have those lips on mine and then around my cock.

Before too much longer, the speeches are over, and the cake is cut, handed out, and eaten. The lights are now dimmed, the bar is still open, and the music pounds through the place. I'm sure I'm not alone in saying this is the part of a wedding that I actually enjoy.

The DJ calls for our attention and then invites the bride and groom up to the dance floor for their first dance as a married couple which gets a huge cheer. The song starts and Cullen and Max sway together, moving across the floor. I watch them and then I feel eyes on me, and I glance along the table to find Harriet looking at me. She doesn't look away when I look back at her. Instead, she smiles, and I smile back at her.

After a minute of the dance, Cullen waves his hands toward us all, wanting everyone to get up and dance. I look at Harriet again and raise an eyebrow and she nods. I get up and offer her my hand which she takes, and I lead her onto the dance floor. I take one of her hands in mine and wrap the other one around her waist and we begin to move to the music. This close to her, I can smell the sweet smell of her perfume and I can hear her humming along to the music.

The song ends and something faster starts to play. Harriet and I release each other, and I turn around to head back to my seat. Harriet stops me with a hand on my arm.

"Umm where do you think you're going?" she says. I open my mouth to tell her I'm going back to my seat but it's clearly a rhetorical question because she pulls me back toward her. "You don't honestly think that you are only going to dance with me once, right? And for half a song at that."

"I'm not much of a dancer," I say, but the fact that she

wants me to dance with her isn't lost on me and I feel like going and sitting down now would be like a rejection to her and that's the last thing I want and so I force myself to move to the music.

I surprise myself because after a few minutes, I relax, and I find myself actually enjoying dancing with Harriet. My self-consciousness slips away when I realize that no one is watching me – everyone is just doing their own thing and having fun.

"You kept this one quiet, Liam," a voice says as an arm wraps around my shoulders. It's my Aunt Dorothy and her other arm is around Harriet's shoulders. "Why didn't you tell everyone you're seeing someone."

"Oh. We're not... I mean I'm not..." I start but Harriet smiles at Dorothy and speaks over me.

"It's still pretty new so we're kind of keeping it quiet for now," she says.

"Got it," my Aunt Dorothy says and winks at Harriet. "Your secret is safe with me."

"What was that?" I say when my Aunt Dorothy has drifted back out of earshot.

"Sorry. Did I overstep the mark?" Harriet says and I quickly shake my head.

"No, not at all," I reassured her. "I just didn't expect it."

"It just seemed easier than trying to explain that we could have brought dates if we wanted to, but we chose not to. Or at least I did," Harriet says with a mischievous smile.

"Yes, me too," I say quickly. "But yeah. My Aunt Dorothy wouldn't have understood that, and I would have gotten the lecture about settling down and so on."

"Exactly," Harriet says. "And she was always going to

think we are together so why not play along? This way there's less chance of her gossiping about it because she thinks she's part of a secret."

"Oh, you're good," I say, and Harriet does a little curtsy, and then we both laugh.

We keep dancing and laughing, stopping only to go to the bar when our drinks need topping up and when we go outside to escort the bride and groom to the car that's taking them to the airport to go on their honeymoon. After that, we drink and dance and laugh and around two am, Harriet fans herself on the dance floor.

"I need some air. Do you want to walk out onto the grounds?" Harriet asks me, shouting to be heard over the music.

I nod, take her by the hand, and lead her through the dancing crowd and then through the tables and chairs. We go into the lobby of the hotel where the reception is being held and then out of the back doors and onto the grounds. The grounds seem to go on forever, all manicured green and flecks of colored flowers. The immediate area as we step outside is a seating area and it is decorated with fairy lights and white roses and just down from the seating area is a water feature with a dolphin rising from the center of it.

"It's beautiful out here, isn't it?" Harriet says as we sit down at one of the tables. A couple sits at one of the other tables having a cigarette, but otherwise, we're alone out here.

"Yes," I agree. "And so peaceful."

"I can't believe bloody Max dragged us to that park for her photos, I mean yeah, the park was nice, but she could have had the photos done here instead," Harriet says, shaking her head.

"It does seem a bit silly," I agree. "I mean surely when they chose this venue, they looked around out here."

"Well, you would think so wouldn't you," Harriet says.

We go quiet for a moment, and I watch the fountain and then I feel Harriet's eyes on me. I turn toward her and smile questioningly at her.

"Don't mind me," Harriet says. "I was just thinking how nice your eyes are. Such a striking shade of blue."

"Is that so?" I say and Harriet nods.

"That's funny because I was just thinking how nice your lips look," I say.

I start to smile but Harriet looks at me and I can see she isn't joking around anymore. On her face is an expression of lust that makes my cock start to go hard just looking at her.

"If you think they look good, you should know how they taste," she says, her voice low and breathy.

Enjoyed the sample?

Pre-order the book here:
Not Yours Yet

About the Author

Thank you so much for reading!
If you have enjoyed the book and would like to leave a
precious review for me, please kindly do so here:

One Bossy Night

Please click on the link below to receive info about my latest
releases and giveaways.
<u>NEVER MISS A THING</u>

Or
come say 'hello' here:

Also by Iona Rose

Flirting With The CEO

Surprise Proposal

Propositioning The Boss

Dream Crusher

Until He Confesses

Insufferable Boss

Strictly Business

Confessing To The CEO

Enemy Boss

The Bride's Brother

The Bet

Made in United States
North Haven, CT
29 November 2024

61146639R00207